VIOLET IS NOWHERE

THE JOLVIX EPISODES

FAITH GARDNER

MIRROR
HOUSE
·PRESS·

*For the person without whom
I would be nothing: me.*

VIOLET

WELL, looks like I get to check something off my rock-star bucket list, and I'm not even a rock star yet: this morning I've woken up in a bed I don't recognize with no idea how I got here.

I prop myself up on an elbow, brain foggy, head hammering, the spins taking me on a nauseating carousel ride. It's daytime and the light hurts my eyeballs. My mouth tastes the way diesel smells.

I lie back down.

This rings like a hangover, but I'm not usually a big drinker. I can barely remember last night though. A gap of time is missing between the show I played and somehow ending up here, in what looks like a cozy cabin and what is definitely not my condo. Above me, a wood-paneled ceiling with dark swirls and a skylight displaying a puffy cloud. Lovely. But not my ceiling. I squint through the air dancing with dust.

"Hello?" I call out, my voice a croak.

Silence.

I'm alone.

Okay, this isn't funny. Did I slam a bunch of cocktails and

go home with someone? That's the most hopeful scenario I can spin right now. Dread swells at the thought that maybe some creep slipped something into my drink. But I'm usually so careful. I buy my own. Never accept favors from strangers.

I close my eyes. Focus, Violet. What can I remember?

Last night, I played a show with Violet and the Black Sheep. I remember loading equipment back into the van with Benzo and Lila when it was over. They were giving me the silent treatment because I talked to a rep from Maxam Records earlier in the evening. Maxam was looking to set up a meeting next week with me alone and I, traitor, agreed. Benzo and Lila thought I was trying to cut the Black Sheep out of a possible record deal with a major label, which ... come on. I was simply trying to seize an opportunity, one I would have turned into something huge for all of us if they'd given me the chance. I guess they're sick of every success we have, every news article that picks us up, every mention we get, being about me. Curse of the frontwoman. Is that what this is about? Did Benzo and Lila lock me up somewhere to teach me a lesson?

"Benzo?" I call out. "Is this a sick joke?"

More silence.

From my horizontal position, I take it all in. This looks far from anywhere Benzo's goth ass would ever set foot in. And it's too drab for Lila and her adorable vintage taste. And it's not like either of them have the money to be renting out vacation rentals or whatever.

This place is something from another century: wooden walls; a table with a chair that could be handmade; a trapezoid-shaped window with bars on it next to the door; a kitchenette of some kind in the corner; and what looks like a doorless, closet-sized bathroom. In Silver Lake, someone would probably slap a label like "rustic chic" on this baby and call it a luxury rental, but Toto, I have a feeling that we're not in Los Angeles anymore.

It's minimal but well kept. No gadgets, no TV, no robot vacuums, no smart speakers. Not a ton of evidence of life here either. There's a cardboard box beneath the kitchen table. My eyes focus on a plaque hanging on the wall that says HOME SWEET HOME. I'd marvel at the irony, but I'm too busy trying not to barf.

"Hello?" I call out again. "I'd love to know where the fuck I am. Anyone?"

I take it slowly this time. Use my hands to push to an upright position and notice, with a little alarm, that my black-painted fingernails are ragged.

What happened?

Did I climb a cement wall, get in a fight?

Standing up, I'm also extremely sore. My worry amps up. One aching step at a time, I embark on the slowest, shortest marathon the world has ever seen, that gold doorknob gleaming like treasure.

It's okay.

We're cool.

I can't remember why I'm here, but I'll soon be on my merry way and figure out how to get home.

After the painful few feet to the door, I clasp the doorknob and turn it, ready for the click of a release. Instead I feel the stick of a lock. I jiggle it harder and harder, desperation mounting.

Nope.

Not budging.

Stunned, a wave of weakness washes over me and I slide down to sit on the wooden floor. Five days a week I'm running miles on end and here I am making a journey across a cramped room, barely able to stay standing.

This is not good, and that is one hell of an understatement.

Blood pounds in my ears like the thump of a kickdrum. When I wipe sweat from my forehead, it's faintly purple on my fingertips. Apparently I didn't rinse the dye out too well.

Cute. Working hard on steadying my breath, I take this weakling minute on the floor to go over what I can remember.

Okay. Rewind, replay again. The show last night, our weekly residence opening for Lady Lithium. Awesome time. Packed house. The lady from Maxam set up an appointment for me to come in on Monday—Violet sans Black Sheep—then later, the argument backstage with my bandmates. Does all that have something to do with this? I don't remember much after that except packing up our gear and getting into Benzo's van. But locking me up in a cabin seems a tad much, even for a six-foot-six drama queen like Benzo. And Lila's sweet as a bunny rabbit.

Focus. I've got to focus. There has to be a reason.

I use the doorknob to pull myself back up to a standing position. Stars twinkle my vision and disappear. I hobble to the window, acrylic, two-paneled and shaped like a house. There's a hook and eye latch that I undo to swivel the window open, examining the thick jailhouse-style bars. I try to ignore the panicked thought that I'm locked up in here. I can't flip out yet.

This can't be as bad as it looks, it just can't.

A warm breeze reaches in and blows my cheeks. Oh, to feel the wind right now is like drinking cold water after walking in the desert. But outside, it's unfamiliar land. It's not my urban neighborhood or anything like it. There's nothing but tall, thirsty grass and a faraway grove of oaks. Beyond that, low, dark mountains piebald with green patches of woods. No houses, no people anywhere in sight. Not even any animals.

I reach and grip the iron bars and hold them, shake them, but they don't budge.

"Hey!" I scream, as loud as I can. My throat feels screamed raw. "Anybody hear me?"

The tall grass hisses with wind.

"Hell-ooooooo!" I yell, voice breaking.

I cock my ear to hear anyone, or anything—a highway humming, the drone of nearby voices. But no.

"Shit!" I yell, kicking the wall with a bare foot. "What is going *on*?"

The light bulb in my brain pops: what if, somehow, I've ended up on one of those shows where they suddenly surprise you on camera and you get a prize for your humiliation? *Psyched Out,* is that what the show on MTV 6 is called? Someone in a band I played with once was on it. There could be hidden cameras here. Hilarious! Must-watch TV! Witness singer/musician Violet Wilde lose it when she wakes up in the middle of nowhere! There could be cameras hidden all over the place. I'm beginning to think this is the most logical explanation when my eyes land once again on the cardboard box underneath the table. I noticed it before but didn't think to open it.

Okay, what are we?

I take a few steps, stoop down, pull the box out, and drag it across the hardwood floor. I plop myself down in a cross-legged position and pull the haphazardly taped top open. Inside, a manila envelope sits atop some white T-shirts and sweatpants in my size and a stack of towels. I push my face inside and note how brand new it all smells. There are even undergarments, but nothing sexy or interesting. I'm talking granny panties. Like prison garb. Boot camp couture.

What the hell is this?

I slap the package of socks on the floor. A box of Tampons. A phone charger. All right, I'm trying to make sense of these items in light of my *Psyched Out* theory. But this is more like something pointing to a long-term stay. *Psyched Out* wouldn't lock someone up in a cabin for days. They'd pop out soon and yell, "Psyched you out!" before cutting me a fat check and then we'd scuttle back to our normal lives.

Maybe this is a special, two-parter episode?

The manila envelope sits on my lap. I tear it open with my

teeth. A folded piece of paper and an old flip phone fall out. Turn-of-the century relic.

Unfolding the piece of paper, I read the words typed in small caps.

HELLO VIOLET.

THIS PHONE DIALS JUST ONE NUMBER.

WE WONDER, CAN YOU FIND HOW YOU'RE CONNECTED TO THE OTHER END OF THE LINE?

NO CHEATING! THAT MEANS YOUR CONTACT CAN'T REACH OUT TO AUTHORITIES OR PEOPLE IN YOUR LIFE TO ASK QUESTIONS ABOUT YOUR DISAPPEARANCE.

IF THEY DO, WELL ... LET US REMIND YOU, WE ARE ALWAYS LISTENING.

AND WE DON'T WANT TO BE DANGEROUS, BUT WE CAN BE.

I MEAN, YOU'RE HERE, AREN'T YOU?

THIS ALL HAS TO BE FIGURED OUT ON YOUR OWN.

IF YOU CAN SOLVE THE PUZZLE IN ONE WEEK, MAYBE YOU'RE SMARTER THAN WE THOUGHT.

MAYBE YOU DO DESERVE YOUR LIVES.

My stomach turns. This is far too harsh for a reality TV setup.

This reads more like a ransom note.

Holy shit. Have I been *kidnapped?*

My hand shakes as I read it over again. On the second read, it's even more ominous. What kind of twisted game is this? Do I even know anyone in my life capable of such playful cruelty, to create a puzzle threatening my life?

Could this be some unimaginably messed-up way for Benzo and Lila to teach me a lesson for possibly pursuing a record deal without them? Or is this some random evil asshole after my money?

Not wasting any time anymore. Adrenaline's pumping. Pulse is pounding. I get up and start looking for something, anything that could help get me out of here or to figure out who did this.

I explore the limited perimeter of the cabin's interior, poke my head into the doorless bathroom, hoping to see a window. Instead, there's a shower head sticking out of the wall like a silver snake skull above a cement floor with a drain in it, and a toilet next to the shower. Fresh toilet paper. A can of bleach powder and a used sponge behind it. How nice of my deranged kidnapper to clean the bathroom before locking me up here. A desperate thirst hits me all at once and I pound warm, metallic-tasting water straight from the sink faucet.

I explore the tiny kitchenette next and open the cupboards. It's filled with spices, condiments, boxes and cans of food. Nothing's been opened yet. The seals are still intact on everything. Why? The caring gesture of stocking the place is even more baffling. Sure enough, I swing open the door of the mini fridge and it gleams with fresh groceries, all Whole Foods brand, available anywhere. Which offers no clues about where in the world I am. I squat to look closer: my favorite sparkling water, Greek yogurt, tofu, pita bread, organic fruits and veggies. Just the type of stuff I keep in my refrigerator. I blow a long breath out.

"You know me," I say, swinging the refrigerator door shut.

There are no mirrors in this cabin as far as I can tell. But there's some aluminum foil in one of the drawers next to the stove. I pull out a sheet and assess my face. So there was a fight. That explains the sorry state of my fingernails. I also have a puffy lip and a crusty cut along my cheek. Purple dye all over my forehead and ears, I guess from the sweating and my half-assed dye job. Could be worse, really.

The thought's still trying to sink in. I've been *kidnapped*. I can't believe I've been kidnapped. But the sight of actual injury makes it all real.

I pull off my black T-shirt and put it on the counter, studying my belly, my chest, pulling up my lace bra momentarily to examine my tits. I press my skin for hidden injuries. My ribs are tender, but that's it. I pull my pants down and do the same. Closing my eyes, I hesitate a moment before plunging my hand into my underwear and putting my fingers inside myself to see if I feel anything tender, anything telling of some trauma I'm not remembering. But there's nothing tender, nothing different. In a wave of relief, I yank my pants back up. Hold my breath a second before pulling my shirt back over my head.

Well, I think bitterly. *I guess I should feel lucky.*

I walk back and forth, eyeing the twin bed where I started. It has a quilt on it that looks handmade, with bright pretty colors—lime green, magenta, turquoise. I stop, stand still, close my eyes and take inventory of what I've figured out so far, writing an imaginary list. I've been kidnapped; I'm locked in a cabin with no idea where I am; there are provisions here; my fridge is stocked like my fridge might be stocked at home; I don't appear to have been sexually assaulted. I have no memory of being kidnapped and no idea who would do this to me.

What if it was a fan? This care, this attention to detail reeks of an obsessed fan. But my fan base is also small potatoes compared to actual famous people. I mean, I've had success, yes, but I haven't even had a major record deal yet. *Yet.* I think that word with a pang and my eyes prickle.

My mom was a doula. My dad was a math professor. Both taught me the importance of problem-solving. Emotions have a time and place. No tears are allowed right now. Save it for a song, Violet. Next hit song right here: "Cryin' in a Hell Cabin."

I take a deep breath, blink the sting away, and sit back down on the ground with the cardboard box.

The note sits on the floor next to me, half folded. I can't bear to read it again. The directions on it, as cavalier as a scavenger hunt, when my fucking life's at stake. I can sit here for a week racking my brain to try to come up with a suspect or a reason, but this will never make sense. And I have a plastic phone in my hand that has the answer. So why waste time?

With quivering fingers, I flip it open. The clock says it's noon. Under "Contacts," sure enough, there's a single number. One with a 940 area code. Not an area code I recognize or have ever called before. Maybe when I press the *send* button, I'll hear a familiar voice—someone who can explain this to me. Someone who can put it all into perspective.

My thumb hits the button and I hold the phone up to my ear.

It rings like a cat purring. It rings and rings and rings.

BUD

DON'T KNOW if it's always been this way or if I'm only now just noticing, but the world seems to be growing and growing with no signs of stopping. Traffic's hell. Can't get a beer without having to fight for a seat at the bar. Driving around, ugly glass skyscrapers are taking over everything. Heard on the radio they're thinking of extending the BART trains to run all the way up to Marin County. I don't know, maybe I'm getting old. Or maybe the country runs too deep in me. All I know is, life's sprouting up around me at bamboo speeds and I'm standing still as a lawn gnome.

Funny part is, if it wasn't growing so damn fast, I'd have more of a reason to leave. But construction work's in high demand. Neighborhoods are gentrifying. Every other house you look at's getting flipped. Bought up, gutted, patched up, and painted with one of those horizontal wooden fences out front—and I'm the guy doing the gutting, patching, and painting. Making a killing. 'Cause a day later, a FOR SALE gets nailed into the lawn and the day after that some tech bro and his family have bought the place for millions. *Millions*, for some crap three-bedroom house with no real garage.

Sometimes I swear the more crowded a place gets, the less

soul it's got.

I'm thinking all this while finishing up a deck at a place in Oakland. Cottage with a backyard so dinky you couldn't turn a tractor around in it. The buzz of a helicopter overhead. That thing's been circling like a house fly all afternoon. I count the planks I have left to seal—four, six, eight—dip my brush in the bucket and try to run it evenly over the wood, hand shaking. Eight planks. I can make it eight planks.

"Hey Bud," a voice says.

It's Margot, burgundy hair twisted up like a big old rose on the top of her head. Bright-eyed and grinning with that gap between her teeth. She waves at me from behind a bush at the edge of the house, sneaking in through the side yard. Long olive-green dress and Greek goddess gold sandals.

"Hey," she says. "I thought I might catch you before you go."

"Ms. Margot," I say.

Margot's in the bungalow next door. This week, since I've been out working on the side yard, fixing up the walkway and finishing the deck, she's started talking to me through the fence each day. Then it moved to her standing up on a ladder so she could take it up a notch, make it face to face. Now I guess she's graduated to coming around to this side of the yard. Probably because I told her yesterday that today I'd be finishing the job. We've talked about all sorts of things: the elderly couple who used to live in this house, the insulting cost of rent around here, favorite beer brands, and she even pretended to be interested in how to mix and pour cement. But I knew all along what she's up to. She's flirting with me. And I'm flirting right back.

She blocks the sun with her hand and comes closer along the brick path. "Hope it's okay I came back here."

"It's fine. I'm about off anyway. Just adding a last coat on the deck here and waiting for the boss to come back around again to pay me."

"Wow." She turns to get a full, three-sixty view of the deck, the back porch, the spruced-up yard. "You've really done a number on this place."

Not to brag, but she's right. Before, the deck was a safety hazard, the concrete path was split and missing chunks, the grass dead and brown and littered with sun-bleached lawn ornaments from another century. Now it's picture-perfect and ready to win over someone's wallet.

"Still got a few pink plastic flamingos hanging around here somewhere if you want them," I tease.

"Not exactly my style, but thanks." Margot's eyes twinkle, the color of lake water on a sunny day. She opens her bag and pulls out a brown bottle. "I thought maybe you'd have a beer with me, if you don't have anywhere to go after this?"

What a sweetheart. Bringing over my favorite beer, the one I told her about last time we talked. And I'm thirstier than a fish in Death Valley.

"Sure, I'd love to."

I drop my brush in the sealant can and stand up, wiping my hands on my jeans. She hands me a beer. I pull my keys out, use my shark bottle opener to pop off the top. Hand the beer to her and then uncork another for myself. We clink bottles, both with little smiles perking up our lips like each of us know a secret but won't say, our eyes locked while we take our first sips. Well, for her it's a sip. For me it's a series of gulps. One that quenches a squirming beast inside me. I've got to keep myself from not downing the whole thing in five seconds.

"The kind of guy who has a bottle opener on his keychain," Margot says.

"They call that kind of guy 'prepared,'" I say, taking another look at it, right next to my Swiss Army knife. "Had sharky here since high school."

"Where'd you go to high school?"

"In Aubrey, little town outside Dallas."

"Texas!" she says. "Your accent. I knew you were from somewhere in the south."

"Funny thing is, whenever I visit home, my family says I've got a California accent."

I put the beer down, grab the brush, and get back to sealing so I won't finish the beer too fast. Margot's barely taken a sip of hers. She sits cross-legged on the grass and watches me work. Asks me about Aubrey. I answer there's not much to tell, unless you're a fan of cows and church. She says she grew up across the Bay in San Francisco. Rattles off a casual resumé while she drinks her beer and picks at the grass: how she was a barista in her parents' café throughout high school, then went to nursing school there. Now she's a home care registered nurse living on this side of the Bay and working with the elderly. Has been for years. Finally, she finishes her beer and grabs two more for us, borrowing my keys to pop off the tops.

"Thanks, sharky," she says, plopping back down on the grass.

I finish the dregs of the last one and down half this new beer and now I'm feeling pretty good. "Takes a special person to do that kind of caretaking work." I put the bottle down, pacing myself. "I don't think I could do it."

"Anyone could do it if you had to. We all care for people at different times in our lives," she says softly.

The sun's moved and now the shade has dropped over her and she looks magazine-girl pretty, the breeze lifting the few flyaways of wine-colored hair around her face. Not to get too carried away, but maybe this could be the beginning of something. Maybe she's just what I need in my life. What a sap. How many times have I said that before? I turn back to the deck and finish up, liking the way we can just be with a silence between us and not rush to fill it.

Bob's voice cuts through the peace like a machete and booms out the open windows. The man speaks in all caps, all the time. You wouldn't guess it's the voice that would come out of him when you see him in his Hawaiian shirt and long white hair and John Lennon glasses. Looks like the type of guy who'd bust out a guitar and sing you "Kumbaya." But he's got the soul of a used car salesman.

"Buddy," he says, coming out the back door and standing with his hands on his hips at the top of the stairs. "Place looks good. This a wrap? Oh, who's this? Buddy's got a Buddy!" He guffaws and stomps down the stairs in his sandals. "Why hello."

"Hi, I'm Margot. I live next door."

"Why hello Margot Who Lives Next Door." Bob stoops down, offers his hand for a quick shake. "I'm Bob, Buddy's uncle."

"He's not my uncle," I say.

Bob stands back up and walks over to clap my back. "Well, this boy's worked for me for, what, going on ten years?"

"Four years, Bob."

"Practically family."

"We're not family."

"Who bailed you out of jail that one time, huh?"

"Give me my money and get the hell out of here, Bob."

"See?" Bob says to Margot. "Only people I let talk to me that way are family."

He takes his wallet out and counts to thirty. Hands me thirty twenties. I pocket it and squat back down to do my last few streaks of sealant.

"He's a good boy," Bob says to Margot. "Even if he acts otherwise."

Margot's eyes are wide and she's fighting a laugh. Bob's entertaining, even if he is a maniac.

"You can go now, Bob," I say without looking up.

Bob heads up the stairs and points his finger at me. "Text you about Monday."

"Yep."

"Don't party too hard, you hear?"

I don't answer him and soon hear the door slam. Then I glance at Margot, her eyebrows up.

"Well, he's a character," she says.

"You're telling me."

I put the sealant away and rinse my brush with a hose.

"He bailed you out of jail?" she asks.

"Long time ago. Drunk tank. They were going to let me out in a matter of hours anyway."

"That was a nice amount of cash he handed you."

"All in a day's work."

"A *day?*" She gets up and gathers up our empties, puts them in her bag. "That's probably more than I make in a week."

"You should ask for a raise."

"Maybe. Yeah." She waits in front of me, touching her hair bun as if to make sure it's still there. "Well. Do you have somewhere to go? Someone to ... meet?"

The beat hangs there between us. I know her real question.

"No one to meet, no," I say.

She brightens up. "How about you come over and I make you dinner then?"

"Dinner sounds nice."

"You like pasta?"

"I eat anything."

"Pesto?"

"Anything."

"Give me a few minutes. Meet you at my place in five."

After locking the place up and gathering up some crap to throw in the back of my truck, I walk the dozen steps to Margot's place, painted a silly periwinkle. Hammock on the front porch. Flowerbeds in the windows. Place is cute. I stand out front, asking myself if this is the best idea. Thing about me is, I tend to screw things up. The things worth keeping, anyway. So the law in my head goes, if I want it, I probably don't deserve it.

I want this.

As I take the two steps up the concrete stairs, I pull out my phone to look at the time. It's barely after five and that's no surprise. But the thirty-six missed calls from UNKNOWN NUMBER are. As usual, I've left my phone on silent all day. Never seen a sight like that on it.

"Hey," Margot says breathlessly, opening the door.

"Hey." I stare at the screen of my phone for one extra second before slipping it into my back pocket.

"You get a call you need to take?" she asks.

"No, no. Probably just spammers."

I go inside. Anyone back home, they wouldn't have shown up as an UNKNOWN NUMBER. I don't know any unknowns.

The inside of Margot's house is thoughtfully put together. You can tell this is a woman who considered the color of her curtains and the color of her toaster oven deeply. She has a pre-printed pad of paper magnetically attached to her fridge that says Lists and a robot vacuum cleaner wheeling around the floor. I feel like a man who stepped onto Neptune.

"Well, this is real swanky," I say, and then realize I sound like someone's grandpa, so I add, "and shit."

"Thanks," Margot says, and then puts her hand out in the air like a waiter with an invisible tray. "Have a seat."

She hands me another beer, which I gladly accept. I sit at her table, which kind of looks like a table from a diner where my mom still works back home. White and shiny with a silver rim. She's even got a napkin holder like the one at my mom's work and I almost say something but then I'm not sure what to say. That's how it is sometimes, I don't know where to begin.

"Sorry the place is a mess," Margot says, plunking a pot full of water on the old-fashioned stove, *snick-snick-snick*ing the gas light on under it. She drops a wooden cutting board on the counter and I jolt. "I haven't had time to really clean this week."

"I'm not seeing any mess," I assure her. "If you saw where I lived, you'd feel better."

"Where do you live?"

"Crockett. You know where that is?"

She shakes her head as she hacks up asparagus.

Something gives me a little surge of pride, to be able to live in a town here in the same metro area, to chat with a local, and have some knowledge she doesn't. I describe my place: a bottom-floor apartment in a strange, spacious building that once was a historic bank. There's only one main street in that town, with a single bar and a few shops. No big grocers, no chain stores whatsoever. At night I used to see the Vegas-bright glitz of the sugar factory under the Carquinez Bridge. It was both so ugly and so beautiful.

Margot's pasta is delicious. We eat with little half-giggles, mouths full of noodles. I'm on my fourth beer now and I'm happy. I imagine what it must be like to have a home like this, not just a place you exist, but a *home*. With art on the walls and furniture you didn't just find on the curb somewhere and plates that match each other. Of course, I can't help but think of Priya for a moment and it becomes hard to shake the thought of her. The way my jaw clenches, it's like I have a muscle spasm. And though we've been quiet, eating, Margot notices, her hand on my arm.

"Everything okay, Bud?" she asks.

"I'm fine," I say, downing my drink. "This dinner's so good, by the way."

It takes a moment for her hand to let go. When she does, she twirls her noodles around on her fork a minute longer and if I were guessing, there seems to be so much she wants to say. But guessing's not knowing.

"What's Bud short for?" she asks.

"Nothing," I say, setting my fork down. "It's not short for anything."

I don't know what it is about me saying that, or maybe fixing my eyes on her, but she puts her fork down with a clanking sound too and pushes her chair out and then she's on me, lips on mine, hands in my hair, straddling me. Not sure what I did or how I provoked her but I'm not sorry for it either.

We move, like one body, some sensual three-legged race, back to her room. It's perfume-heavy, her bed's oddly high off the ground and has curtains on the sides. A bowl of potpourri sits on a shelf above her bed next to a book that says *Bedtime Meditations*. She apparently takes sleep very seriously. She gets on top of me and leans over, fluttering her lips on mine. Pulling my hair with her hands. Hate to say it but I'm still hungry, still thirsty, and that's the energy I kiss her with. I run my hand along her curves, shoulder to waist to hip and up again. Her hands are on the belt of my jeans. In one second, I flip her over to her back.

It happens so fast. Don't get me wrong, it's great, it is … but then it's over. And though I'm panting half-naked in her bed, holding her, I'm left dizzy, wondering what happened. Wishing I could rewind it. Not sure if it was good enough. She looks over at me with shining eyes and asks if I liked it. I'm not lying when I say I did. I'm not sure what I am.

"Got any more beer?" I ask, my arm under her neck.

"Sure, sure." She gets up, naked and jiggling, and heads to the kitchen. And damn me for feeling sad at a moment like this. She comes and brings me back an uncapped beer. "Here you go."

She kisses me on the lips and climbs into bed with me, under a duvet. Rests her cheek on my chest. It's comforting, that weight on the place my heart should be. I drink the rest of my beer and then another. She talks. My mouth moves and my ears stay open, but I'd be lying if I said I shared or heard anything.

Next thing I know, the morning light's accusing rays are on my face. My head's pounding, my stomach's sick. And she's still got a hand on my chest, her face on my shoulder, sleeping angelically.

It takes a lot of care to let her down easy—to let her face fall unknowingly to the bed. She's beautiful there, wine-colored hair, milky skin. And everyone's at their most innocent when they sleep, aren't they? I head to the kitchen and root around the cabinet for coffee, but don't find anything. In the bathroom, I rifle around for headache medicine but don't find anything. I stand in the hallway a moment, not sure where to go from here. I can hear her snoring.

I realize I'm staring into a room in the hallway. Another bedroom, door open. There's a twin bed and a rocking horse. Toys on the ground. The word LOUISA spelled out on the wall, in cutesy letters.

Well, shit.

I sneak back into her room. Slip my shirt and my boots back on. Grab my keys and my wallet. And she's snoring until suddenly she's not—she's up, with a sleepy, hurt gaze, the sheet pulled up over her body. Yesterday's makeup smeared underneath her eyes.

"Where are you going?" she asks.

"Just—you know. Heading out. I'm an early riser."

"Early riser." Her hand goes to her mouth. "Were you going to—?"

"No, no, not like that, not like that."

She sits up straighter, pulls the pins out of her bun one by one. "Okay. Good, because—anyway."

We exchange smiles. She shows off that cute gap between her teeth. I squeeze my keys tighter in my hand.

"You want to maybe get together again this week?" She tosses her merlot hair, running her fingers through it.

I look away.

"I don't think that'd be a good idea," I say. "Sorry. The extra room you have there?"

I try to drop it like a question. I don't know why, questions seem to hurt less.

Margot draws the sheets up tighter. Her expression goes on ice. "What about it?"

"Well, I just … I don't do kids."

She closes her eyes like I slugged her or something. She shakes her head.

Oh hell.

"Get out of here," she says quietly.

"I just—I mean, I had a great time—"

"Get the *fuck* out of here."

I oblige. Out in my truck, I run a hand through my hair and exchange a red-eyed glance with myself in the rearview. On the way home, I stop at a drive thru for an egg sandwich and the liquor store for a twelve-pack. Pop a warm beer open and chug it parked in the truck before heading home. At the intersection before I get on the freeway, a sunburnt homeless man stands in the sun with a cardboard sign that says, HUNGRY. A LITTLE HELP? Across the street, an encampment of countless tents, broken furniture, litter. It's such a shit world that that guy's there and I'm here helping flip houses for millionaires.

I roll down my window. "Hey!" I shout.

The guy ambles over to where I'm waiting at the intersection, no expression on his face.

"Here you go, man," I say, handing him the wad of bills in my back pocket.

He stares at the money in his hand. "This a joke?"

"No, I'm a crappy comedian." The light goes green and I take my foot off the brake. "Have a good day."

In the rearview, he's still studying the money in his hands, wind blowing his hair.

The drive home's long and stop-and-go. I turn up the radio and try not to think about the look on Margot's face at the end there, like I'd turned to garbage before her very eyes. Then again—didn't I? And she deserves better. In the long run a woman like that would lose interest in a guy like me. So it was all for the best. Save us both the hurt. Ripping off the bandage and all that.

Back home, that stray cat's meowing outside on my back porch. When I kick the door open to air out the funk, she comes running in like she owns the place and hops up on that spot on the couch she likes so much.

"Funny girl," I tell her.

I pop open a beer and rub her behind her ears. She purrs loudly.

"At least one female on this planet likes me," I say.

After plugging in my phone again, it lights up. My jaw about drops when I see I have over a hundred missed calls and sixteen voice messages.

"What in hell," I say.

I press play on the most recent one. A woman. A shaky voice I don't recognize.

"Please. Please pick up. Don't ignore my calls. Pick up."

I play the one before that.

"Don't ignore me. This is serious. Help me!"

"What in hell," I repeat to the air.

At that moment, my phone lights up in my hand, ringing silently with UNKNOWN NUMBER. I let it ring a moment. Is this a scam? I've read stories about scammers faking emergencies and calling your cell. The desperation in her voice sounds pretty convincing though. Maybe it's a wrong number. This lady's in trouble and she's got a wrong number. That's some crap luck for her. I shake my head and plop on the couch next to the cat, who gets spooked and shoots out my back door. Finally, I press a button to accept the call.

"Hello?"

VIOLET

I SPRING up from my position lying on the bed and jump to my feet, pressing the phone into my ear, hand to my chest. The relief that comes at the sound of a human voice is practically a drug.

"Finally!" I can't help but nearly shout. "Oh God, I was beginning to think I'd never reach you." My voice catches at the end. "Hello?"

"Hello?" the guy says slowly again.

With a few steps, I go to the window. The same window I've been peering out of now for a day. Still nothing to report but a bunch of grass and mountains and far-off trees giving me the cold shoulder. In the pause, I take a breath of fresh air and gather my thoughts.

"Hi. This is—this is going to sound insane. Because it is. But my name is Violet and I've been kidnapped. I'm locked in a cabin in the middle of nowhere. I don't know where I am."

"Right," he says.

"I—" The words dry up in my mouth and I backpedal a moment. "What is that supposed to mean?"

"You've been kidnapped," he says. "And you're out in the

middle of nowhere. And I guess you want me to wire you some money, right? And you're related to a foreign prince—"

"No no no." I turn and pace the room, the dozen steps it takes to cross from the front door to the kitchenette. I've had the time to count them and check my work many times over. "No, it's not like that. I don't want your money."

"Then what is it you're after?"

He doesn't even ask it, he just says it, like there's already no hope of him believing me. Somehow, when I'd imagined how this phone call might go—and I've now had many hours to imagine all sorts of scenarios—I didn't imagine that the person would immediately assume I was a scammer. Though now that I think about it, I can understand.

"I don't even know," I say. "I don't know. Look ... I'm trapped. In some kind of game."

"I thought you were kidnapped."

"I was. That's how I ended up here. I can't remember exactly what happened, my memory's super hazy, but I think I was drugged and roughed up. Then I woke up here. And all they left me with was a note and a flip phone that has one number in it. Your number."

The sounds of gulps, like he's drinking something and thinking this over. "That's a crazy story."

"It's *true*. It *happened*."

I spin on my bare heel, continuing to pace across the wooden floorboards. Pretending I'm on a balance beam and I have to stay on a single plank.

"So ... who are you then?" he asks skeptically. "What's your name?"

Right. That. Names, introductions. "Violet Wilde."

"Violet Wilde," he repeats, like he doesn't believe me.

"Look, my parents were new-age weirdos, but I'm a real person. Look me up."

"I'm too lazy to right now. I'll just give you the benefit of the doubt." His honey-slow drawl is aggravating. He's not taking this seriously.

"And who are you?" I ask, stopping to catch my breath in the middle of the room. I don't know if it was the pacing or the situation, but my pulse is hammering. "What's your name? Where are you?"

"Bud Atwood. In Crockett, California."

"The Bay Area?" I ask, surprised.

"You know Crockett?" he asks, equally surprised.

"I'm from the East Bay. You don't sound like you're from the Bay Area. And you don't have the area code, either."

"Born and raised in Texas."

"Okay. And I was born and raised in Berkeley. Very weird."

"And where are you at now?"

"I told you, I don't know where I am."

"I mean, where'd you live before ... you got kidnapped or whatever?"

"LA."

"Huh."

He seems to be buying this a bit more. I close my eyes, trying to imagine this stranger I'm talking to.

"Bud," I try, because it means so much more to connect with a name than it did to a disembodied voice. "Would you mind? There was a note I got here. I want to know what you think ..."

"Read it off, sure," he says, with the breeziness of a man who's watching TV or reading his mail right now. I have no way of knowing what's going on with him. I have to sit at the table and stare at the disturbing note as if it's life or death, but to him, there are no stakes.

"Okay," I say. "It starts, 'Hello Violet. This phone dials just one number.'"

"What phone?" he interrupts.

"The one I'm talking on," I tell him. "It's a burner phone with one number in it: yours."

"This is really the only number it dials?" Now he's eating something crunchy, like movie popcorn and I am his movie.

"Yes," I answer, annoyed.

"What happens if you dial another number?"

"The call won't go through."

"Have you dialed 911?"

"I can't. It's complicated. I'll get to that, it's coming in the note."

"Fire away."

"It says after that, 'We wonder, can you find how you're connected to the other end of the line?'"

"'We?' Who the hell is 'we?'"

"I don't know," I say, my finger circling that word on the note. "But good point."

"What's next on this note of yours?"

"Says 'No cheating! That means your contact can't reach out to authorities or people in your life on your behalf.'"

"Who's your contact? Me? So I'm not supposed to reach out to ... anyone?"

"Anyone," I declare at the same time. "And it says they're always listening."

"But why?"

I try to fathom this actual human being on the other end of the line. I try to fill him in, this slow-talking man who sounds my age. My mind colors in a skeleton with olive-skinned flesh, muddy-colored eyes and a lazy beard. He sounds quite possibly stoned.

"What the hell do I have to do with this?" he goes on.

I clear my throat. "The note ends with, 'If you can solve the puzzle in one week, maybe you're smarter than we thought. Maybe you do deserve your lives.' And over a day has passed since I probably got dumped here, which means it's closer to five days. I have to figure this out in five days."

"And this isn't some joke," he clarifies. "This is real."

"Dude, I'm stuck in a cabin out in the middle of nowhere," I say, my voice catching. "And I'm terrified. I don't know why this is happening. What if I never get out? What if I die out here? Or what if the guy comes back and kills me?"

"How do you know it was a guy if you can't remember how you got there?"

I explain to him that, last night as I paced and my brain ate itself alive in here, I started remembering some details. Not scenes, just still frames. My bedroom. A man in a ski mask. I think I was kidnapped from my condo after the show was done, though I'm not positive how it all went down. It's all blurry when I try to make sense of it.

"Shit, man," he says. "I don't know how to help you."

I lie my head on the table, cheek to the cool wood, a swell of fear and desperation rising in me. My eyes burn and I try to hold it in, but it becomes unbearable, the pressure, it rises up and I cry, tears spilling on the table. I put the phone down for a moment and sit up, palms to my face. How did this happen? Why to me? What is going to happen if I don't figure it out in the next five days, like the note said? Who is this person on the other end of the phone in some tiny town in the East Bay?

God, the loneliness. The devastating loneliness. It aches and it brings up the worst memories. It reminds me of how it felt to receive the news that my parents had died in a car accident when I was twenty-two. My mind racing and fighting it, the disbelief, *this can't be happening, no, it can't*—but then in the days after, having to accept reality over and over again. I'm orphaned again. The whole world is out of reach and I'm here and I'm stuck and there's no way out. Violet is alone. Completely alone.

"Hello?" I hear the man saying on the phone on the table. "Hey, you still there?"

I sit up, wiping my face, sniffling. There's the tiniest flicker of hope seeing the phone there, knowing there's at least one person in the world I can reach.

"Sorry," I say, picking it back up again.

"You don't need to apologize."

"I'm trying to be strong. This is just so confusing and overwhelming."

"Listen, whatever all this is … we're going to figure it out, all right? I don't know how we're connected but let me tell you something about me: I've always loved playing detective."

I stand up, pluck some toilet paper from the bathroom and blow my nose. "Thanks."

"So if they're always listening, you think that means they can hear us right now?"

"Maybe. Hey, creeps, if you are listening, fuck you."

"Not sure how much that's going to help."

"Well, makes me feel better to say it."

"Listen." He pauses a moment. "Violet, the good news is, there's no work today. Saturday. Schedule's clear. Schedule's clear the whole weekend. So I got all the time in the world to talk to you."

Back to the open window. I stare out at the open land, the high, golden grass. It looks like California. But who knows? So many hours passed while I was drugged, lights out. For all I know they could have crossed state lines.

"Tell me about yourself, Bud," I say softly. "Let's start there so we can figure out how we're connected."

A long sigh. The pop of a can opening, a slurp. "There's not much to tell. I'm a simple guy. Like I said, live in Crockett. Do construction jobs for a living, helping my boss flip houses."

"What's your boss's name?"

"Bob Sorvino."

I run my hand along each of the eight bars on the window,

pulling. "Don't recognize that name. Tell me more about yourself."

"I like long walks on the beach."

"You're joking right now? Come on."

"Sorry. Like I told you, I'm from Texas. Dallas area."

"I played a show in Dallas once on tour. Maybe that's how I know you? The venue was called ... let me think ..." I close my eyes and try to imagine the venue. It was a dive bar. They all blend together when you've played so many shows across the country. The crowds, the late nights that bleed into dawns, the strangers who are your new best friends for a day when they let you sleep on their couches and feed you dinner. Oh, world. Please let me out again. Please tell me I haven't played my last show. I was just getting started.

"Played a show?" Bud asks, his voice jerking me back into the here and now.

"I'm a musician. My band's called Violet and the Black Sheep."

"Never heard of you. No offense."

I'd hoped he knew us. Would make connecting the dots much easier. Plus, it's always flattering.

"None taken." I go back to the made bed, sit on the patchwork quilt. "Okay, well what brought you to California? When did you get here?"

"After high school. Came on football scholarship."

"What school?"

"Cal Berkeley."

"Damn," I say, impressed. Even I, ignorant about all things sports, know that team is a big fucking deal when it comes to college football. "That's amazing."

"Eh, don't be too impressed. I dropped out the first semester."

"Why?" I stop myself. My curiosity's pulling me in directions that aren't helpful right now. "Never mind. Focus, Violet. So how old are you?"

"I'll be thirty this year."

"Me too." A common thread. I make a mental note. "So that means by the time you came to UC Berkeley, I had already left the Bay Area."

"Where'd you go?"

"Michigan. I went to college there. After that, I moved to LA to chase a music career and have been here ever since."

It always feels like a lie to me to have to summarize life into something like a resumé or an elevator pitch—a series of events, a checklist of places. It doesn't capture the poetry and sweat and the funny haircuts and smell of ten thousand cups of coffee and the delicate difference between all the half-drunk kisses and a few brushes with danger and the hot air balloon feeling when a crowd sang along with my song lyrics and the tears that rained on my pillowcase late at night and dried by morning. You know, *life*. How can you explain that to someone?

"Never been to Michigan," Bud says. "Never been to any state except Texas and California—and the states you drive in between, but never spent time there."

This guy and his underwhelming existence, I swear. Never been anywhere. Never done anything.

"Okay, Michigan's not the connection," I say. "It's got to be the Bay Area. Unless—have you ever spent time in LA?"

"Oh, I've been down a couple times. Dated a girl who lived in Long Beach. Spent a couple months down there with her."

Restless, I braid my hair. I don't have a ponytail holder and it's been maddening to not be able to put my hair up, especially in the afternoon when it gets sticky hot. "What's her name?"

"Emily Morgan."

"Emily Morgan," I repeat, trying hard to find any semblance of familiarity.

"Doubt you knew her. She died of a heroin overdose years ago."

My jaw drops. My heart drops along with it. I know the pitfall of grief all too well, the sick burying weight you have to keep dragging everywhere with you.

"Oh my God, I'm sorry," I say.

"Yeah. We were a mess back then. I'm surprised I didn't die too."

"You're a recovering addict?"

"I guess you could call me that. It wasn't for that long—it was a weird phase. Sounds bizarre to put it that way but it was that for me. A phase. I don't touch drugs anymore."

"I dated a woman in NA. Maybe you knew her—Alex?"

"Didn't do the whole twelve-step thing. Wasn't like that." I hear water running. "So you're gay?"

"Sometimes," I say, brushing my fingers through my hair to loosen it again. My fingertips are purple. "I'm pansexual."

"Never met a pansexual before."

"Well, now you have."

In the moment of silence, I wonder if he's a homophobe. But then he answers, "That's cool."

I get up and open the fridge, pulling out some strawberries and cheese to assemble a snack plate.

"Violet, I'm thinking we should call the police."

My mouth goes dry at the thought. "No. Not yet. You heard the note—what if we do and they come and kill me?"

"What if this guy—these people—what if they're just bluffing?"

"But what if they're *not*?" I take the plate and sit at the table. "I mean, this is my life. And maybe yours too, Bud, who knows. I'm not willing to take a fucking risk with mine."

On his end, some dishes clank together. I imagine he's doing his dishes while we talk, or preparing to eat something, too. I try to visualize his space but all I see is my condo and I miss it so badly. My shag rug and gorgeous couch. My plants, who all have names and must be thirsty. My Gibson Hummingbird that hangs on my bedroom wall next to her sister, the pool-blue Gibson Les Paul. What I wouldn't give to just have a guitar here, just a guitar. It's always been my answer to the desert island question and I must say, the answer holds up.

"Hey, would you mind calling me back in a few minutes?" he asks, breaking the silence that lapsed between us. "I got something I need to do."

"Oh," I say, my throat tightening. "Yeah, I can do that."

I stare at the food on my plate, arranged in a little circle. Cheese, strawberry, cheese, strawberry, cheese, strawberry. Suddenly, I don't think I have the appetite for it.

"How long?" I ask.

"How about a half hour?"

"Sure." I drum my purple fingertips on the tabletop. "You're not calling the police, are you?"

"No."

"Swear?"

"On my mama's life."

"Just … please answer when I call back, okay?" I ask, clasping my hands and squeezing until it hurts. "You're all I have."

"I will. You got my word."

We hang up. Appreciate the promise, but it does nothing to erase my worry. I don't know what his word means. I don't know who he is. I have to trust him—what other option do I have? But it's unsettling to have my life resting in the hands of an invisible stranger.

What if he doesn't answer?

What if he calls the police right now?

What if the man comes back and kills me?

What if I run out of food?

What if I never get out of here?

What if I die alone in the middle of nowhere?

What if five days pass and then … and then …

I put the plate of food back in the refrigerator for later. Back to pacing, arms crossed, heart pounding. I hurry my pace to try to outrun this horrible feeling. Jumping jacks. Pushups. Squats, lunges. I break a sweat. Collapsing on the bed, out of breath, I close my eyes. Run through a list of people in my life who could have done this to me. That's where I'll start when I call Bud back: go through a list of possible suspects. Who knows? Maybe there's some overlap. Maybe we have that person in common and the connection will be obvious.

So, Violet, who could have done this and why?

The first person who comes to mind is someone on Insta-gratification named puppydawguys. I always assumed it's a guy but the profile pic is actually of me so I have no idea. This puppydawguys person is obsessed with Violet and the Black Sheep. Every post from our band account, every post from my personal account, gets several comments from puppy-dawguys almost instantaneously and is reposted to their account. They've written me long screeds in DM about how they think we were meant to be together because of sublim-inal messages in my songs. They talk a lot about how the universe connected us and that soon we'll be one. It's the only fan I've ever had who creeps me out. But according to their profile, they live in Raleigh, North Carolina. That's a long way to go. Then again, if you're hellbent on kidnapping someone, what's three thousand miles to stop you?

The second person who comes to mind—and I feel guilty even thinking this—is still Benzo. I mean, he was so angry with me at the show. So was Lila. Though Lila I just can't imagine having anything to do with this; she cries if she has to kill a spider. But Benzo? He has a temper. I've seen him get in a physical, punch-throwing, bloody-nosed fight over whether or not The Cure was the greatest band of all time. But despite his temper, Benzo's also a giant goth teddy bear.

He's forty years old and has a daughter in kindergarten. I can't see him calculating this whole plan and carrying it out. And why? How would it help him in any way?

This has to all end somehow with a ransom. If that's what this is about, it could be anyone. Between the settlements from my parents' death and the money they left me, I still have quite the nest egg, even after buying my condo. But so far no money's been mentioned. Why would they bring Bud into this if it's just about squeezing money out of me?

Checking the flip phone, I see it's been thirty-two minutes, so I call Bud back.

"Hey," he says, answering after the first ring this time. "Violet?"

I let out a giant breath. "I'm so glad you picked up."

"Told you I would."

"I know you did. But I don't know you."

"Thing is, if we're going to figure this out, we've got to trust each other. Right, Violet?"

"Yeah."

"Because I'm having a hard time trusting you here."

I sit cross legged on the bed and pull a pillow on my lap. The white pillowcase is now smudged purple from my hair. "Why would you have a hard time trusting me?"

"See, I just looked you up online. That's what I was doing. Some research."

"Okay," I say slowly. "And?"

"And I found you. Violet Wilde. Violet and the Black Sheep. You've got a lot of followers."

"I mean, yeah. But back up—why do you have a hard time trusting me?"

"Because, *Violet*." He says the word like it's a lie. "You posted a picture to your account just this morning."

I squint at the dust in the air, letting the words settle in my mind. "What? I did not."

"You did. At 8:46 a.m. this morning."

Rising from the bed, I resume my pacing. Purple panther in a cage. "I don't have my phone, man. What's the picture of?"

"You, in a robe with purple dye in your hair. Looks like in a bathroom."

"I took that Thursday afternoon before I was kidnapped," I tell him. "But I didn't post it. Someone must have my phone."

"How do I know you're not lying to me?"

"Hey, weren't you the one who told me we had to trust each other?"

"I said that 'cause I don't trust you."

The heat of the room has become musty and unbearable. I go to the kitchenette's sink and take a paper towel, run it under the water, and wet my face. Then I sit at the table again, resting my elbows, closing my eyes, the air cooling my damp skin. "Look, did you go to the Violet and the Black Sheep account? There you'll see a pic from our show Thursday night. My hair's bright purple in it. I dyed my hair before the show. I'm not lying to you."

"All right," he says after a moment. "I did see that picture. Guess it makes sense."

"What was the caption on the photo of me dyeing my hair?"

"It said 'The future is bright ... violet, of course!'"

Cute.

"Sounds like something I'd write," I admit. "Did you by chance look at the account of my bandmates?"

"No. Why?"

"I don't know. Just ... there's been friction between us. I mean, I know they'd never do this. But I don't know. Just grasping at straws."

"I can look for you, if you want to call me back again—"

"No," I say. "Not yet. Later."

Another pop of a can, another slurp. "I want to help you, okay? If this is for real, I want to figure it out with you."

"It's real," I say, irritated. "How am I supposed to convince you?"

"You're not, it just—it might take some time."

"We don't have time. I'm locked in a fucking cabin and I need to get out."

"Tell me about the cabin," he says. "Maybe that'll help."

I paint a picture of the place for him: a cross between a cute vacation rental and prison. The wood ceilings and floors. The twin bed with the quilt. The bars on the windows, the grassy plains, far-off trees, hills that jut up behind it all. As I look out to describe it, some crows fly by, cawing as they glide through the air and land in an oak tree. The sight of them—of some glimmer of life out here, of some moment of unpredictability—gives me a flash of hope.

"Oh!" I say. "I just saw some crows. A bunch of them. They're the first birds I've seen."

"A murder," he says. "Isn't that what they call a bunch of crows?"

"Not helping," I say, my brow furrowing. "Don't say that."

"I'm sorry. I shouldn't've said that word."

I bite my lip, a shadow of superstition passing over me. It seems like a horrible sign to see a fucking *murder* of crows. But Violet, you are not superstitious. You don't believe in such things. Get it together.

"It's okay," I say, my breath steadying.

I turn from the window and head to the kitchenette next to describe it to him. Like a realtor in hell: stainless steel mini-sink! Plenty of cabinet space! Open the fridge and squat in front of it, closing my eyes to appreciate the cold air. Oh, what a relief it is. This place is so suffocatingly hot during the day. When I give him a list of the contents of my refrigerator, he stops me.

"Sparkling water?" he asks incredulously.

"Yeah, my favorite kind."

"You're shitting me. Your kidnapper stocked the fridge with sparkling water? That's better than a hotel."

"It's very weird," I agree. "Also, it's all my favorite foods." I pull out the ice tray and put it to my forehead, close my eyes. And the Instagrat post that rang like something I'd post myself. "They know me well."

"Okay, so who are you close to in your life? I'm sitting here with a pen and paper, by the way. I'm going to write this stuff down."

It strikes me as sweet, this effort he's putting in, though there's a grip of fear on my throat. "The note said you can't contact anyone."

"Doesn't mean I can't write it down so we can rule stuff out."

"Just making sure you know."

"I know. I hear you. I won't do anything 'til you tell me to."

So polite, so Southern. I imagine a rugged man with gentle eyes and a cowboy hat, chewing a piece of straw. "I mean, my whole life is music," I say, eyes still closed, trying to answer his question. "Violet and the Black Sheep is so close to finally breaking through. In fact, we were—I was—going to meet with a record executive at Maxam about getting signed next week."

"That seems like it's worth writing down. When was that happening?"

"Monday. I talked to a rep from their label Thursday night, at our show. Her name is Nora Zats."

"And what are your bandmates' names again?"

The thought of them rings with regret. "Lila Gutierrez. And Benzo."

"The hell kind of name is …"

"His real name is Benjamin Dworkin. His socials are all under the name Benzo though, one word."

"Benzo," he repeats. "Who else? You got a boyfriend?" You can hear the way he catches himself. "Or girlfriend? Or …"

"No, not dating right now."

"Why not?"

"Focusing on my career. I'm a woman turning thirty this year, Bud. Breaking into the music scene's just an uphill climb from here. I have to make this happen now if it's ever going to happen."

"Whatever you say. What about exes?"

"Alex Janairo. J-A-N-A-I-R-O. Bass player I dated a few years back. She's not in LA anymore though."

"Where is she?"

"She moved back to Honolulu, which is where she's from." I get a twist in my chest, imagining her bright smile, her mischievous eyes. "She got married and started a family."

"You sad about that?"

"No. It's what was best for her. I never wanted kids. It was … the insurmountable issue for us."

"I'm sorry," he says. "I can relate."

"Yeah?" The fridge's fan gets loud and I close it. Don't want to burn the thing out. "Tell me about it."

The silence on the line is long enough for me to panic, wondering if he hung up.

"Hello?" I ask.

"I can just relate," he finally says. "Let's focus on this list for now, all right?"

I push myself to my feet, stretch my legs, and go sit on the bed again.

"Honestly, that's about it," I say. "I share a practice space with a few bands. I have a lot of followers online and I try to reply to them and interact with them … oh, there's this one creepy fan. I'd write them down on the list for sure—puppy-dawguys." I spell it out for him.

"I noticed they posted a few comments on your picture today."

"Yeah? What were the comments?"

"Don't recall it word for word, but it boils down to, you're hot. I mean, they think you're hot. Nothing that jumped out at me."

We go on like this. I backpedal and rattle off my neighbors, ex-bandmates, flings. I describe a time an old apartment was broken into, a cousin who went to jail. On and on until my throat hurts from doing all the talking. Bud diligently writes it all down.

After a while like this, I'm sure we've wasted our time, there's still no common ground found. It's just shallow information, names and places. The room has cooked even hotter and the sweat is pooling in the small of my back. I feel like I'm melting. I tell him and Bud gets on his phone, looking at temperatures, but he says it's not too hot near him in the Bay Area. That there's a heat wave going on in southern California. Great. That sure narrows it down.

I wipe my face with the bottom of my shirt, stain it purple like the rest of me. Me, the grape-colored woman. My shitty dye job is under my nails, the palms of my hands, fingerprints on the countertop like I dipped my fingertips in ink.

"This isn't working," I say. "We're getting off track here. We're supposed to be finding how we overlap, Bud, not conducting some junior detective investigation of the weather and random, irrelevant questions about my life. We have five days. Five days, or my life's in danger."

It's unbreathably stuffy in here. I get up and go to the window but the breeze just shoots hot air on me like a blow dryer. I remind myself about deep breaths. Deep breaths, like my mom taught me when I was a nervous little kid. I squat and close my eyes, dizzy.

"We're going to get this," he says. "Hang on."

"I'm so tired, Bud. So tired." My voice cracks. "I'm baking in here and I can't get enough air and my brain's in a loop. I'm delirious."

"Look—I know you want to go ahead rapid-fire here but maybe, just maybe, it'd be good for both of us to get off the phone for a little while. Okay?"

"No."

"Hear me out. Might be best for you to take a nap. 'Cause no one does quality thinking when they're delirious."

"I can't nap. I have to figure this out."

"We're probably not going to figure this out in the next hour. We got five days. And I do much better if I can think in silence for a while. Listen, I'll go through your socials again, further back, see if I recognize anything. If anything looks familiar."

I remain in my squatted position, just pain, a human container for pain. My heart breaks like he's abandoning me. Oh, Violet. Ever dramatic. Cue the violins! I know, logically, he's probably right. A break would be good for both of us. We can't stay on the phone every moment of every day. But, man, I don't want him to go.

"When can I call you back?" I ask in a small voice.

I resent that this dude, this slow-drawling stranger, is my lifeline. If I could, I'd tell him to just leave me to solve this mystery solo. I do not require emotional support from others. I was always the one in school who completed the group projects by myself. And aced them too! Unlike unhinged damsels in old black-and-white movies, I despise the thought of depending on the kindness of strangers.

"How about at four?" he asks. "That's two hours from now. Long enough for me to do some research and for you to get some rest."

"You have to answer," I say. "You have to."

"Look, I just turned my ringer on and up as loud as it goes. I'm giving you practically my whole day. All right?"

How nice of him, to gift me his Saturday, after I was kidnapped and left for dead in a cabin-oven. But I bite my tongue.

"Four o'clock," I repeat. "Guess that means we're in the same time zone. As if knowing that means anything."

"Hey," he says. "Hang in there, okay, Violet? We're in this together. You're not alone out there. You're going to be all right, you hear?"

"Sure," I say numbly. "Bye Bud."

I hang up the phone and hold it in my sweaty hand. Even the phone is overheating. I open the fridge, do a quick inventory of what's in there, and wonder if I should be rationing my food or something. I eat some strawberries and cheese, chug a sparkling water, let out a huge satisfying burp, and splash cold water on my face.

Two hours. What can I do for two hours?

If I were home, I could play through my set three times. My left fingers dance a moment as I imagine playing the first chords of our opener, "Not Nobody." What I wouldn't give for a guitar, a pad of paper and a pen. Or even a place to run—to get this all out of me. I'm a hamster without a wheel.

"All I can do is feel/I'm a hamster without a wheel," I sing into the air, belt it out, and then bust up at how stupid that line is. I laugh so hard I cry a little and then I'm just crying and I don't know anymore, I guess I'm losing my mind. Which isn't promising. I thought I'd last longer than this.

Maybe I do need a nap. Not that I can nap. But I lie back down on the bed for a rest and close my eyes, my pulse a relentless, frantic techno beat. And I swear there's no way I'll fall asleep, not in heat like this, not under these circumstances, but then I must, because the next thing I know I'm woken up again by the sounds of crunching gravel and an engine.

A dream? Or ... ?

I bolt upright, slick with sweat, at first confused about where I am—then realizing yet again that I'm still here in the nightmare cabin. And there is a sound, a vehicle parking, outside the window. Which means someone is here. Which means someone is either here to rescue me, or it's my kidnapper.

Every muscle in my body tenses up. My thoughts become flashes—hide? Where? Rescue? Danger?

Standing up too fast, I start to black out and immediately sit back down, my low blood pressure striking, my limbs shaking as the room colors back in. I go slower this time and hear the sound of a car door opening—*fuckfuckfuckfuckfuck*—and make my way over to the window, where I peek out to see a man with shaggy blond hair tying a bandanna over his face like a bandit not ten feet away. A white T-shirt, baggy jeans, hiking boots.

Who's this guy?

Ski mask man?

Or some hero who heard me screaming pointlessly out the window hours ago, toward the tree-spotted nothingness?

The car is a white windowless van covered in dirt, mud on the tires. There's no license plate on it. No stickers. Nothing worth remembering and reporting to the cops later. I'm pretty sure I've been sneaky here and he has no idea I'm watching him until he pulls a handgun out of his pocket with the ease of a cowboy and whips around, pointing the nose of the gun right at my face and walking toward the window with the bars I'm looking out of like the prisoner I am.

My stomach drops. Guess we can rule out this man being my rescuer. The scene from the other night, the blur of the kidnapping, it roars back in a horrible memory that has no visuals, just a sick animal feeling that I'm about to die again.

This must be how a mouse feels when it's dropped in the snake cage.

"Turn around," he says, in a low voice—almost unnaturally low, like he's pushing his voice down to sound different. Maybe I know him? Maybe that's why he's trying to change his voice? "Walk to the back of the room right now, put your hands on the countertop, and don't move until I tell you to move."

I remain frozen, desperately trying to place him. *Do* I know him? Is there anything familiar about him, other than the déjà vu to the other horrible night? As I stand here with my jaw unhinged, scouring the top half of his face that's visible for anything, anything at all—noting his muddy-colored eyes, his receding hairline and wavy shoulder-length hair, a small birthmark peeking up on a cheek, mostly hidden by the bandanna—he clicks the gun's safety off. I will myself to contain the contents of my stomach, which seem to be rising up in my throat.

"Now!" he screams.

I turn toward the back of the room like he told me to and sprint one single step before terror wins and I puke strawberries and cheese all over the floor.

BUD

DON'T WANT to be cynical. That's the last thing I aim to be, I swear. But this whole thing stinks to high heavens. Can't be blamed for thinking it, can I? Sincere as the girl sounds, whole story about being stuck out in the middle of nowhere —and I'm not saying I don't believe her, I'm not, but—why's her social media tell another story? Why am I forbidden from calling the police, or reaching out to anyone who can back up the fact she's missing? How would me and a stranger lady with a music career and pretty purple hair and green eyes be connected?

Okay, maybe I am cynical. But I've got reasons. Plenty. I'll rattle them off, simple as a shopping list.

I've been lied to before. Lied to packaged up with a big old ribbon of truth on it, so you feel crazy for calling it a lie. The worst kind. Like the time Daniel Barber said it wasn't him who lit my mama's car on fire in the parking lot of the diner where she works, where he looked me in the eye and said he didn't do it, when I saw the burns on his fingers for weeks afterward. All because my mama was dating Daniel's dad the preacher and Daniel didn't know how to take it. So he took it out on my mama's poor battered sedan with some squirts of gas and a lighter. And now my mama and the preacher are long married and Daniel's my family, my other-mothered brother, and he still lies to my face and says it wasn't him who lit that car up like Independence Day way back when, and everyone shakes their head at me like I'm the sorry one at the dinner table, "Oh, Bud, not that again. It wasn't Daniel who torched that car. It was so long ago." I can hold a grudge, but don't lose sight of what I'm saying here: I've been lied to.

I mean back when I went down to visit Emily Morgan, she lied herself a whole personality. Said she was successful, worked in the movie business, she was a grip. She was a grip, all right. The second I entered her basement apartment I felt like I had entered a zombie underbelly, pale, sweating strangers sleeping in odd corners, food out to rot on the table-top, the sick smoky barbecue sauce smell in the air. And then she put her hands on my cheeks and led me to her room. She opened a little bag on her skirt and told me she loved me. Those glassy green eyes. Long hair she wore in a sandy braid like a rope. A long, loping laugh, a guitar she played some-times in gentle strums. We didn't leave her apartment for weeks, a month, months, a stupor's what it was. I was stupid, chasing the lie that was Emily Morgan. Ignored the gas and fire. Pretended it was fun. I knew, deep down, this was bad news, very bad news. Turn around and never look back kind news. But somehow, despite the mess of her, I believed she would turn it around, that she was the success she had sold herself as in our messages, the airbrushed headshot, an odd thing, I guess, for a grip to have anyway.

Emily Morgan was the one and only dating app experi-ence I ever had. Why we were matched, hundreds of miles away, I'll never really know, because I never really knew her. After she ODed, I left quickly, scared to die myself, as if her condition was contagious. (Though—wasn't it?) Reached out to her family back in Missouri to lend my condolences but was shocked to hear them call her Emerald, her name was Emerald. A woman died by the name of Emily when she was born an Emerald, I just—I'm still baffled by the twist and who that woman really was, when all I knew was her demise.

Those aren't all the lies I've been on the receiving end of, though. There are more. Many more. Like being told I was the only one—but, hell, I'm dwelling now, stewing into old emotional debts that'll never get repaid and what's the point anyway.

I pop open another beer and lie back on the couch. My back door's still kicked open in front of me, the trees shaking with wind, and the cat licks her paws up on my kitchen counter. I'm too lazy to yell at her to stop it. On my phone, it's unnerving to see the missed calls in the triple digits. I tap it to make the notifications disappear. I look her up again, Violet Wilde; even her name sounds like a lie. But I'm not going to say I don't believe her.

I just don't get it.

For instance, if she's stuck in some cabin in an unknown location, why'd she just post another picture of a shimmering lake surrounded by buildings and palm trees? My bullshit alarm's screaming. I scroll back through her pictures—the hair dye one from earlier, yesterday there's a picture of a cactus in a planter pot and the words "My son" and then there's a picture from a show, there she is onstage with a blue guitar hanging from her neck, singing soulfully into a microphone. Where's the real Violet begin and end, then? And I can't call anyone to ask their opinion. I've just got to trust this woman's voice on the other end of the line that she's who she says she is.

I scroll back, far back. Swipe, swipe, swipe. This lady's life in reverse—her fan-packed shows, to recording sessions, to excitement at buying her condo, to a long string of tours through cities I've never been in, to a backlit photo kissing that woman Alex that's pretty hot, I must admit … guitars and brunches and beaches. Snippets that suggest a life. I don't know, though. I don't see a lot of overlap between us, besides our passion for fresh fruit and sunsets. The places in LA she's taken pictures of have no overlap with my hazy time there, besides us both having visited the Hollywood sign. And she doesn't appear to have any record of having lived up here—nothing in the Bay Area save a single show she played at a place called the Happy Days Pavilion on the Jolvix campus nearly six years ago. I know that name, Jolvix, the tech company that makes all that futuristic crap.

I'm flipping through this stranger's life with an ache of déjà vu, and I don't know if I've dreamt it up or if it's real, that déjà vu. It's easy to feel like someone's familiar when you've stared at their frozen, photographed face long enough.

I don't know, man.

It's exhausting, really. That and all the beer. I put my phone down with a clunk on the floor and just let my eyes rest a moment. Let it all settle, maybe into some kind of sense. Because right now there's not a ton of that. And it's a warm afternoon, the sun hitting my legs right now. And I hear the cat's purr, a rumble like a sweet engine, and the world feels so heavy and light at once.

Next thing I know, I'm sitting up in the cold dark, wiping the drool from the corner of my dry mouth, crickets loud through the open door.

"Shit," I say.

Heart's hammering in my chest. I push myself up and go to the kitchen sink, drink and drink and drink. When I wipe my lips, I pull my phone out and see it's dark and dead. Of course it is. I've overslept, ran out of juice, and missed her call by a long shot. She's probably freaking out. Though what's the point? Of us talking, I mean? What'd I even find, and what could she possibly figure out if she really is stuck in some cabin somewhere? This whole thing makes me feel like there's a jackhammer in my skull. Or maybe it's dehydration.

In the bathroom, I swallow three ibuprofen and have a bloodshot staring contest with myself in the mirror. Disgusted, as usual. I divert my eyes and go back to the kitchen, grab a beer, and head back to my room, where I plug my phone in and lie on the bed. When my phone glows again, I see it's almost midnight. There are notifications that I missed eleven calls, but no new voicemails. I tell myself she's settled down. This space is good for us. Gives us time to think it through, though I'll be honest, as I stare at the dust doing its ballerina dance in the lamplight of my bedroom, I've figured nothing out. But it's nice to have the silence to think it through.

I search her name online. There are a ton of music blogs reviewing her band's latest album. Buried many pages deep I find some more personal stuff—a pic of her probably fifteen years ago, having won some local poetry contest. She had bleached, pixie-cut hair then. She's reading behind a podium. At that same time, I was that age too. But I was in Aubrey and my whole life was football. If we'd gone to high school together, there's no way we would have crossed paths. Girls with pixie haircuts, girls who wrote poetry, they were like another species. I run across a defunct YouVid account of hers from seven years ago called Wilde Tunes filled with dozens of videos. Almost all of it is her talking direct to camera and reviewing albums from bands I've never heard of. I try to watch one but zone out. It's just not my cup of tea. And I don't think there's much here anyway.

Strange to think about the graveyard of the internet, the dumb records we leave behind us. Forgotten video accounts, images of brunches—that's what's left of us. That's how we're searchable, remembered.

I go back to Instagrat, click on that weirdo commenter she talked about, puppydawguys. But when I go all the way back to the first couple photos posted to their account, selfies, it's clearly a kid that can't be older than thirteen. Add that to the fact he lives three thousand miles away and I think we can pretty safely rule that one out.

Back on Violet's account, I stare at her picture. Zoom in with two fingers. Her ever-shining eyes, rosy cheeks. I watch a music video of her and her band, though most of the video's focused on her with the band blurred behind her in the shadows. A song with a somber, catchy hook. I close my eyes, taking in her throaty voice, her lyrics. *I never knew how lost I was/ til I found you/ and I never found myself/ til I lost you.* The way she strums the guitar and sings so soulfully to the camera, her faded purple hair falling over her closed eyes, it catches me with emotion. I don't know why. I guess that's how music is, it captures the parts we can't find the way to say ourselves and says it.

She's good. Real good.

I buy her album online with a click and listen to it, getting the bright idea that maybe I should ask her to sing to me when we talk again so I can be sure it's really her. The cat comes up on the bed and nestles into my armpit and purrs and we both fall asleep that way, together, and though a tiny part of me rings a little alarm bell—get up, Bud, get up, wait for the poor girl to call back—I'm just so tired, so relaxed, I figure it's all right. We've got time. There's nothing left to say right now. Whatever I could say, I could say it better in the morning.

———

"You motherfucker," she says when I pick up my ringing phone, groggy, the sun just starting to shine through my window.

"Hello?" I say again, as if I didn't know who the unknown number was.

"You fucking motherfucker," she repeats.

And I wish it were the first time I'd been called such a

thing, but it's far from it. I sit up in my bed, sweaty and stretching, unsure what time it is.

"Sorry," I offer. "I fell asleep."

"I'm kidnapped in the middle of nowhere," she says, her voice cracking. "Losing my mind! And there you are, *sleeping*. Soundly. God, what a *shit* you are."

"Not disagreeing with you."

She blows air into the phone. Her voice is shaking and I can hear movement, like she's pacing or moving around. "Do you even care?" she almost yells. "What happens to me? If I live or die?"

"Course I care, I just—"

"Two hours. You said I could call you in two hours."

"Sorry, I lost track of time—"

"It's been almost *sixteen* hours. I called you, Bud. I trusted your word. And your voicemail box is full and it just kept ringing and ringing—"

"Full? Oh. Shit. Probably all those messages you left—"

"So now it's my fault?"

"No, I just—"

"Fuck you, Bud," she says.

I shake my head, heavy, swollen with something nearing a headache. "Listen—"

"No, you shut all the way up right now and *you* listen. A man came here—my kidnapper—he came here yesterday after we talked and Bud, I was scared, I was so scared, and when he left I called you and called you and I got nothing." Her voice wavers. "I was so terrified you'd never pick up again. Don't you get it? You're all I have. I don't know why and God knows I'd do anything for this not to be the case, but it is the case and—and—"

"A guy came there?" I ask, sitting up straighter. Standing to my feet and going to my kitchen to make some coffee. "And—shit. What happened?"

Soft sobs fill my ears and flood me with guilt as I put a

pod in the coffeemaker with a crunch. This is real, I decide, hearing her. It's definitely real. As the coffee cries into my mug along with her I get a sick twist in my gut, that little voice in my ear, *You worthless sack of crap. How could anyone rely on you?* I try to shake it off because, right as it is, it can't help now.

"He had a bandanna over his face, but I'm sure it's the same guy who kidnapped me. He put a gun to my head, made me turn around and put my hands on the kitchen counter, and he—he—"

I brace myself, shaking my head, waiting to hear some horror. "It's okay, Violet. Go on. You can tell me."

"He—brought in groceries, restocked the fridge. Lugged in two fans and plugged them in. Asked if that made the temperature better."

Her words settle between us, bewildering me.

"Wait … what?" I ask.

"Then he was gone. He said 'Take care' and left. I watched him drive away, screaming after him. He didn't stop."

I wait all twisted up for her to explain how he beat her, assaulted her, hurt her. But the silence drags on as she sniffles on the line.

"That's it?" I ask slowly. "He restocked your groceries and brought you some fans and … left? I mean—'Take care?'"

"I was so scared," she says.

"Sounds terrifying," I say, then bite my tongue. Shouldn't be a jerk. I mean, he had a gun. But you've got to admit, this sounds more like a polite hotel concierge than it does a serial killer. Luckily she doesn't seem to notice the sarcastic edge to what I said. I guess being strangers obscures sarcasm, which is probably a plus when it comes to me.

"I hate this," she whispers. "I don't understand."

"I'm so sorry," I say, walking to my back porch and plopping down on the wooden steps. The bees are buzzing around the overgrown passion flower vines on the brick wall, the knee-high grass is bent back with a breeze, the sky's clear and blue. And I feel bad, being somewhere so pretty and free when this girl is locked up, crying in my ear. "Look, anything you can remember about this guy? You catch a glimpse of his car, I don't know, anything stand out to you about him that might be a clue?"

"Nothing. He drove a white van, no license plate. Blond shoulder-length hair, blue bandanna. I didn't know if I knew him. There was—it looked like some kind of birthmark or mole on his face, but it was half-covered. I couldn't catch a full glimpse."

"That's something," I say. "A mole or whatever. Which cheek?"

"His left. It's not enough, Bud. It's not enough to figure anything out. Unless—does that ring any bells for you?"

I close my eyes, sift through pictures of people I know, who I've met, flipping through years of frozen memories, try and imagine the man with the blond hair and some mark on his face. But I come up empty, opening my eyes. "Not off the top of my head. I'll keep thinking."

She sniffs. "I'm so—I'm still so mad that you didn't pick up."

"I'm real sorry about that."

"What were you even *doing*?"

Embarrassed, I sip my coffee. "Just relaxing."

"Relaxing."

"You know. I work hard all week slinging a hammer. Saturday comes and I drink some beers and lay out on the couch."

"So I'm here with a guy with a gun to my head, scared I'm about to become a pile of blood pudding, and you're there lying around on your ass and getting drunk in the middle of the day."

"Look, I apologized. Multiple times."

"Hope you enjoyed yourself."

Lord, this girl's a live wire.

"I did, thanks," I say, unable to help myself. "And I hope you've enjoyed your fresh stock of sparkling water and fans."

She blows a sigh into the phone. "You truly are an asshole. But yes, the fans have helped."

"I'll have you know that while I was 'lying around on my ass' I did a deep dive back into your Instagrat account. Someone's still posting pictures, by the way."

"Of *what*?"

"A little cactus."

"Barnabus," she says. "He's my—"

"Your son?" I ask.

A beat passes. "How'd you know I was going to say that?"

"Because it's what the caption says on the picture."

"I guess anyone who knows me or follows me knows that I'm a plant daddy."

"A what?"

"You know, I'm very into my houseplants. No kids, no pets, I have to dote on something."

"Plant daddy," I repeat.

"What else did they post?"

"Pic of a lake surrounded by buildings—"

"Silver Lake Reservoir. That's right near my condo. So, interesting—this week I took a couple pics there and a pic of Barnabus. This person has my phone. They have access to my phone somehow, even without the passcode. They're using pics I took but never posted. Why?"

"I don't know. To make it seem like life's easy and breezy and you haven't been kidnapped?"

"Well, all that's going to come to an end soon because we have practice tonight and Benzo and Lila will for sure worry that I'm not there and that they can't reach me. I *never* skip practice. They'll call me and realize that something is seriously wrong when I don't pick up."

"Let's hope so."

The sun's baking my arms already so I head inside for a UV break. I put Violet on speaker and set the phone on my kitchen counter so I can go through some mail on the counter. Copy of a bill I paid online. Statement I could get online. Advertisement for DashDrone. Early birthday card from my mama—I put that one aside. Violet asks what I'm doing and I tell her. Real exciting, isn't it? Listening to a man go through his mail.

"Cute that your mom sends you birthday cards," she says.

"Mama's big on cards," I say, chucking everything but the birthday card into the trash. "She paints them herself."

"Awww. How sweet."

"Yeah. Watercolors. She's real good at it. The diner she works at has her paintings up and she's even sold a couple."

"Sounds like you're close."

"We are. We're just different."

"How so?"

"Well, when I was young, I didn't want what she has. Saw more in life than staying in one small town and marrying someone and popping out little carbon copies. You know? I saw big things for myself. Never had much imagination— never really imagined exactly what those big things were— but I figured they were out there."

"And were they?"

"I don't know. If they were I never found them."

"I mean, you got into a really good school on scholarship. That's something."

I open my fridge and stare at it. A lot of condiments and beer, some eggs and bread. I should eat something. Instead, I grab a beer.

"I went to college less than a week. Sat in there looking around me at all these smartass kids from all over the country and I could barely read the syllabus. Went to practice and all these players on the team were pros, I mean, they were abso- lutely killer players. And I knew right away there'd been a mistake in bringing me here. Wasn't right. There was no way I could swim with these big fish. I thought, to hell with this. And so I just stopped going."

"You stopped going."

"I did."

I pop open the beer and sit on a stool at my counter, taking a sip.

"Is that—did you just open a beer?"

"Sure did."

"Is it even noon yet?"

"Somewhere it is."

"For the love of God, don't drink a beer right now!" she almost shrieks. "Yesterday you just ditched out on me because you got so sauced in the middle of the day. Did you learn nothing?"

"I learned to keep my phone plugged in. If it hadn't have run out of batteries, I'd have heard it."

"Bud, I'm serious. You care about me living and dying? Do you?"

"Course I do."

"Pour that beer out right now and don't make the mistake you did yesterday."

I sputter out a laugh, squeezing the can in my hand with a slight aluminum buckle. "Oh, come on."

"I'm serious," she says, in a quivering voice. "I'm trying so hard to hang on right now, to be strong—I need you to not be the person you were yesterday. I need that from you."

The sound that leaves my mouth is like the hiss of a pressure valve. I pound a few gulps of the beer and then eye it in my hand again in the silence of the line. Annoyance creeps with tiny feet along my skin and I'd like to swat it away. The truth can feel that way. I drain a few more glugs of it and get up, pour the rest out theatrically, as if she were here to see it.

"I'm pouring it out," I tell her. "Happy now?"

"I am, Bud," she says, her voice lighter, surprised. Been a

while since I've made a woman sound that way. "You really did that?"

"Yep."

"Well ... thank you."

"You got it," I say, sitting back on my stool, trying to fight the resentment. Petty of me. Ridiculous. When there's someone in my ear stuck out in the middle of who knows where with her life on the line? It should be the least I can do. Even though I know it would have been fine and it was stupid of her to think—but I let it go.

We keep talking. I describe my apartment because she asks me to. She tells me about the dreams she had last night. But I'd be lying if I said I didn't lose a bit of my gusto as the clock creeps past noon. She goes around and around about the man who came yesterday, about the kidnapping, the details just a soapy muck circling the drain. Repeating herself over and over again like a junkie—the mark on his face, the concern he expressed for her, his vehicle, did she know him? She's not sure but she's pretty sure she didn't. I settle into a lot of *uh-huh*ing, which I do well. I'm a good listener if the word "listener" has quotation marks around it. I know how to perform it. Real thing? Not so much. Funny because I've never considered myself a performer, but when it comes to real life ...

I still have two beers in the fridge over there, that fridge humming and gleaming at me from the kitchen.

"Am I boring you?" she asks. "Tell me if I am."

"Course not," I say, getting up from the stool and leaning away from the receiver to let out a yawn. "This is important."

"We have to keep talking," she says, as if she can hear me slipping. "We're on day four now. You know? We're halfway through the time the note says. And we've still found nothing that links us."

"Well, we've figured out we both love fresh fruit and sunsets."

"Come on, I'm serious. Talk to me about when you lived in LA. Your turn, fill my ears."

Even though the sun's not on me anymore, I swat a prickle of heat from my neck. "'Living' is a generous word for what I did down there."

"Well, tell me about it," she says.

"Not a lot there," I admit, getting up and opening my door for the thumping of cat paws. She flounces onto the couch like it was made for her, curling up and licking her tail in seconds.

"Tell me about your apartment, the area," she says. "Start there."

"There was no 'my apartment,'" I say darkly, pacing the room a few seconds before deciding to do something with this ugly energy. I direct myself to my hamper and pick it up, head out the back door to the machines under the deck in the back. *Thump* and the top of the machine opens up like a white mouth. *Plunk*, dirty laundry falls in. "Who knows if it was even Emily's apartment. Can we talk about something else?"

"Sure. Of course. What about other serious relationships you've been in?"

"What is this, therapy?" I ask, annoyed.

"I guess?" she says with a strained laugh. "Unintentionally?"

I ball up jeans and socks and T-shirts and deposit them into the machine each with a *ping*.

"Look," she says, more seriously now. Her voice shakes like a woman on a brisk walk. "You think I want this? To be picking the brain trust and the heart scabs of some stranger I've never met?"

"Brain trust and heart scabs," I say, stopping a moment to savor the words before pouring in the detergent that, I'll be honest, I'm stealing from my landlady. But I do pull her packages into the foyer, I do move her patio furniture into her shed every time it rains.

"My point is," she says, panting. "I don't want this either. But we're connected. And I'll find it if it takes all fucking day and night. I'm not going to die this way, Bud."

"What the hell are you doing?" I ask, stepping into the yard, the sunshine, where a couple of squirrels are chasing each other over the fence.

"I'm talking to you frankly," she says.

"No, I mean … you sound all out of breath."

"Oh," she says. "Running in place. To get exercise. So I don't lose my mind or my muscles."

"Okay," I say, plopping my ass on the step again and wishing I had a beer. The sun's at that perfect afternoon angle of the day—not too hot, not too cool. A beer just fits the moment.

"Bud," she says, catching her breath. "I feel like you're not willing to tell me anything. I ask you about LA and you skirt it."

I shake my head. All that, the whole time there, is a pit of bad memories. The kind that give you the cold sweats and make you double back in fear and disbelief—holding Emily dizzy on the bed, both of us too wasted to speak, strangers who yelled in the halls as they came and went, tin foil and lighters and beautiful blond hair full of perfume, the smell of amber incense on the windowsill and vomit on my shirt, selling blood and doing weird brain scans for cash and everything short of prostituting, that was really my life? There's no point in talking about any of this, the dumpster of details. There was no overlap between all that and Violet. I didn't leave Emily Morgan's apartment except for a handful of instances, and it was only to get some money and drugs—in that order. And the last time I did, I came back to find Emily cold and stiff and just a body, just a body, not a girl anymore.

"How hard is it," I say, in as level a voice as I can, "to understand that some shit you don't want to talk about? And isn't worth talking about?"

"My life is—"

"Look, unless you were a junkie in Long Beach those couple of months I lived there we have no overlap, you get it?"

"Fine," she says, her voice a bit softer. "But that was a long time ago. Tell me about your other relationships since then."

"My other relationships," I say. "Plural? Since then? I only ever had one real long-term relationship, and it was before Emily."

Priya. Priya, as dead to me as Emily, yet alive as ever in London. I push her out as quick as a door shutting—she's not even in the goddamn country, what the hell would she even have to do with this. The rage that rises forms a taste in my mouth. I close my eyes to forget her. Will myself, as I do, issue it like a self-imposed threat: *forget her*. I peer behind me back in through my back door, into the apartment. The cat's sprawled out in the middle of the wooden floor in the spotlight of sunshine, eyeing me with a look of satisfaction.

"Nothing worth going into," I say in a voice that sounds surprisingly at ease considering I feel like I could smash a fist through something. Wouldn't, of course. Just a thought. "And she lives in another country."

"What about—"

"What about you," I ask, getting up from the porch, taking a glance at my phone's clock on the way in—way past noon, way way past noon. How long's this going to eat into my Sunday, anyway? The refrigerator's white with promise in the corner. Soon as this call's done, I don't care, I'm popping both those beers and sitting on that couch and not moving for at least an hour. "You haven't told me anything."

"I've told you a *ton*."

"Can't help but notice how the only people you think might be worried about your disappearance are your bandmates," I say as I go to my room and make the bed, tossing the plaid quilt across with one arm and the striped pillow on top of it with my other arm. "You telling me no one else is going to call you and wonder why you don't pick up?"

"I'm not a phone person."

"Neighbors?"

"They—we keep to ourselves."

"Friends?"

"I don't have time for that lately. I've been so focused on music."

"Family?"

"No."

That's all she says, *no*. A red light in word form.

"No," I repeat, I don't know, just to make sure.

"I don't have family."

"None?"

"My parents died in a car crash years ago. I'm an only child." Her voice cuts out—not the connection. Her voice. It just drops for a second. She clears her throat and it returns. "That definitely isn't how we're connected."

"Well, gosh, I'm so—so sorry to hear that."

I get a pang in my chest and head back to the living room, drop on my wood floor next to the kitty, rub my hand on her belly. Because awkward as my family is—my mama with her long meandering voicemail messages, her embarrassing red-faced preacher husband, and Daniel in his choke-me ties, receding hairline, and bragging of all he knows about insurance policies—it's still a family. When I come home to Aubrey for holidays, I'm a goddamn celebrity. I can't imagine life without all that. It's the unsaid security that's boosted my confidence all these years, the people I knew I could always count on or fall back on if I had to. Imagine not having that.

"Maybe we know someone mutually in the Bay Area," she says, breezing over my sympathy. "Have you ever lived in Berkeley?"

"For a time. And I've done jobs all over the place."

"Okay, let's try this for an exercise. Ready? List everyone.

Just shoot it off, list everyone you know, especially anyone near Berkeley."

`"I've lived in the Bay ten years, you expect me to just ... name everyone I've ever met?"

"Whoever you can remember, yes. Just rattle it off, stream of consciousness, you can do this, go, go, go!"

I shake my head. She says it with the pep of a workout instructor. I find her energy, even over the phone, too much. Not that she doesn't have every right in the world to be too much given the circumstances. But man, racking my brain for every contact I've ever had with the pressure of some stranger's life weighing on me? Not the mellow Sunday I was looking forward to.

What a dick I am, to even think that.

The room's heated up and those beers keep beckoning me. I'm going to stick to my word though. I've made a habit of disappointing women all my life, but this has to be different. It could mean life or death—though it's hard for the stakes to feel that high with the whole sparkling water and fan thing. Can't get over that.

I take the broom out of my kitchen closet to keep myself busy. Sweep the whole place as I talk to Violet on speaker and try to name off anyone who comes to mind from the past few years—my buddy who owns the local dive bar, my neighbors, my landlord, ex-roommates, the old carpenter Andrew who took me under his wing and apprenticed me, rest in peace. Relationships, hours spent together, disagreements and understandings and handshakes and pints drunk together reduced to names, sound bites: Pete, Amy, Travis, Shannika, Ian, Antony, Denise, Tan, A.J., Margot. Life, compressed. I move on to scrubbing my bathroom and try to remember names connected with the bigger jobs I've worked in the area —the McMansions I painted next to the train station, that rich family's guest house on their vineyard up in Napa, friends of Bob's, all the while Violet's on the other end of the line running in circles around her cabin prison and *nope*ing me to exhaustion.

By late afternoon, my laundry's done, folded, put away. My apartment's clean as a hospital and my throat's sore from all the talking. Over a decade I've lived in the Bay and there's no overlap with Violet's former life, except obvious stuff like we've both walked the Golden Gate Bridge and shopped on Telegraph Avenue. When she asks me about my ex again I open the fridge and stare at the two beers there, heart pounding. God, I know it's awful, but I want to get off the phone. Get off this call and be left alone and not hear a voice in my ear buzzing like a relentless little bee.

But she persists. "Other than Emily—sorry, my condolences, I'm so sorry to bring her up again—you keep avoiding talking about, you know. Your other serious relationship?"

I push my tongue to the top of the roof of my mouth and slam the fridge shut. Damn it. This again. Plus my stomach's gurgling and I need something to eat. "Priya Patel," I mutter.

"Priya Patel," Violet repeats, then says it slower. "Priya Patel." She gasps. "Bud, that's it! That's the connection! Priya Patel—grew up in Berkeley, right?"

"Yeah," I saw slowly, sinking onto a stool at the kitchen counter. "You know her?"

"I mean—we weren't close or anything. But we went to high school together. Graduated the same year. She was class president!"

"Of course she was president. Priya's always got to be on top."

"Bud! We did it!" Violet laughs. "We figured it out!"

I rub the stubble on my chin, mystified at the connection. "But—I don't ... I don't get it."

"Neither do I, but that's what the note says—that we need to figure out how we're connected. And we figured it out. You hear me?" she shouts, and I pull the phone away from my ear. "Yeah, you assholes who did this—*we won*. Listening? We won! We won your stupid, fucked-up little game! Now you can let me out!"

A long silence expands between us. I shake my head, unable to celebrate quite yet, because none of this makes sense. "So you were, what, friends with Priya in high school?"

"Not *friends*. We were in a couple classes together. Didn't really interact much. But what matters is, I know her. We both know her. I could sob like a baby. I'm so relieved!"

"So then what would the significance be?" I ask. "This doesn't add up, Violet. What would Priya have anything to do with your kidnapping?"

"I don't have a clue, but she's the link. And all the directions said was that we needed to figure out the link and we did it. We did it!" She sniffles. "Oh my God, oh my God, I'm so happy right now, I'm just—I need to sit down. I'm shaking. Dizzy. Oh, I can't believe it. I'm not going to die. I'm going to be okay!"

"Listen though," I say. "Priya's—she's in London, she has a whole life over there. She's a bigshot editor at a magazine, she's a mom, she's not about to get involved in some bizarre crime here in the states. What would she have to do with the kidnapping?"

"We didn't need to solve the whole mystery, Bud, just figure out the connection."

"Yeah, but why?"

"Bud," Violet says again, her voice steadier. "Just be happy. We did it, okay? We figured it out."

But I can't be happy. It makes no sense. I ask Violet if she wouldn't mind giving me an hour to process this and get some dinner or something, because it's a lot to take in, and something about it isn't sitting right with me.

"You want to get off the phone?" Violet asks in a small voice.

"Violet, we've been talking the entire day," I say as nicely as I can. "I need a break. We figured it out, right? So you can rest a little while. Maybe your gun-toting sparkling water delivery boy's on his way back right now to let you free."

"You think so?"

"I mean, it's possible."

She's quiet. "Will you promise to pick up the phone in exactly one hour?"

"I will."

"Promise not to get drunk and pass out and forget about me?"

"'Course I wouldn't."

"I can trust you," she says, almost like she's trying out the phrase.

"You can."

I can sense how much she wants to hang on, but we hang up.

And I open the fridge and crack a beer and drain the whole thing in one go.

VIOLET

PRIYA PATEL. *Priya Patel.* My heart drums the rhythm of her name.

I'm gazing out the stupid window again, hands gripping the bars that have warmed in the late afternoon sun. Waiting. Waiting for the roar of a vehicle, for the man to come back. My legs are cool, the fan pointed right at me. Thanks for that, kidnapper dude. Outside, the hush of high grass and faraway trees. Same picture I've stared at now for hours on end. I'm getting ready to lose my mind, shaking the bars like an ape at the zoo.

Priya Patel, Priya Patel. A girl I knew in passing as a teenager. How does she fit into this?

Doesn't matter, Violet. I wasn't told to solve a mystery, just find a connection. And that's what I did. I take puffs of air in and blow them out, cocking my ear for the sound of human beings: the roll of tires, an engine hum, but nothing yet. This nightmare will end soon. Bud and I cracked the code, we figured out the connection. The game is over. I read the note again. I have it memorized. Come on, masked jerk! Come back and fulfill your end of the deal.

It is the worst feeling in life, being at the mercy of a

stranger. Having to trust the universe to save you. I've never had much faith in the universe. I want to save my fucking self.

"Come on, prick!" I yell out the open window. "Come on, Priya Patel!"

Priya Patel. The connection. But my kidnapper? I mean, she's not the *actual* kidnapper, obviously. But is she the mastermind behind all this? Did she hire the guy to do this to me? Why? The girl with shiny black hair to her waist and flawless brown skin, the girl who sat up front in every class and raised her hand and got her papers handed back with big red As on them? I can't remember ever exchanging a single word with her, honestly.

In high school, I was the opposite of Priya Patel. Class president? Pffft. I was an anarchist. I slouched in the back row of class and doodled on my quizzes and wrote poems in a special notebook covered in skulls. I was the girl who brought her guitar to school every day. The girl in heavy eyeliner who pierced her own nose with a safety pin and cut all her hair off in the bathroom and bleached it nearly white. The girl who teachers thought had real "potential," which is an insult in disguise, isn't it? That word "potential," it implies something's not put to good use, something's wasted. Speaking of which, I got wasted a lot in high school, too. There was this parking structure a couple blocks away from school where I'd hang out on the rooftop with other misfits and drink peppermint schnapps stolen from someone's parents' liquor cabinet. I wrote songs with titles like "Sad Little Witch" and "You Can Hurt Me If You Want." I was such an adorable teenage cliché.

One would think this is rebellion, right? But no, my parents loved the shit out of me.

"Vi, that song of yours called 'Men Are Scum' is so damn *catchy*," Dad said. Bright green eyes, salt-and-pepper beard, a long-sleeved button-up shirt he wore to work to cover his tattoos. He stood there in my bedroom doorway, eating a popsicle—his addiction. "It's been in my head all day."

Mom popped up behind him and put her head on his shoulder, ever cute with her dyed red curls and cat-eye glasses. "I think 'Burn the Fucking World Down' is better. You're a force to be reckoned with, flower girl."

"I'm trying to do my math homework," I sighed from my bed.

"Need help?" Dad asked, passing Mom the popsicle so she could eat it.

"Just some quiet," I said pointedly, accompanying my tone with a look.

"Message received," he said with a bow.

"Don't work too hard," Mom said as she handed Dad his popsicle back. Then to me, "By the way, I cleaned your bong. It's back in your closet."

My parents were stoners. They met in a commune. They grew weed in the backyard next to the elaborate vegetable garden and did mushrooms together on their wedding anniversary.

"Thanks," I said.

They closed the door and I could hear them murmuring about me, about what a good girl I was. No matter what I did, I was a good girl to them.

They're so gutting, memories I have of them like that— every time I told them to leave me alone. Every time they asked me to go somewhere with them and I stayed in instead. Every time I shut the door so I didn't have to hear their voices. The journal entries from that time, filled with a longing to leave home forever, to go far away from them and from Berkeley and all of it and start a new life, find out who I really was. Alone. I wanted to do everything alone.

I got my wish. I fulfilled my potential. I was accepted into a decent university in Michigan. My parents never pushed college on me, but they were glad for me. Whatever made me happy. So I went, with my guitar and not much else. Back-pack. A couple boxes. Grew my hair out, back to its mousy brown color, tossed my eyeliner, took the ring out of my nose. Fit right in with all the normals, as I used to call them in high school.

Fell in love with this boy Alex Lee at a poetry reading on campus.

He was devastating.

Jet hair just slightly overgrown, falling over his eyes. His eyes. I'll spend the rest of my life mentally tracing the sleepy shape of his eyes. The color—you know sand wet by the rain? Warm and shadowy and gold? That was the exact color and sentiment of his eyes.

Oh, Alex.

We loved hard. We were such softies, such emotional animals at the core of it, yet our relationship was barbed and full of an alluring kind of almost-violence. The way we'd stop, mid-fight, and make out mean in a dark, stinking alley-way. The way I'd write a minor-noted thing about him that I'd sing and play for him, that would then provoke him to disappear for days until he reappeared with a thing he wrote on his own. He played the keyboard, sassily and moodily. His voice wasn't half-bad. And then, oh the sex. Next level. So electrically charged. So new every time.

Until one night, that infamous night. How stupid, yes? How predictable. Drama at an open mic night. I sang my first song ever in front of a crowd. Me and my guitar. Played this dumb song I'd written, was warmed by the applause like a cold-blooded creature. It was weird. I changed that night, transformed. I even saw it in the scratched-up bathroom mirror of the venue. My hair, still growing out, was a plum waterfall—I'd recently tried purple for the first time. My green eyes were bright as a traffic light. There I was. Was that me? That girl was new, was different.

What that girl was, was a beginning.

When I came out and the crowd surrounded me hive-like, bee-like, humming-with-love-like, this shift happened. I saw the future laid out before me in wildly different directions, with crooked path-lines. And oh, I wanted not to be the mousy girl majoring in English with the Michigan boyfriend and the question mark future. I wanted to be the girl with violet hair, Violet, headed out of here like a girl-shaped rock-etship. It was weird, it made my lips hum and my skin buzz the way that strangers loved me so instantly. Bewilderingly. Really?

Alex accused me of being superficial, to pursue a career based on one stupid show. To almost graduate with a degree in English at a respectable university but then drop out and leave for Los Angeles immediately, for what? Was I a dog? Wave a bone at me and away I went?

I went.

As the bus rolled into my new destination, the smog painted the cityscape a mysterious tan-gray, and my pulse rolled like a drumline at the sight of it. It looked apocalypti-cally beautiful. It was real. I thought of my parents, of my mother telling me I was talented and I could make it some-day. They were so freshly dead I could smell the dirt of their funerals. Meanwhile, Alex sent me text after text. If texts could weep, his were wet with it.

I'm a chasm. Why am I thinking of Alex again?

Out the window here in my hell cabin, everything's still the same. A blah slice of nature. Tedious. Still. It could be a photo for all I know. A cloud has spread across the sky, cotton stretched and pulled apart. I pace the floorboards and hum a tune, one that seems to rise up from nowhere and come out. A sad one with a twist of hope.

Priya Patel. Priya Patel.

So Bud is Priya Patel's ex. Priya is the connection between us. Bud—who I can't even picture. I've never even asked him what he looks like because who cares. He talks with a honey-drawl like a man who's never had a reason to hurry in his life. Which is aggravating. He doesn't strike me as anyone special. Just some dude parked on his ass all weekend downing beers, his to-do list blank. No motivation for doing anything greater with his life than fixing up houses. Who lives like that? At thirty? That seems weird, now that I think about it.

I go back to the window, peering out, but nothing's changed. I blow out a big sigh.

"Come on," I say to the air out there. "We found the connection. It was Priya Patel." A flame rises in me and my voice rises along with it. "Play fair, you dick!"

That's the worst part of this. I'm being rational, I'm following rules, I'm complying—all assuming that this person is going to hold up their end of the bargain. I count the days on my hands again, whispering, "Thursday, Friday, Saturday, Sunday." I don't know if this game started Thursday or Friday, but I'd rather be safe than sorry. I have three days left. Are they going to let me live the three days out here regardless? What about Bud? Why is he free to lie around like a sloth-man guzzling brewskies and I'm locked up like an animal? How does that make sense? Misogynists.

"Sir," I yell through the bars. "I'd like to speak to your manager!"

I laugh for a minute until tears prick my eyes and then I sob a little sob into my hands. I'm so mixed up. So very mixed up. And at the bottom of all this—underneath the rage, the bewilderment, the sick nerves, the circular illogic that grips my mind—I'm just a simple creature who doesn't want to die.

I don't want to get shot by that gun.

When the guy came here yesterday and I saw a gun pointed at me again like an ugly promise and I spewed all over myself and the ground, it was the nightmare of the kidnapping all over again. I walked to the kitchenette like I was told and turned around and I begged him to please spare me, to not hurt me, not touch me. I scrunched my eyes closed in nauseated anticipation of what was next and my mind worked at about a thousand miles an hour making movies of all the possible horrible scenarios. The noise of a gunshot; a painful blow to the back of the head; the pull of my clothes coming off; or worst of all, nothing—absolutely nothing.

Goodbye Violet.

But instead I heard rattling and the sound of a man whistling. *Whistling.* Derp-dee-derp, just whistling like a care-free man getting a job done. I was dying to turn around and peek, but I didn't dare. So instead I stared ahead at the spice rack—the fucking spice rack, like I'd be locked up here whipping up extravagant meals for myself while in captivity. After a minute or two I started breathing closer to normal again as I remained there untouched. Finally, I cleared my throat and closed my eyes and asked, "Who are you?"

I felt a cool breeze on my legs at that moment and a croaking sound. The feel of it was a surprise, a relief, and I stood there uncertain why I was feeling it.

The man didn't reply to my question. Instead he asked, "That feel better?"

I swallowed. Though it did, it truly did, sweat ran down my face and my back in salty rivers, I wasn't about to give him the satisfaction of answering.

"Why are you doing this to me?" I asked.

I heard the rustle of paper. "Coming up behind you," he said. "Don't move."

I seized up, tensing every muscle of my body, expecting him to grab me, grope me, hurt me. But after a moment, there was nothing, just some bumping, whirring sounds to my lower left. I opened my eyes and looked down. There he was, fridge ajar as he restocked sparkling water and a new plastic container of strawberries, gun in his other hand. I studied him intently, trying to gather anything that stood out about him in this glimpse. He glanced up at me and, as if he knew what I was doing, pulled his bandanna up right as I noticed the spot there on his cheek. He dropped the strawberries and pointed the gun at me again and said, "Eyes ahead. Don't look at me."

There was something about that moment—the way he gripped the gun again, almost clumsily. The way his hands shook as he did it. It made me feel like this, whatever this was, didn't come naturally to this man. I pointed my gaze at the spices again, reading their labels as he finished restocking the refrigerator. Marjoram. Oregano. Paprika. In alphabetical order, no less.

"I don't understand what you want from me," I said. "I—I don't know what I did to deserve this." My voice broke. "I just want to go home. Please let me go home and I swear, I'll never tell anyone about this. I'll pretend it never happened."

He didn't answer. He shut the fridge and then I heard the rustle of paper again behind me, I assume paper bags.

"Do you want your life ruined?" I asked him. "Because when this all shakes out, that's what's going to happen. Is this worth ruining your life?"

A moment spread between us. I heard his rubber soles squeaking on the floor, heard him go into the bathroom and rummage around. Some movement. My heart thundered and my mind lightninged with a thousand questions.

"What happens if I don't figure this out?" I asked. "Am I going to die?"

The fans whirred. The room seemed so empty I wondered if he was gone already.

"Take care," he said.

The sound of footsteps and the door closing and locking with a beep. He was leaving. I grew frantic listening to the sound of it but remained still. I stood with my hands glued to the counter because I was scared. I didn't want to give him a reason to shoot me. I wanted him to go away forever and at the same time I wanted to run after him and yell for him to take me with him.

I cried for a long time. When I finally turned around, my face swollen, my soul shrunk, I noticed that not only did he plug in two tower fans that oscillated and cooled the room, he also cleaned up my vomit from the floor.

"Thanks, champ," I said weakly to the air.

Then I went and looked out the window like I'm doing right now.

I think I finally understand the pampered misery of an indoor cat's life.

A rush of wind blows through the thirsty meadow grass. I check my phone: still thirty minutes until I can call him. I mean, wouldn't want to bother the free man out there by calling back too early, right? He needs time to "process" this. When my life's on the line. I hate patience so much I kick the wall again and stub my poor toe.

And don't forget—when my kidnapper showed up yesterday, Bud, that useless helper I've been tethered to for unknown reasons, didn't pick up the phone all night. So there I was, left with my brain repeating the bizarro scene over and over again as I called his number and called his number and called his number and the loser was too wasted to pick up. Come on, man. Deal me another savior please.

And as the wind outside dies back down and the grass stills, a thought shocks like a static touch—what if the reason Bud didn't pick up was because he and the guy who restocked my groceries are *the same person*?

Holy shit. I clamp my hand over my mouth.

It would make sense, wouldn't it? Wherever I am is clearly out in the middle of nowhere. I'm guessing it takes some time to drive that van out here. I can't even see a road, though who knows what exists on the other side of the cabin where there are no windows. So Bud is MIA all night and misses my million calls right at the same time kidnapper man comes in to accommodate me with a gun to my head? Bud acts nice on the phone, his slow drawl dripping with sympathy, but you know, kidnapper dude is acting nice too. And now that I think about it, their voices could maybe sound similar. From the glimpse of his eyes with no signs of crow's feet and his spry movements, my educated guess is that kidnapper dude is somewhere around my age and Bud's age too. Wouldn't that be a funny trick to play on someone you're kidnapping? Pretend to be someone on the other end of the line, just to mess with their head? Put some stupid mental wild goose chase together trying to find a connection?

I'm dizzied by this upside-down theory and go sit down on the bed. The bed with the homemade-looking quilt. Imagine that—some grandma stitched this together and probably never realized it would end up in a hell cabin out in the middle of nowhere. I lie down and close my eyes, let the thoughts swirl like a neurotic merry-go-round. Going back over everything with Bud, all we've talked about. So much personal stuff I don't usually divulge until I know someone well—past lovers, the fact I'm a grown-up orphan, the names of everyone in my life. He knows so much about me now. And isn't that brilliant, really? Kidnap a woman and then make yourself her only contact, masquerading as an ally when really you're the villain?

I don't know what Priya Patel has to do with any of this, but I've back-burnered her for the moment and Bud has become my prime suspect. If Bud is his real name. It makes so much more sense now. Why would I only be allowed him as my contact—*him*, a nobody I have zero connection with? Maybe he's a sick fan of Violet and the Black Sheep and this is his way of keeping me in captivity but also his good graces. A way to befriend me while being my enemy.

I pick my phone up and check the time. It's been an hour. An hour, and kidnapper dude hasn't come back to set me free. I'm getting a sick feeling in the pit of my stomach that it was a false flash of hope believing that Priya Patel was the simple answer. There's likely a lot more going on than I thought. Including Bud's role in this.

Getting up and stretching my legs, I take a deep breath and dial his number. Unlike yesterday, he picks up on the second ring.

"Hey Violet," he says through what sounds like a mouthful of food.

"Hi," I reply.

"How's it going?"

"Well, I'm still locked in a fucking cabin, so not so great, Bud. Not so great."

"Yeah, probably a dumb question to ask." I hear the sound of a beverage being sucked through a straw, that sound when you've reached the end and all that's left is ice. In the background, unintelligible music. Sounds like country. Yuck.

"Where are you?" I ask.

"Sitting in my truck, finishing my dinner."

I sit up and rub my temples, ignoring my own grumbling stomach. It's been so hard to eat here. "What's on the menu?"

"Burger and fries."

"Healthy. From where?"

"Mr. Droidburger."

Mr. Droidburger is the first set of chain restaurants staffed by robots. It's the cheapest, most unethical, and probably unhealthiest fast food that exists.

"Gross."

"I think it's pretty good. Got a double-patty with cheese for five bucks. Can't beat that."

"Again, gross. You do know Mr. Droidburger is setting a trend that's going to end up putting a lot of other restaurant workers out of a job? And that they have their own ranches where their beef comes from that is also staffed with robots and the company's been slapped with numerous violations on how they treat their cows? It's disgusting."

"I might've heard something about that. So where do you recommend I get my burgers then?"

"Nowhere. I'm vegetarian."

"Well then."

"Yeah. You should try it sometime." I spring up and pace the room, my anger rising. It's not about the burgers, of course. It's about the fact he very well could be the person responsible for me being locked up here. "Clean conscience. Highly recommended."

"Does it come with a side of self-righteousness?" he asks.

"Shut up," I tell him, annoyed, stopping to look out the window again. The sun's out of sight. It always sets on the other side of the house and rises up over the mountains, which means, I guess, that I'm facing east. The blue smile of a crescent moon is faint, a promise that night's coming. "You're such an asshole."

I can't believe I have to bear another night here.

"Look, I grew up in Texas, all right? Beef was on our table almost every night growing up. I'm not of the belief that cattle have the same thoughts and feelings as we do until they can prove it to me."

Honestly, I'm feeling a touch of hatred for Bud. Possible kidnapper. Typical carnivore. Beer-guzzling lazy yokel. Whether or not he's my villain, I'm truly in hell having this person as my only contact.

"Humans for a long time have decided we know what other creatures feel and don't feel," I say. "It's one of the greatest, worst, most self-serving lies in the history of life as we know it."

"Let me ask you a question. You think the cashier at Mr. Droidburger has feelings?" he asks.

"Maybe," I say. "I would never pretend to know what's inside the mind of another creature."

"What about drones? They have feelings?"

"This isn't fucking high school debate club, Bud. It's my

opinion. No matter what I think, I'm still locked up in a cabin out in the middle of nowhere. Why are you torturing me?"

The crickets have started chirping outside the window. I close my eyes. It's really true, isn't it? The man probably isn't coming back tonight. Unless he comes super late. But my heart has been doing a slow-motion sink over the past hour. I've been naïve to assume this is simple and he will play fair. And I might even be talking to him right now for all I know.

"Torturing you?" he asks. "I'm not … I'm sorry you feel that way. I was just curious what you thought."

"It's you, isn't it?" I ask, scanning the darkening sky for the first shy blinks of stars. "Just tell me. Stop messing with my head, I'm so tired of this."

"Is what me?" he asks, baffled.

"You're who kidnapped me," I say, not asking, just stating it.

There's a long silence. I hear the music in the background get quieter, like he turned it down.

"Why the hell would I kidnap you?" he asks.

"I don't know, man. Why are you the only contact in this phone?"

"I have no idea."

"Why, during the one stretch of time where you were MIA, was that when the kidnapper showed up?" It's starting to get chilly as day bleeds into night, so I turn around and turn off my two tower fans and grab a zip-up hoodie left for me in the mysterious box. It still has that new store smell. "The only way this makes sense is that it's you. I'm not an idiot."

"I don't even know what to say, that's so ridiculous."

"Come on. Don't fuck with me. I'm already locked up, okay? I did what the note asked of me—I figured out the connection. The real connection. The connection is *you*."

"Violet, listen." Now the sounds on his end have shifted to the swish of traffic, a honk, humanity, and my soul yearns for it. "I know you've been locked up there. I know it's hard. But now you're losing it a little."

"Tell me how this isn't the most logical explanation."

"Okay, well, what about the Priya Patel connection we already found? That's out the window now?"

"Probably some stupid connection you put in there to throw me off."

"Wow, I'm really a genius," he says sarcastically.

"Not really, because I figured out your game pretty quick here."

"You think I'm the dumbass who brought you sparkling water and fans? You think that guy is me?"

"Yeah, I do."

He's quiet, but lets out a long, dramatic sigh. "I don't know what to tell you. I was beginning to form this whole theory—but then it sounds like you wouldn't even hear it anyway."

"What theory?"

"You really want to hear it?"

"Fire away, champ."

"Priya's brother Zayan," he says. "You know him?"

"No," I say, preparing for incoming bullshit. I plunk myself on the chair at the table where the note sits and flatten it out with my palms, staring at the words again, the message tattooed into my brain at this point.

"Well, he's a real piece of work. Grade-A sociopath, I'm talking straight-up evil. Lies, cheats, steals, by the time he was twenty he'd been to jail for assault and battery on his land-lord. Who was a senior citizen, a woman, by the way. Even his parents want nothing to do with him, at least last I heard."

"Okay."

"So—I'm saying, if Priya's the connection, this has Zayan written all over it. He's a conniving prick. I could imagine him learning that Priya went to high school with some famous musician and deciding to kidnap you for ransom, easy. Or hiring someone to do his dirty work for him."

"Except number one, I'm not *famous*," I say, unable to help the flutter of flattery his assumption provokes. "And number two, there's no ransom."

"*Yet*. There's no ransom yet. What if this is just the first part of the game? And next comes a demand for money?"

"Why though? You kidnap someone for the money, you ask for the money. Your theory is stupid. And probably just something you're pulling out of your ass."

"Okay, Violet," he says, sounding annoyed. "Whatever you say."

He's making me feel crazy. He really is. The blood rushing to my face is warm and my hands shake. I bite my tongue a moment, trying to figure out how to move forward with this conversation, with this person who could be the only way out of this nightmare or the reason I'm in it. And I can't decide which he is.

"Look," he says. "If I'm your kidnapper, if you have this all figured out, can I get off the phone then? Can I have my night back? Because I'm sitting here on the phone with you all weekend and I could be living my life."

"Your rich life full of beer and hamburgers," I spit.

"Fuck off," he says.

"No, you fuck off," I shout.

And I hang up on him. With the push of a button, I end the call and then the anger rises up in me and I raise the phone up in the air, so close to throwing it, so close to smashing it to pieces on the floor. Instead, I plug it into its charger and get up and ball up my fists and scream and scream and scream so hard that I start gagging. I fall to the floor in a ball like a toddler dissolving into a tantrum. I do this until I feel empty, until my throat is scratched dry and I have hardly any voice left.

If I were playing a show this week, I'd probably have to

cancel it after what I just did. But I'm coming to the realization that I'm not playing any shows in the near future. In fact, I'll be lucky if I get out of here alive. And if I don't die, if I survive, who knows—will I be like one of those cases you read about? A woman locked up in captivity for years? My future is black and not in my hands and it's the worst feeling I've ever had. The only comparison is when I got the call that my parents had driven off a dangerous highway and died.

When I stand up, stars sparkle my vision. I need food badly. I've barely eaten all day. I walk weakly to the fridge and pull out some pita and hummus and sit at the table again, numb, empty, shoving the food in my mouth but tasting nothing, feeling nothing. My outburst scraped all the me out of me and I'm hollow.

Because I've been waiting, waiting, in a constant torment of waiting, I haven't showered in days. My hair's greasy, my palms stained purple, the sweat is caked all over my skin. After eating, I stare out the window into the darkness like a dog waiting for its owner. No sign of life out there, except the crickets and some faraway frogs. Which I guess means water is nearby, but what good that does me, I don't know.

"He's not coming back tonight," I say hoarsely to the air. "Accept it, Violet. This day is done. Tomorrow is another day."

I let myself shower in the stall for the first time, unwrapping a tiny bar of soap from its wrapper like something you'd find in a hotel bathroom. Lavender. How nice of you. Thanks, Bud. But even as I think it, I have my doubts. Can I really imagine a guy like Bud shopping for sparkling water and cute lavender soaps? Not that I know him super well, but from the small bit I have gotten to know him, it doesn't add up. Nothing adds up. I'm so tired of thinking, of being left alone with my brain. I step into the warm shower and lose myself in how good it feels. I stay until the water starts to cool and then get out, toweling off. The white towels are stained purple from my hair dye, but my skin is clean. I use the miniature bottle of lavender lotion left in the bathroom with the soap and then change into the other pair of sweats left for me in the box. The last pair of sweats. What happens after that? What happens after this?

I'm exhausted. I peer out at the night one last time before closing the windows and dropping the latch to keep the room warm. The days here are unbearably hot, the nights shockingly cool. That's why I guess I'm far from LA—because at home, I often run my AC all night long.

I sit on the bed, calmer than I've been in a while. The phone is in my palm. I consider my options. *Options.* As if they're plural. There's really only one path forward from here.

"Hey," Bud says, picking up after the first ring. "I was afraid you wouldn't call. I've been worried about you."

I don't answer for a moment, getting under my covers and then staring up at the ceiling.

"Violet?" he asks.

"Yeah," I respond, my voice husky from my screaming session earlier.

"Listen, I'm real sorry," he says. "I shouldn't have told you to fuck off. That was shitty of me."

"I said it first," I say. "I'm sorry too."

"You don't have to apologize. You're the one locked up and alone. I can't even imagine how it feels."

"It's the worst," is all I can manage.

"What happened to your voice?"

"I screamed a lot."

"Wow. You sound pretty blown out."

"I never let myself scream like that. I take good care of myself, honey and tea before every show. I'm afraid of damaging my singing voice. I guess it just goes to show how hopeless I feel that I wrecked myself screaming like a baby."

"I'd do the same if I were in your situation."

My eyes fill up. I don't even try to stop them. My face stays still but they sting and fall down my face.

"Listen," Bud says. "It's okay if you suspect me. I was thinking about it. Of course you would. Honestly, I've had moments where I didn't believe you too. It's natural. We can't prove anything to each other, you know?"

"Yeah," I manage, reaching up to wipe my face.

"So … you just do what you need to do. Believe what you need to believe."

I hear the pop of a can.

"Beer?" I ask.

"Yeah. I won't check out this time, I swear. I only got a six-pack."

"It's fine. Who cares. Get drunk. Live it up."

"Don't sound so down, Violet. I have a lead. I think I got something to investigate."

"Priya's brother, I know. Sure."

It seems so farfetched, so pointless.

"I'm going to do some research into him tomorrow," Bud says. "We got this, okay?"

I close my eyes, which are growing heavy. "Sure."

"Don't give up, you hear?" he asks.

"I was supposed to get a record deal tomorrow," I say blankly. "My whole life was supposed to change. I wanted my whole life to change. But not like this."

"The record deal can wait," he says. "It'll be there when you get out. And you know the news'll be covering this story when you're back and it'll end up making you even more famous. Your career will skyrocket."

"Wouldn't that be something," I say.

We're quiet a moment and I hear a meow on his end.

"You have a cat," I say.

"Well, she's not mine. She just kind of ended up here."

"That's how it always starts."

"My mind's racing. How about you?"

"Somehow, I'm tired. So tired."

"I'm thinking about Zayan. I hate that bastard."

"When I can't sleep, I listen to music."

"How about you sing me a song?" he asks softly. "I want to hear one of your songs."

"I sound like a toad after screaming myself raw."

"I don't mind toads. Please, would you?" he says, his voice sounding loosened, probably from the beer. "Sing me one?"

I sigh. Part of me wants to chide him for being buzzed again—he sure seems to drink a lot. But I've always been a moth, drawn toward the light of anyone's attention. Even now, even here, even in this state, I'm lifted by the thought that someone wants to hear my voice.

Clearing my throat first, I start singing a new song I've been working on called "Wicked Hope," an acoustic song about how painful it can be to think things will get better and then to have them not. Which, right now, feels so tragically on point it could be the soundtrack to my life story. As I sing the words, softly into the phone with my eyes closed, I disappear into the music. I am swallowed whole. I love that part of music—its vastness. Each song contains a universe. And, surprisingly, my voice sounds damn good, like a whiskey-throated blues singer from some bygone era.

By the time I'm done we both get quiet. So tired. So done with this day. I slip into a pool of sleep. When I wake up, I see we've been on the phone for over two hours. We both drifted off. I can hear him snoring on the other end of the line. I could hang up, but I don't. There's a comfort in hearing him there. So I plug the phone into its charger and close my eyes again. I reach out and put my hand on the warm phone and fall back asleep.

BUD

THAT FAMILIAR DULL pounding in my head rings in the morning. Three ibuprofen, a shave, and a quick shower later, I towel off and pull on some jeans and a T-shirt. My phone died in the middle of the night and it's charging again. Hope that doesn't piss her off but hey, couldn't help that we fell asleep on our phones like a couple of middle school kids. The sun's blazing already out the window. I brew a mug of coffee and sip it on the back porch, petting the cat. When my phone's charged up again I call Bob and tell him I've got a bug and can't come in today.

"A bug," he yells over the sound of traffic. "Is that what the kids call hangovers these days?"

I hang up and then say, "Fuck you, Bob."

I have a love-hate relationship with Bob: love his money, hate him as a person. We met long ago through Andrew, the carpenter I apprenticed with for years. He told me Bob made his money originally from suing a craft store that he stubbed his toe in and then went into real estate, flipping houses in gentrified neighborhoods, multiplying his millions. American dream.

After looking up Zayan online, I lock up and stretch on my front porch, double-checking my ringer's all the way up. Violet still hasn't called. Not too far away, construction workers are tearing down the sugar factory that sits on the bay so they can build upscale housing right on the water. Upscale housing, tucked right underneath a bridge that leads to the North Bay. Rich people'll buy anything you sell them.

I get in my truck, which smells like leather and stale fries. Most people buy self-driving cars nowadays but they're not for me. I've always loved driving, actual driving, and had an affection for beat-up old cars. Growing up, my grandpa had this Chevy with an engine that rumbled when he revved it and it made my bare feet tickle when they touched the floorboards. Some of the only memories I have of my grandpa are in that Chevy. So when I moved out here, I bought a similar truck that had been converted to biodiesel even though it cost a fortune and biodiesel is a pain in the ass. I wasn't paying for a car, I was paying for a feeling.

On the road, engine humming under my feet, I swing through a Mr. Droidburger for a cheesy eggwich and hash browns and eat them in the parking lot. I check my phone again, a tickle of worry that she hasn't called yet. Across the street, I run into a liquor store and get a beer, just a sixteen-ouncer, and drink it in the car while listening to the headlines. It's all bad. Another pandemic's spreading in China. Some companion bots are getting recalled for rebelling against their owners. A woman in the South Bay shot her husband's face off and left the country. I turn the radio down and stare at my phone as I finish my tall can.

"Come on, Violet," I tell the air, my pulse up a little.

Finally, when I'm finishing the last warm sip, my phone rings with UNKNOWN NUMBER and I let out a breath of relief.

"There you are," I say.

"Here I am," she says.

"What took you so long?"

"Why'd you hang up on me in the middle of the night?"

"Forgot to plug my phone in."

"You know, you really need to get better at the little things if you're going to be my savior. You're so aggravating. And you snore."

"I do not."

"You do too. The point is: plug your fucking phone in when you're a kidnapped girl's only contact. Is that too much to ask?"

"It isn't."

"Anyway, I'm fine, thanks for asking."

"You sure woke up saucy."

"This is nothing, Bud."

"I can imagine." I put her on speaker and start the car. "So how'd you sleep?"

"Surprisingly well considering my life is hanging in the balance."

"I was thinking about something, Violet," I say as I pull out onto the road. "I was thinking about the sparkling water and fans and the 'take care' line. Isn't that what he said to you? 'Take care'?"

"Yes, those were his parting words."

"Well, that just makes me think this is Zayan even more."

"Why?"

I head toward the 80 south signs and wait in a long line of cars. Traffic's going to be agony. "Just think about it. Why would you abduct someone and treat them well?"

"I don't know." She sounds like she's got her mouth full. "Enlighten me."

"Because what he's after in the long run is your money," I say. "You can't get money from someone who's dead."

"So again, if it's ransom, why not ask for ransom money?"

"I don't know, maybe he's waiting for something to pan out. Maybe he wants to make you feel scared and isolated and shook up in the meantime."

"Walk me through this Zayan theory," she says. "Why would he want you involved?"

"Because he hates my guts."

"So you're thinking this is a two birds, one stone situation —he wants my money, he hates you, he comes up with this wacky idea to get my money and mess with you at the same time?"

"Maybe even implicate me," I say, finally pulling onto the on-ramp as we inch toward the freeway. "Maybe in the end he's going to blame all this on me."

She keeps chewing. "Okay, I'm entertaining this theory. Better than anything else we have at the moment."

"What are you eating?"

"Stupid yogurt."

"Why's it stupid?"

"Because it's hell cabin yogurt, Bud. Everything is stupid here."

"How've you been spending your morning so far?"

"Oh," she says, her voice brightening. "It's been great. Just staring out the window like a sad little pet, waiting for my abductor. Doing pushups and running in four-foot circles to try to not go insane." Her voice drops. "'How've I been spending my morning.' For fuck's sake."

"Look, sorry. Trying to make conversation."

"And don't think you're off the list of suspects, either, just because you've thrown Zayan in the mix. I don't even know if there is a Zayan. You could be making him up."

"I'm almost flattered you think I'm that much of a mastermind," I say, honking my horn at a car that won't let me merge into its lane. Not that there's much point in getting mad at a self-driving car. "Look, I called in sick to work today so I could go chase down this shitstain for you."

"Oh, did you? How *kind* of you, big man."

I roll my eyes.

"You do realize your life might be in danger too, right?" she asks. "That you're a part of this? You might be free at this moment, but who knows—you could end up in a hell cabin soon too. Or worse. May I remind you that the note said 'maybe you do deserve your lives.' Plural. *Lives.* So this is all self-serving as much as it is ... wait a second. You called in sick to work?"

"I did," I say, turning the music up a notch as I enter the river of bumper-to-bumper traffic. Some old honky-tonk tune.

"To chase down Zayan?"

"He's in the South Bay, Santa Clara. I'm gonna find him and smell him out for us."

"No, no, no." Her voice climbs. "Remember the note? You can't go around asking questions to people in my life about my disappearance."

"But Zayan wasn't a person in your life, he's a person in mine. You never met him."

"I don't like this, Bud."

"Well, what the hell am I supposed to do? Just sit around?"

"We found the connection. They're listening to us. We just have to wait. Kidnapper dude's probably coming back today. Honestly, if he's coming back, I don't even care who did this anymore." She's still hoarse. "I just want to go home. I won't even ask any questions. I won't even call the police."

"And what if he doesn't come back?" I ask.

"Please don't screw this up for us," she says. "I'm extremely uncomfortable with you going and talking to Zayan."

"I won't even mention your name, I swear."

I can almost hear the wheels of her brain turning.

"You won't mention me, you won't mention the kidnapping, any of this?" she asks.

"Nothing. I'll just ask general questions. It's not even about what he says. I can read the guy. I can tell when he's up to something." She's silent for a long, long moment, so long I think the call might've gotten dropped. "Hello?"

"This is my life," she says quietly. "My *life*, Bud. In your hands. It makes me sick to my stomach to think of you doing this. And for what? What could you possibly learn that will help?"

"All I know is we can't sit and take this," I say. "We found the connection and nothing's happened. We need to go deeper. And if that means I have to go talk to this shitstain, well, I'm doing it. Carefully. I wouldn't do anything to hurt you, Violet."

She moans a fed-up moan. "Or you're tricking me."

"I'm not—" I shake my head. "Why would I—"

"You say it's Zayan. But if Zayan's Priya's brother—if Zayan exists, because I knew Priya but I never knew her family—then he's Indian-American. And one thing I do know is kidnapper dude is white. Blond, in-danger-of-a-sunburn white."

"Okay. But the note says 'we.' So this is more than one person we're dealing with."

"What if it's you and Zayan?"

"Look," I say, annoyed. "I don't know how to convince you it isn't me, or that I would never, *ever* do anything to help that sociopathic shitstain as long as I live."

"Geez. You really hate this guy."

"The feeling's mutual," I say. "Believe me, I don't want to be driving down to see him right now. I would have happily lived the rest of my life without even thinking his name. But if there's a chance he can give any hint as to where you are, or anything else—maybe it's worth it."

"I want this to be over," she says.

"Me too."

"I keep hoping the dude will come back," she says. "Live up to his word."

"C'mon, you think we're dealing with honest people here? If you're going to get out of there, we're going to have to figure it out ourselves."

"You *swear* you won't mention my name or my kidnapping."

"Swear on my mama's life."

"You'll be ultra careful when you talk to Mr. Shitstain."

"Like I'm walking on eggshells and carrying fine china."

Finally, finally, the freeway opens up just a little and I'm able to kick the truck up to thirty miles per hour. This'll be how it goes, the whole drive down.

"Why the hell do you hate this guy so much anyway?" she asks. "What did he do to you?"

"Long story."

"Well, I got news for you, Buddy—hey, can I call you Buddy?"

"No."

"Well, I got news for you, Bud: I've got nothing but time on my hands."

———

I've always been a settler. Don't expect too much from the world, hold a special suspicion for anything that brings me hope, and don't bother with big dreams, because big dreams aren't for small guys like me. Football was the anomaly. I played fiercely in high school, shocked by what my body could do. Shocked at the wins that piled up. I was sure I'd get injured. I played hard, knowing it could be over any second. I'd seen it happen to guys, tear their knees up at sixteen and poof, there go your big dreams.

"You never seem excited about anything," my girlfriend Kimmy Nguyen said to me. She was a wide-eyed cheerleader who wore her hair in pigtails every day and had energy like a large coffee with three shots of espresso. "You're so *brooding*. Even after you win, we're all partying and celebrating and you're wandering off somewhere all by yourself."

I had that reputation at parties. Drink too much and I'd disappear on long walks, go incommunicado. I liked the way the world felt to me, a lonesome tipsy ghost stopping to gaze at half-lit houses in dark neighborhoods. I don't know why I'm that way.

I didn't believe Kimmy really liked me. I thought she deserved better than me, which was why I shut her out so much and didn't treat her well. When I was getting recruited by schools my senior year I didn't believe it, didn't trust anything would happen. I'd seen other guys wooed by bigshots and treated like kings only to have things fall through. When I got the acceptance from Berkeley, I figured they had made a mistake. I worried about it as my family celebrated and I worried about it on the plane ride to California and I worried as I unpacked my suitcase and introduced myself to my new roommate and I worried as I walked around campus feeling like a roach that had crawled into a palace. It seemed like at any moment someone would find me out, realize the fraud I was, that I didn't belong there. So I dropped out. I got a job hauling junk for a while, then moved on to carpentry work. I didn't love the work, but I felt I deserved it. I didn't love the Bay Area, but I didn't feel like I had any reason to leave it either.

I settled.

One time, *one* time in my life I stretched my arms for the stars and didn't settle. And her name was Priya Patel.

When I first laid eyes on Priya, I was standing at a stoplight where Telegraph Avenue meets Bancroft and bleeds into UC Berkeley. A funky, colorful strip of shops on one side, the spread of campus on the other. I had a sub sandwich wrapped up in my hand, on lunch break. Andrew and I were working on custom shelving for a smoke shop up the street. Priya sat on a patch of lawn in front of a white building that looked like it was from another country, another time—a touch of ancient Rome, maybe. The henna in her long hair caught the sun. She had lunch in a to-go box and a textbook splayed in front of her and she seemed to be looking at me through her bug-eyed sunglasses, grinning brightly. As if to clarify, she pushed her glasses up and then waved at me. I did that corny thing where I looked behind me to make sure she was waving at me and then, when I saw no one behind me, I waved back. There was something magnetic about the moment. Like I was in one world and she was in another, and there was a door that opened between us. Heart jackhammering, a brave surge pushed me toward her. I walked on over, jumping over a short wall so I could join her on the lawn.

"Oh my God, I'm so sorry," she said, putting her hand over her mouth and laughing. "I thought you were someone else."

"I wondered why you were waving at me."

"So embarrassing," she said.

Up close, she was even more beautiful. Her hair was lifted up in the breeze, a fiery halo around her. Instantly I memorized the beauty mark on her chin, the dimple on her cheek, the cowlick at her hairline.

"My name's Bud," I said. "I'm on a lunch break. Mind if I join you?"

"Sure. Since I lured you over here under false pretenses," she said. "I'm Priya."

I plopped down on the soft grass and, snap of the fingers, we fell into easy conversation. She was a journalism major and it blew her mind when I told her I'd come here on scholarship and dropped out a few years back. Immediately, she started trying to figure out how to get me back in, trying to tell me I'd wasted my education. I liked how comfortable she was pushing me, chiding me, as if she knew me well when I was just a stranger. She wasn't judgmental about it—she was just curious, she didn't understand how a person could turn down an opportunity. She had worked so hard to get in, and then there I was, throwing all my potential away. We would spend the next two years riding that merry-go-round. It would get old, and dizzying. But I didn't know it yet. All I knew was the magnet of my want. Every day that week and the week after that the scene would repeat: me spotting her on the lawn during lunch hour and joining her there. It's not often in life I click like that with someone—that ease where there's a lot of laughter and no space between sentences.

"You're my favorite distraction," she told me with a wry smile. "I'm supposed to be studying, you know."

"Well, if you give me your number and let me take you out to dinner, I'll stop pestering you during your study time," I said boldly.

We went out to dinner. We went out for drinks, both of us freshly twenty-one. Too many drinks. I took her back to her house and we slept on her bed together. Fully clothed. Cuddling. Her place had so much taste. Tapestries, bookshelves full of antique books, Tiffany lamps and Persian rugs. And it had order. Calendars, to-do lists, robotic feather dusters and vacuum cleaners. She reeked of family money. The whole place did. It was a two-bedroom Victorian cottage she shared with her "baby brother" who I met in the kitchen the next morning as he stood there in nothing but tighty whities and the gold chains on his hairy chest, eating Cheerios out of the box like a toddler.

"Who the fuck are you?" is how he greeted me.

Zayan had piercing brown eyes. His hair was going prematurely silver at the temples. It gave him an air of sophistication that was an outright lie.

"I'm fucking Bud," I said.

"No," he answered, stuffing cereal into his mouth. "I believe you're fucking my sister."

Priya came in and gasped. "Oh my God, Zay, put some clothes on."

"Nice to meet you, Bud," Zayan said as he sauntered out of the room.

"He's between jobs," Priya told me, as if that explained anything. "I'm so sorry."

"It's fine," I said.

I was willing to put up with anything, *anything* to be with Priya. I knew from the get-go she was too good for me. I knew she deserved better. But for the first time in my life, I was willing to fight for something. I told myself I would step it up to be with her, work on myself. Enrolled in city college. Cut down on my drinking. Started lifting weights and running. I was sweet with her. Brought her flowers and took her out to nice dinners, like a grown up. Wrote her notes that she kept in a special box. Moved into her house with her, shared her bed, shared her room, dared to dream a future.

I soon learned that Priya had projects. Beyond her studies, she tutored underprivileged students. She rescued abandoned houseplants at the side of the road and took them home to bring them back to life. She had a three-legged blind cat named Tripod who she'd adopted because no one else wanted it. Zayan was another one of her projects. She was constantly looking for opportunities for him, scouring the internet for job prospects, giving him to-do lists to make him useful around the house. He was always asking her for something—to spot him money, or give him a ride somewhere, or bail him out of jail. He lied all the time, and about stupid shit that didn't even matter. He shoplifted. He was mean to the cat. I'd never known a loser like him in all my life. Priya told me he had antisocial personality disorder, which sounded bad. A disease and all. I felt sorry for him until I looked it up and realized it meant he was a sociopath and had no feelings. What's the point of sympathy for a man with no feelings?

It took me two years to realize that I was also one of

Priya's projects. That she loved me, but only under certain conditions. When I dropped out of city college after two semesters and went back to carpentry full-time after Andrew got sick, she was disappointed in me. When she saw a twelve-pack in the refrigerator, she was disappointed in me. When I went to parties with her at school and wandered off down hallways to escape the boring conversations about academics, she was disappointed in me. Whereas she used to claim opposites attract, that I was the yang to her yin, she started telling me she thought maybe we weren't a good match after all. And it made me bitter that, meanwhile, Zayan got her unconditional love and forgiveness.

Then she got into Oxford University for grad school and told me she needed to go alone.

It felt out of the blue. I didn't even know she had applied to schools so far away. We had talked about staying in the area. We had talked about marriage, kids, a fixer-upper I could work on with my own two hands. I was stunned.

"I've been trying to tell you," she said, tears rolling. "I just —I think we're better off going our separate ways. Clearly you want your freedom. You want to bounce around doing odd jobs and drinking beer and—I want more than that. I want kids and I want them to have good role models. I don't think you're there yet."

To say our parting broke my heart would be a lie. It's too weak a phrase. It broke me in my entirety. Broke my whole being. It was as if my spirit were hit by a bus. I didn't see it coming, I really didn't, though she said she tried to tell me, she had been thinking of breaking up. But I'm not a psychic.

She left. I moved out. Found a cheap room in a house full of idiot frat boys. Made furniture in the garage and learned to repair my truck. Drank and drank and drank. And what finished me off was about six months later, when I saw that Priya, in Oxford now, posted a picture of her baby on social media. Her baby with blue eyes. My baby. Our baby. She had to be our baby—do the math. And when I reached out to Priya, she said I wasn't father material and she wished me well. Then she blocked me from her pages. She gutted me with the cool disregard of a serial killer. I had to wonder if she was a sociopath just like her brother.

———

"Bud," Violet says. "That is the most fucked-up story I've ever heard."

All that history, me vomiting the worst shit that ever happened to me, and I'm only in Newark. Road work has made traffic even more unbearable than usual and it's stop and start now.

"So you have a kid out there you've never even met?" she asks.

"Yeah. Arabella. I think she's six. They live in London now, Priya's married to some hoity-toity professor. Sometimes I go incognito and look at pictures of her on Priya's account. That sounds creepy, doesn't it?"

"Um, *no*. It's your kid! Did you ever try to … I don't know. Get a paternity test? Sue for custody?"

"She lives in England. And she's right, isn't she? I'm not father material. I'm a wastoid who fixes up housing. Kid's better off never knowing me."

There's a long silence.

"I don't even know what to say," she finally answers. "I'm so sorry that happened to you. I don't think you're a wastoid. You sound like you drink too much, but … you also sound like a nice person. A kind person. I mean, you're helping me, a stranger, and we've never even met."

I force myself to say, "Thanks."

I hate that my eyes are stinging right now. I wipe the wetness away. I let the feelings blaze through me, just burn me to a crisp, just have their way with me. Then I'm numb.

Then there's nothing left. My eyes dry. I keep my hands on the wheel, my gaze on the road.

"I do wonder now if Priya has something to do with this," says Violet. "Because she's the connection. And if she is a cruel as you say—"

"It's Zayan," I say. "Priya's on another continent. She has a career, a family. She's too important to dirty her hands with trash like me."

Violet is quiet, but I hear a faint sigh. "Be careful today, Bud. Don't let your emotions get the best of you."

The best of me. I only gave one person in my life the best of me and it was the worst decision I made in my life.

———

Zayan works as a vet tech now. I guess the office he works in doesn't care much about criminal records. And I find it disturbing that the diagnosed sociopath who used to yell at a blind, three-legged cat now works with animals. But okay. Here we are. Nearly three hours with traffic and here we are. I park in the lot for Sunny Hills Vet Hospital and get off the phone with Violet.

I was never a meditating man, but I try real hard right now to close my eyes a moment and ground myself. Because I know even the sight of Zayan's face is going to set me off. I need to keep focused. I'm not coming here to rehash the past. I'm coming here to sniff out if there's a connection, if Zayan's up to something. Because the thing about Zayan is, he's a terrible liar. He gets a shit-eating grin on his face whenever he lies about something. I don't know why he'd be behind this, but nothing he did ever made sense. I remember once going bowling with him and Priya and he stole three bowling balls and I asked him, why the hell would you do that? And he just smiled and said, because he could.

Because he could. But could he do this? Is he even clever

enough to cook this scheme up? That's what I'm here to find out.

The vet office smells like wet pet hair. Linoleum and plastic chairs gleam under fluorescent lights. I get in line behind a woman with a panting chihuahua in a sweater and take a long gander at a fish tank. Big old clownfish stares back at me and blows bubbles. Try to calm the hammer of my heartbeat. Steady there. Just here to say hello to an old enemy, ask a few questions. Measure his response.

"Why hello there!" says the chipper receptionist when it's my turn. "How can I help you today?"

I take a look at her pupils to make sure they're black and not silver—robots are looking creepily human these days and popping up in a lot of customer service positions. But this one's are black. Human.

"Here to see Zayan, if I can."

"Do you have an appointment?"

"Afraid not. But I can wait."

"Is this regarding ... a pet?" she asks, eyeing my empty arms.

"Yeah. My cat. Her name's Tripod."

"And where ... is Tripod?"

"Back at my house."

She raises her eyebrows. "All ... righty. I'll see if he can spare a few minutes after this appointment he's in right now, 'kay?"

"Sure," I say. "I'll wait right here."

I sink into a plastic chair near the aquarium. The chihuahua across the room starts barking at me and her owner, a woman in a kaftan who looks like she hasn't had a good night's sleep in a decade, claps and hisses, "Stop it, Inkypoo. Stop it now."

Inkypoo. What in God's name are people thinking sometimes, I swear.

After an intense staring contest with the clownfish, one of the doors opens and a voice says, "Tripod's owner?"

I stand up. Zayan stares back at me, clipboard in hand, lab coat on. He has thick glasses and a goatee now which makes him look like even more of a douchebag. I approach him. It takes him a moment to place me, and when he does, his brows furrow and a grin spreads on his face. "Well," he says. "Yes. *Tripod.* Come right in."

We go into an examination room that reeks of bleach. His eyes are wide behind his glasses as he closes the door, as if the sight of me is so shocking it's brightened his day. Behind him, a poster for different worms that can infest your dog. I don't know why, it just seems like the perfect backdrop for him. I snicker.

"What the fuck are you doing here?" he asks, his smile stuck like a mannequin.

"Just came to say hi," I tell him, perching myself on the examination table.

"Why? The fuck?" he asks.

"Nice job you got here," I tell him, crossing my arms, eyeing the walls and the digital picture frames featuring all the happy animals that have come in here to get treated by a sociopath. "Not where I would have imagined you ending up. But sure."

"And you look exactly how I'd imagine you," he says cheerfully. "Same greasy hair, brooding look, wrinkled shirt. And now you have a beer gut. Let me guess: you're still a carpenter. You rent, don't own. You live alone."

"Stupid asshole," I say.

I hate that he's right. Is he right because he's been following me? Because he's kidnapped Violet and is listening in on us? It seems more likely he just made an educated guess, which, ouch. I sit staring at him, trying to envision how he could be listening in on our conversations and serving as the mastermind behind the kidnapping and also apparently holding down a full-time job. Then again, he has a partner, the white guy who's visited Violet.

"Again, what the fuck are you doing here?" he asks. "I have patients to see."

"Bought any sparkling water and fans lately?" I ask.

He starts laughing. "What is going on, bro? You got the DTs or something?" He steps closer. "Or are you here about Priya? Because you know she doesn't even *think* about you anymore. You're nothing to her." One step closer. I can smell his minty breath. He drops his tone. "I was just there visiting her and the family last month. They're so happy, man. Got this big, beautiful house in the country. So much room for Arabella to run around."

At the sound of her name, I snap, pushing him hard, so hard he falls back into the door. I have a good four inches and forty pounds on him, and suddenly you can see him see that. The smug grin's wiped off his face and he stands up straighter.

"Get the fuck out of my office and never come back here," he says. "My family doesn't want anything to do with you."

He exits through the back of the room, closing the door behind him. But I spring forward and catch the knob in my hand and pull it back open. I follow him into the room that lies behind the examination room, which is filled with dogs and cats in kennels. Guess this is where they board them. Zayan turns around with his hands in front of him to keep me away.

"Out, I said!" he yells. "Employees only. Fucking neanderthal."

I lunge and shove him back into a kennel with a huge dog inside it. Zayan's back hits the cage and he falls onto it, cursing. The dog starts barking and then a bunch of dogs join in from their cages, yipping. One's howling. I feel like I'm one of them.

Violet told me not to get emotional. To be careful. Her life is on the line. *My* life is on the line. I tell this to myself as I grab the front of Zayan's shirt and yank his face close to mine. It takes far more strength to contain my anger right now than it does to pull him close to me.

"Tell me what you did to her," I say, yanking harder, hearing his collar tear a little.

He pants, gazing straight into my eyes and smiling, almost like this excites him. Animals whine in the background. "I told her that you told me that if you ever got a woman pregnant you'd make her abort. That you secretly hated kids. I told her you were a sleaze and I'd seen you in bars with other women. I told her she was better off leaving you behind and starting over. I convinced her to leave you and cut you out of her life. I'm so convincing, bro. I could have been a fucking actor."

Everything he's said, it doesn't make sense at first. I'm still stuck on Violet, trying to make what he says make sense about Violet, because that's who I was asking about. But then it sinks in that he's talking about Priya. And it's like someone shoved me into the middle of the cold, deep ocean. I can barely breathe. He pushes me away from him and I let go of his collar. He stands up and straightens his shirt out, looks down at a rip. "Fuck, bro. This is designer."

I remain frozen in place, processing, still underwater and unable to catch my breath. It was him. He lied to Priya. Said things that weren't true—I *did* want kids someday. I would never have told her to have an abortion. I never, ever cheated on Priya. How could she have listened to Zayan? And not even asked me my side of it? Why in hell did she always give him the benefit of the doubt? Trust him over me?

A cat yowls from a cage.

That old broken feeling returns. The wound remembers itself. My fists shake at my side and the rage, it's hot under my skin as Zayan adjusts his collar and gazes back at me with sadistic curiosity. I make a decision to control myself. I'm not going to stoop to beating the shit out of him about the past right now when Violet's locked up in a cabin somewhere. That's what this is about.

"I'm going to be needing you to MyCash me for this damaged shirt," Zayan says.

On second thought, this is too much. I can't.

I step forward and pop him in the nose with my fist—not even that hard, I'm not aiming for lights out. Just to shut him up. But Zayan's such a featherweight he topples backward onto the kennels again, dogs banging around and barking, and screams, "Ow! Fuck! You fucking punched me!" He pulls his phone out with one hand, holding the other one out at arm's length, something like fear flashing in his eyes. "I'm calling the cops right now. Help! Bethany! Shit! Anyone!"

I can't help but snort at how pathetic he is. Yeah, I should have controlled myself. But this is satisfying enough to numb the pain a little bit. Just a taste of vengeance.

"There's an intruder in my office," he tells the phone.

I lean down and pull his phone from him and toss it in a kennel. It lands in a Pomeranian's water dish and the dog yips loudly.

A door behind us opens. I turn around.

"What's going on?" the receptionist asks, popping her head in. She clasps her hand over her mouth. "Oh my God."

Zayan's bloody lip has smeared red into his goatee. Looks a lot worse than it is.

"He fell down," I tell the receptionist. "I was just helping him up."

I pull him up by his collar, ripping the collar more and yanking off the stethoscope with it. When I turn around, the receptionist flinches and closes the door.

"Call the police!" Zayan screams.

I blast through the door we came in through, the examination room, and the waiting room, high on adrenaline. Go out to my truck muttering "shitstain" under my breath. Once I get back into my seat, I pant like I've run a 5K and realize my fist is still clenched over the stethoscope. Ripped it off his neck and stole it. Whoops. I toss it on the passenger's seat, rev the engine, and drive the hell out of there.

Speeding up the boulevard, my pulse settles back down and a sick hurt rises up. It starts in my middle and spreads outward from there, ending tingling in my fingertips and burning my eyeballs. I miss the freeway entrance, the world blurring. I wipe my eyes and try hard to hold it in but I sputter. Pulling into a lot, I park the car and then I explode. Tears and snot and screaming and hitting my steering wheel. Why're humans build this way? To carry hurt around like it's so fresh and new when it's been years? It shouldn't hurt this bad to find out that Priya left me because of lies her brother told, because Priya's been gone now for so long, for most of my twenties she's been gone. It's just not fair that pain doesn't have an expiration date. It's not fair.

There's a stockpile of Mr. Droidburger napkins stashed in my glove compartment, so I use those to wipe myself up. To the rearview, I say, "You look like hell." Bloodshot eyes, swollen pink cheeks, in dire need of a shave. But it's a comfort to know Zayan's looking worse. I get out of the car and walk to a liquor store at the corner of the lot, get a cold six-pack and bring it to my car with a bag of barbecue chips. After a couple beers, the animal in me is tamed. I don't feel as mad anymore. Sure, it hurts, but screw it right now. I've still got a life to live and a mystery to solve.

Soon I'm back on the freeway, window cracked, air in my hair, the country station turned all the way up. I check my phone again—nothing from Violet. I expect she'll be calling soon. Traffic isn't nearly as bad as before and it feels good to pick up speed and get into fifth gear. I go over what happened, rewinding it to watch the movie again and again in my mind. And besides the fact that I wish Zayan would fall into a pit of alligators, I'm having a hard time drawing any conclusions about his role in Violet's kidnapping.

Violet was right, this was stupid and pointless. I can't think of one thing I learned about her disappearance. Instincts are telling me that Zayan's not the right thread to pull here. For one, he was convinced from the get-go that I was there to rehash my breakup with Priya. If he was Violet's kidnapper—or one of them—he wouldn't have acted that way. He would have been smug and coy. When I asked him to tell me what he did with her, meaning Violet, he misunderstood me to mean Priya. And I know Zayan thinks he's a convincing actor, but I've always seen through him easy as glass. I didn't catch any glimpse of a man hiding something. Just a man openly parading my pain. Then there was the fact he called the police without hesitation, at intergalactic speed. First call he made, first thing he thought to do. If he were in on this, would he really want to be inviting the police to come in and question me?

Doesn't smell right. Don't know that Zayan has anything to do with this.

I stop by Mr. Droidburger on the way home. Think I'll start cutting down on it soon. Maybe tomorrow. Violet was right, it is the worst of the worst. That news story, I remember it vaguely, something about them getting slapped with fines for animal cruelty at their ranches. Like there's any surprise there. You staff a slaughterhouse with robots and what do you expect will happen. Yeah, tomorrow I'll try and get some groceries and eat healthier. Maybe start cutting back on beer too. I order a bacon double-patty Droidburger with cheese and bring it home, eat it on the back porch while working on my six-pack of beer, giving the whining kitty little crumbles of hamburger.

A little long to go without the phone ringing, but I'm sure Violet will call soon. Hell, maybe the kidnapper came back and lived up to his word and now she's packing up and going home. Wouldn't that be something? But I doubt that's the case. I ball up my fast-food trash and let out a big burp. The cat comes and settles on my lap. I guess I'll be parked here awhile, so I take out my phone.

Good thing I'm not eating anymore, because I'd have choked at what I see there when I start to scroll.

VIOLET

THIS MUST BE ABOUT RANSOM.

What else would it all be about? Someone out there knows I have a lot of money and they want it. They know about the settlement. Or maybe it's someone who lives near me and they see how I live, on my own in an expensive condo with no "real" job, and they put two and two together. Or some idiot who just assumes musicians are rich. Maybe Bud's right, maybe this is the work of Zayan and some other person and they're trying to psyche me out and show me how serious they are by locking me up in hell cabin and making me play some stupid game before demanding the ransom. Well, guys, I played it. Game over.

Come back now.

"I'll give you all my money," I yell out the window, my voice pathetic and hoarse. "No questions asked."

My heart thuds in my aching chest and I grip the bars. I shake them as hard as I can, but they never budge. Just like I've kicked the door as hard as I can and taken a chair and hit it hard as I could and nothing happened except a pitiful dent. Thing must be made of steel behind the wood. Every day is the same, every minute the same; I can hardly stand it in here anymore.

I check the phone. It's been two hours since Bud went on his fishing expedition with Zayan and I regret everything. Bud doesn't strike me as the smoothest operator and I could see him saying too much and getting us in even more trouble than we're already in. And what's he going to do? Find out where I am from a single conversation, come ride out here on his white horse and use his superhuman big man muscles to bend the bars open or Hulk-smash the front door? We're screwed no matter what we find out and our best bet is to wait and hope that the promise the note-writer made is honored.

I'm about to call Bud when something stirs in the air. Something underneath the wind—a hum. Right? A mounting buzz. I tilt my ear up and close my eyes and sure enough, it's there. An engine, getting louder by the second. Nausea and the urge to cry rise up in me and I peer out the window whispering, "No no no, yes yes yes," not knowing what to feel but feeling something at least other than boredom and like things are happening, they're *happening*, it's so loud now, rumbling, gravel crunching under tires. The van peels around the corner, dust-covered white with no license plate, and parks just ten or so feet away from me out front of the cabin.

I gasp, hope bursting, nervous fireworks inside me. It's him again. He's back. I'm going to be freed. He steps out of the van into the dirt cloud, appearing somehow shocked that I'm gaping at him from the jailhouse-looking window, and hastily ties a bandanna around his face. I push my hand out and wave at him from between the bars, hating myself for the cheerful way I yell, "Hello! You're back!"

"Hello," he says, stiffly, suspiciously. What the hell do *you* have to be suspicious about, you ass? My life is in your hands. But soon something else is in his hands—a gun. Pointing at me. "So, same deal as last time. I want to see you put your palms on the counter back there and keep them there until I leave. No funny stuff."

The desperate grin on my face suddenly hurts and though I nod, I don't understand. I don't understand what he means. I turn around and walk to the back counter in the kitchenette in a sick déjà vu trance and put my palms there like he said and study the spice rack. Cumin. Curry. Dill. Why is this just like last time? It should be different. Something's wrong.

"Hey," I say as politely as I can, hearing the door open behind me. "Excuse me. We—we found the connection. Have you been listening?"

He doesn't answer. I hear the crinkle of paper bags and realize he's brought groceries again. Fighting tears of frustration, I will my voice to remain steady.

"Priya Patel," I say.

He's leaning down to my left now, opening the fridge.

"I don't know what you're talking about," he says.

"The connection," I say, daring to look down at him as my hands remain glued to the countertop. "The note said we had to find a connection. And we did. Priya Patel. She's a girl I went to high school with and she's someone Bud dated. We both know her. The connection is her."

"That's ... not why you're here," he says, then sharper, "and stop looking at me."

I turn back to the spice rack in disbelief. "Then why? What is it?" I can hear the bang of a plastic drawer closing and opening. Fresh fruit, yippee. I want to kill him. "Is no one actually listening to us? I don't understand."

"Oh, they're listening. But that's not my job. I'm simply here to check on you and keep you in good shape."

"So—if Priya's not the connection," I say, pitch climbing as I hear the fridge door shut and fear he's going to leave soon. "If it's not her, is it—is it something else? Is it her brother?"

He ignores my question, disappearing behind me again. "I left you some fresh clothes in the box."

"I don't want clothes, I want to get the hell out of here!" I shout.

"Look," he says, paper bags crinkling again. I assume he's folding them. Imagine him being conscientious enough to recycle, but not conscientious enough to, you know, not kidnap a fucking person. "You're never going to guess it."

"Guess what? So it's hopeless?"

"Just take good care of yourself, all right, Violet? Everything'll make sense soon."

The sweet way he says my name, as if we're friends. His assurances. Fresh fruit. Clean clothes. The words "take care" repeated again. What he said not one minute ago about keeping me "in good shape."

It occurs to me that he's invested, very invested, in my well-being.

I have no idea why. None of this makes sense. As I hear the beeps of the locks, I'm filled with such desperation, a chest full of wild birds. This is what a woman must feel like seconds before she spontaneously combusts.

I scream, deep and guttural, more beast than human being, and turn my head to see him frozen there with the door ajar, his gun up, eyes wide. In a swift movement, I grab a fork that has been sitting on the counter in front of me and stab myself in the face, dragging it hard along my cheeks with a roaring sting. I stab my other cheek, feeling insane and not giving a shit, the horrible pain a blessing because it's changing things. It's different.

The man is rushing toward me and I hear a clatter to the ground, spot the gun, and drop my fork. I'm about to sprint and lunge for his gun when he pins my arms behind my back, surprisingly strong. It hurts my shoulders and my face burns and I'm laughing and crying at the same time.

"What has gotten into you?" he says, as if he knows me, as if he knows what I'm capable of. "Your face! Look what you've done to your face!"

The screeching sound of tape. My hands are being tied and taped together behind my back. I go limp, closing my eyes. It's coming back to me, that night—the night in my apartment. He taped my wrists just like this.

"It was you," I say.

"I don't understand why on earth you would do that," he says, chiding me. "That's—that's going to be a problem for them."

"Oh is it? Is it going to be a problem?" I ask, opening my eyes just so I can glare at him. "Damaged goods, is that it? You going to sell me on the black market?"

I've seen documentaries about women who go missing and end up sex slaves or whatever. I'd rather die. I'll fork myself in the heart next time if that's what my fate is.

He pulls me like a cop pulls a handcuffed person, by the arms, not exactly gently. He pushes me down into the chair and duct tapes me to it, the tape screeching as he loops it around and around. It pinches me and I can barely move. My face burns in pain.

"I don't want to be a sex slave," I cry.

"You're not going to be a sex slave, for Pete's sake." He holds up a phone. "Sit still."

"What are you doing?"

He ignores me, taking my picture, then typing on his phone, brow scrunched. The top of that mark on his face is peeking out the top of the bandanna again. Just as I fixate on it, he pulls the bandanna back up. His phone brightens, makes him sigh.

"Great," he sighs. "Suicide watch."

"Excuse me?"

He shakes his head and goes out the front door with a *beep-beep*. I sit in stunned silence. Did he leave? What does that mean, suicide watch? The locks beep again and the door opens and he's back, tiny plastic suitcase in hand. Though my cheeks are throbbing and I'm now immobilized, I can't help but shake the idea that I think this is an improvement over where things would have been if I hadn't acted out—at least I've broken the spell of same, same, same.

Kidnapper dude crouches, puts the gun at his feet, and opens the plastic suitcase. It's a first aid kit. I can't help but sputter a laugh.

"Yes?" he asks, almost hurt.

"What the fuck is going on?" I ask.

"I'm going to treat your wounds. We wouldn't want an infection."

"No, we wouldn't want that," I answer sarcastically.

I don't know if this man is fluent in sarcasm. He doesn't acknowledge my remark. He takes out a cotton ball, douses it in rubbing alcohol, and gently wipes my face.

"Ow!" I yell.

"Man, you really cut yourself deep," he says. "Why'd you do that? You don't want scars, do you?"

"How purdy my face looks is the last thing on my mind," I say, working hard to control the shake in my voice. "I don't even know if I'm getting out of here alive."

"No one's going to murder you," he says, as if it's silly to even think it.

"Then what are you going to do with me?" I ask.

"There." He screws the cap back on the rubbing alcohol. This close, I can see the dot of yellow in his dusky blue eyes. I can tell he's wearing contact lenses, the barely discernible transparent halo around his irises. There's no cruelty in those eyes. Just something like care, or pity.

"Do I know you?" I ask.

He doesn't reply. He breaks eye contact to put the first aid kit back together, clipping it shut.

"It's not an easy question with an easy answer," he says.

"Meaning …?"

He picks the gun back up. "Mind if I sit on the bed?"

Are you kidding me?

"Yes, I 'mind' that. I also mind you fucking kidnapping me. I mind, dude."

He sits on the bed anyway, on the edge. "I have to sit somewhere."

This guy is so weird. He's somehow non-threatening even with a gun to my head. Despite the threat he poses, he's … soft. There doesn't appear to be anything creepy or lecherous about him. He seemed genuinely disturbed by my face-forking incident, genuinely concerned for my well-being. Then how he seemed to be taking orders from someone from his phone. And his vague answers. He watches me, refixing his ponytail.

"How long am I on suicide watch?" I ask.

"Until you seem cooled down."

"I'm cooled."

"If I were you, I wouldn't try to pull any silliness like that again." He rests the gun next to him. "Unless you want to just forfeit."

"Forfeit what? I don't even know what game we're playing. Doesn't seem like I'm going to win anyway."

He continues to stare at me glassily, like a man lost in his imagination. Then his phone vibrates, startling him out of his reverie, and he reads the text.

"What does it say?"

"Next steps," he says, standing up, grabbing his gun like an awkward soldier.

He steps back to the table, next to me, and opens the first aid kit again. He pulls out something wrapped in plastic and a little bottle. My pulse skips a beat when he tears the plastic open and I spy the gleam of a needle.

"Why are you taking that out?" I ask.

He plunges the needle into the bottle, sucks liquid into it, and holds it to the light. "I hope you know now you need to behave from here on out."

"Behave?" I say, stomach turning. "What is that?"

He stoops and touches the inside of my arm. I try to squirm, but the duct-tape is too tight. I can't move an inch.

"No!" I screech.

"It's just a mild tranquilizer," he says.

I look over at the table, read the word *xylazine*. What the hell is that?

"I'll give you all my money," I say hurriedly as he taps my arm in search of a vein. "All of it. I'll give you money I haven't even made yet."

He raises his eyebrows, needle poised. "It's about more than that."

The bandanna has fallen just a little. Just enough for me to see that he has a brown birthmark there, shaped like a bird in flight.

"Please," I beg him. "I could give you so much money. More money than what I have now. See, I was supposed to get a record deal today." Tears fall and send a new burn to my fork wounds. "Everything was going to be amazing."

"It's still going to be amazing, Violet," he says, his eyes shining with something resembling sympathy as he sticks the needle in and warmth blooms in my arm. "Don't worry. You have your whole life ahead of you."

Then it all goes black.

––––––

It's strange, if you think about it, that we fear death. Why? Death is just that vast nothing-sea where we came from. It doesn't hurt; there's no sadness, no fear. Whenever I've thought of death in life, I imagine being trapped in endless blankness, me alone with my thoughts. But being trapped and alone is a state of life, not death.

To be drugged into oblivion is probably the closest we ever get to dying. In sleep, dreams await us. Our imaginations keep flickering. The stillness of the anesthetized, though, is to rest like the dead. And to wake up from it is a special eeriness—finding myself confused, dry-mouthed. Heavy-limbed and in a different place than I remember.

It's as if no time or possibly a hundred years passed since my eyes were last open.

I was strapped to a chair. Taped to a chair. Now I'm lying in my bed. Well, not *my* bed. My hell cabin bed, wrapped up in a hand-stitched quilt in the middle of a nightmare. My head hurts.

"Hello?" I croak.

The man appears to be gone. I scan the room for signs of him. No grocery bags, no gun, no first aid kit. As I sit up, the blood flows to my face along with a rush of pain. I touch my cheek. Puffy, scratched.

Shit.

I remember the fork and everything.

"Ow," I whisper.

Maybe I'm sorry I did that. Maybe not. I don't know what good it did. Was that stupid? I guess if I ever get out of here it will give me character. Be a wild story I tell one day. "So there was this time I was kidnapped and I stabbed myself in the face with a fork …"

I try to get up but I'm a noodle. This again. It's like how I felt that first day here. Kidnapper dude shot me up with a drug. He called it a tranquilizer. I read the bottle. Xylophone?

The window's dark and it's cold in here, so it must be nighttime. Which means hours have passed. It's an inexplicably gross feeling to know a man was left alone in a room with you and your passed-out body. I pull my shirt up, my pants down, feel around. But I really don't think he touched me. He's very odd. Seems calm and kind, yet shoots me up with drugs and duct tapes me to chairs. He cleans up the wound on my face yet he points a weapon at it. He gives the impression somehow he's just following orders, that a part of him is rooting for me.

But he said Priya wasn't the connection. And I'm still here.

After a ridiculously long, groaning push, I sit up and breathe a moment. Man, that xylophone shit really messed me up. My phone's on the kitchen counter and I need to go get it, which at the moment feels about as feasible as me swimming across the Pacific.

"You can do this, Violet," I tell myself.

I'll bet Bud's worried about me. Either that or he's blissfully passed out next to a mountain of empty beer cans. Takes me another pep talk to push myself to a standing position and hobble to the kitchen counter.

Once I'm here, I catch my breath again and hold onto the countertop and pray to the universe that I don't pass out. I take the phone and lower myself to a cross-legged position on the floor. Opening the fridge, I grab a sparkling water and hold it against my head. Even though the room is cold, I feel sweaty. Hot flashes or something. I screw open the bottle and have a drink. With my eyes closed, the blackberry aftertaste transports me to home. I'm sitting at my kitchen table, guitar on my knee, playing in my favorite spot of the house where the acoustics sound the best.

I could cry. But I don't this time.

My phone tells me it's after ten. Damn, I was *out*. I dial Bud. It takes him three rings to pick up.

"Hullo?" he says.

"Hi. It's me, your favorite unknown number."

"What the hell happened? I've been worried."

"It's been a wild ride, Bud," I say with a forced little laugh.

"So? You okay?"

"Well," I say, taking another swig of blackberry sparkling water. "Other than stabbing myself in the face with a fork and a throbbing headache from a tranquilizer given to me by my kidnapper, yeah, I guess so."

There's a long silence. "I sure hope you're going to unpack that for me a bit."

Indeed. I open up my verbal luggage and unpack.

There's so much to revisit. It all comes bursting breathlessly out of me. The kidnapper dude, the conversation, the impromptu self-inflicted violence. Bud is preoccupied with the fork incident, but what is much more important for us to explore is the fact Priya Patel is not the connection after all. Kidnapper dude's remark about how we'd never figure it out. The person he called—or people? Didn't he pluralize them? Which would mean there are at least three people involved, right? Then there's how upset he was when I stabbed my face.

"Well, yeah, I would expect anyone would be upset by that," he says. "Do you think you're going to have scars?"

"What the hell do I care?" I ask. "At this point, if I have to worry about scars for the rest of my life, yippee, that means I live to get out of here."

"What's the guy look like? You sure you don't know him?"

"Same guy as before. Blond. Tall. Blue eyes. He covers his face. Oh! The mark I mentioned seeing before? It's a birthmark on his cheek. Looks like a bird in flight."

I've been recapping it all to him while eating cheese on the kitchen floor now for a while. And though we've gone over the facts like dogs chasing our tails, neither of us seem to know how this affects our futures or the game we're trapped in.

"So he said Priya wasn't the connection," Bud repeats, going over it again. "But did he say Zayan wasn't?"

"No," I say, sitting up and returning the cheese to its home in the fridge. "He acted like we were way off. What happened with Zayan?"

So much happened today in hell cabin that I forgot about Bud's fact-finding mission, which rings petty now in comparison. He explains it to me—slowly, agonizingly, like a man sitting around a campfire, coloring in unnecessary details including the staring contest he had with a clownfish in an aquarium at the vet's office. Man needs to learn some self-editing skills. Finally, he gets to the meat of the story and the whole thing gets derailed into some drama about how Zayan was the reason Priya left him all those years ago and I have to interrupt and tell him to focus.

"We can 'dearly beloved' your love life later. Did you get the vibe it was Zayan or not?" I ask impatiently.

"Gut feeling? No, I don't think it was him. Even though he's a shit—"

"A shitstain, yes, I know, we've been over this."

"Plus, Violet, you're never going to believe what I found when I got home."

"What, Bud?" I ask, not holding my breath, expecting some long-winded story about not much at all.

"I went to check your socials."

"'Your socials.' Okay, gramps."

"I'm serious."

"Listening."

"It's everywhere," he says, and his voice gets louder, closer to the receiver. "There are even a couple articles about it in the news."

"What?" I ask, now all ears.

"You quit Violet and the Black Sheep."

I don't know why, but those words cut deeper than a fork to my face. I've been playing with that band for years. It's as if a part of me grew up with them. We went from playing for five people in dive bars to having a residency with Lady Lithium. Benzo and Lila, they're like my siblings. Sure, we squabble. Things weren't left on the best terms. But I had high hopes that I would be able to score us a deal somehow through Maxam. That it wasn't over yet. But now, like this, I find out it's over.

It's all over.

I'd cry, but I've run dry at the moment. Instead I shake my head and steep in the pain. The grief. The loss. Even if I get out of here, life's never going to be the same again.

"Who'd this come from?" I finally ask. "Who posted the news?"

"You did."

"You mean, whoever has my phone did," I say quietly.

I push myself up to a standing position. My legs are still a little wobbly, so I walk carefully to the bed and plop down on it. I massage my arm where kidnapper dude stuck the needle in earlier. Asshole.

"It's an audio recording," he says.

"Of what?"

"You."

I punch my pillow a couple times and then lie down, frowning at the ceiling. "What do you mean, me?"

"Listen," he says. "Hold on. I have to figure out how to play it for you."

Clicks and mutterings of "how the hell do I ..." and "where's that window again, I had it open..." Seriously, he's an old man trapped in a young man's body. Finally, a recording plays. A recording of a voice.

My voice.

Saying words I've never said.

"Hi my little lambs," the recording says. It's me trying to sound chipper, me sounding slightly tired, eerily familiar. "I've got some news for ya. Violet and the Black Sheep are parting ways. It's been so much fun. So many amazing shows we've played in towns all over the country. So much beautiful music we made together. But I've decided to spend some time on me for a change. I'm going on a hiatus from music and taking a social media break. It's time for me to really ... find myself. Thanks so much for all your support."

"That's it right there," Bud says.

The feeling, it's like being shoved off a cliff.

So many thoughts race through my mind at once.

How the hell did they get a recording of me saying something I never said? Was this something I recorded while drugged or something and then forgot about? I was out for a good seven, eight hours today so who knows what happened during that time. The thought of which is appalling. Why a voice message then? Why not a video? I usually posted videos and not audio recordings to my account. And what does that mean, a hiatus? 'Finding' myself? A 'social media break?' The whole thing makes me sick.

"They're going to kill me," I whisper.

"Don't say that."

"They're covering up my disappearance so no one comes looking for me." I can barely speak the words. I close my eyes. "You heard it. You know it. I'm never coming home."

He doesn't answer for a moment, which isn't exactly reassuring. "Well, I hope you're wrong."

I don't answer. It's as if my whole body, my whole being, has turned to stone. Somehow this whole time I had this wind of hope lifting me up. I kept my focus on getting out, on solving the riddle. I was convinced I still had some level of control. But now it's clear that whatever is happening is so far out of my hands, so bizarre, so unexplainable, that kidnapper dude was right: I'll never guess it.

I'll never find my way out.

"You think your bandmates might be behind this?" he asks. "I noticed Benzo and Lila locked their personal accounts up soon after that was posted."

"It was my *voice*, Bud. Explain that."

"What if you recorded that when you were drugged?"

I inhale deeply. "I thought that too. But I didn't *sound* drugged."

"Guess that's true. You'd've been slurring your speech."

"Right. Something, at least."

"You had any issues with your bandmates recently?"

"Well, after our show last Thursday, we didn't exactly leave on good terms."

God, was that just Thursday? And today was Monday? Just one long weekend separates normalcy from agony.

It's mind-blowing.

"Well," Bud says, and I hear the crack of a can. "I mean, there you go."

"Drinking beer this late?"

"A little nightcap always does me good."

"Can I ask you something? No judgment. But are you an alcoholic?"

A beat passes. "I wouldn't call myself that. I just drink to make the world a better place."

"Wow, so charitable."

"I try."

"I'll be real with you: that sounds unhealthy."

"Look, the world's sad, all right? Why not let yourself be happy if you can?"

"You ever think it's you who's sad and the world's just there?"

He sighs. "All right. Okay, Violet. We don't have time for psychoanalyzing. Look, I had an idea. How would you feel if I drove down to LA tomorrow and just … poked around?"

"I'm really not sure what the point is of you playing Sherlock."

"What am I supposed to do instead? Just live my life, go to work? Sit here on my ass and talk to you all day? And come on, how closely do you really think they're following and listening anyway? Did you get the feeling from that dude today that they're hanging on our every word?"

"No. In fact, I got the impression he was totally out of touch with what we'd been discussing. Like he had no idea about the Priya connection, nor did he seem to care. Then again, he also seemed like he was just … following orders. Like there were other people listening. So I don't know, Bud.

But what was the point of you visiting Zayan today? What good did it do?"

"I sure feel like it made it clearer that it might not be him, so it was worth it. You know?"

"Meh."

"Otherwise you and me would be sitting here spinning our wheels assuming Priya was the connection."

"She still could be, for all I know. I don't know what the fuck is going on."

"But the band announcement. Your recording."

I'm quiet a moment, getting goosebumps. The sound of my own voice saying words I've never spoken. It's a feeling unlike anything I've ever had. I almost wonder for a moment if I'm me, if I'm really here, or if that voice somewhere is the real Violet.

"I'm tired," I say. "This day has been a flaming pile of toxic waste. I need to rest."

"Sure, sure."

"You should get some rest too, dude. Lay off the beer and go brush your teeth."

He sighs. "All right."

"Going to need your brain cells when you go to LA tomorrow," I say. "I'll call you back in the morning before you leave, give you my house code so you can get in. Who knows, maybe you'll find something there? The note said you can't ask people about my disappearance. They never said you couldn't snoop around my house."

"So … you're saying I should go?"

"Why the hell not. They're probably going to kill me anyway."

"Violet, don't say that. Jesus."

"Dark joke. Sorry. Have a good night's sleep."

"You too. You sure you don't … want to stay on the line like last night?"

"Nah. I'll call you if I need you."

He pauses. "Okay then. Talk soon."

I guess the misery well has refilled itself, because as soon as I hear the click of the line, I burst into tears. Deep, guttural, rolling sobs like a child. The not-knowing. The lack of control. The sound of my own voice that also sounds like a stranger. The news that I quit the band. The drugs I was shot up with today. The lost hours with a man I don't know. Alone. I'm alone. There's one number I can call, sure, but really I'm in this alone. The pain, the fear, they're consuming, and I'm infinitesimal, insignificant: a violet in the middle of nowhere.

BUD

BEEN a while since I've gone on a road trip.

I used to go camping with Andrew when he was still alive. Drive up to Mendo in his van thick with weed smoke blasting music with wailing guitars. We had some fun up there, me and him. Andrew was stoic all week long on the job but when he was off, he was the king of stupid jokes and tall tales and card games and whiskey. And he loved me with no conditions, even if he was hard on my ass. Only my mama ever loved me that unwaveringly. In some ways, I owe what I am today to Andrew. He trained me, taught me not just skills, but craftsmanship. Lots of people think of carpentry as this functional thing—building walls, fixing shit. But he taught me it's an art form. And he wouldn't let me screw up and walk away from a job, which had always been my instinct. Mess up and run, that's the Bud way. Nope. He made me stay and get it right.

When Andrew got diagnosed with stage four pancreatic cancer, he tried to turn his clients over to me. I wouldn't take them. Even when he was shrinking in that bed at that hospice center, I couldn't believe Andrew was dying. He wasn't even sixty. There'd been some mistake. He tried to have these talks with me about how he wanted to see me happy, have a family, a successful business. How at some point I needed to start taking care of myself and not party my life away, unless I wanted to end up like him—alone, with no one but your apprentice there to say goodbye. I nodded and listened, but none of it made a difference. Because no matter what his advice said, the man I most wanted to be like in my life was Andrew.

As I drive down 5, air conditioner whirring, stereo singing me some country music, I reflect on the fact that life's given me warnings again and again that I've never heeded. My coach back in high school who told me that the only thing holding me back was my lack of self-confidence. Priya, who told me in various ways that she needed to see me step it up more than I did. Andrew dying and warning me against a fate like his at the end. And then Emily ODing—her death was beyond a warning, it was more like a threat from a higher power. This is what your fate is if you don't change what you're doing, Bud. And yeah, I backed off shooting dope. But I went right back to my lonely life of beer, TV, and fixing shit. That was a hard couple of years, losing Priya, Andrew, and then Emily. You'd think it would change me more. But honestly, I feel a lot like the same man who drove this same highway years ago for a girl, for a shot at something new. Vague memories twinkle as I pass the scorched brown flatlands of the Central Valley, fast food joints and strip malls, digital freeway signs.

I know I said I'd try to eat better today but once I'm in the Mr. Droidburger drive-thru line I decide I'll start that tomorrow. Know what? I'll join a gym, too. But for now I eat double bacon patties with cheese. I stop by a liquor store and get a coffee and a beer, just a twelve-ouncer, and drink it in the parking lot to take the edge off. Then I down my coffee and keep driving.

There's something kinda ominous about Los Angeles,

alien. The city juts up in the center of the spread, back-dropped by mountains, surrounded by a sickly haze of smog. The freeways, a tangled mess of concrete snakes. It's an easy place to get lost in. I do like the palm trees. Iconic. Funny though that we all think of palm trees when we think of the city, when they're not even plants native to that area. Andrew told me that. Bunch of monks brought them over from abroad centuries ago. Now Los Angeles wouldn't be Los Angeles without its palms. Makes me wonder if there's any such thing as a genuine self.

My GPS takes me to the Silver Lake neighborhood where Violet's place is. After parking on a hill, I hop out. Sling my backpack over my arm, put my sunglasses on and stand a moment in the sunshine. The lake's blinding from here, surrounded by houses and tufts of green trees. I'm admiring its beauty in a peaceful moment on the sidewalk when a DashDrone whizzes by not two feet above my head and scares the living crap out of me. Then a guy on an electric unicycle drives by, blasting hip-hop music. A robot lawn-mower's spinning circles in front of a bungalow.

This world baffles me. I don't think I was made for these times.

Violet's condo is in this impressive Spanish colonial-style complex that sits at the top of a hill. It's got an old Hollywood feel to it. White with green trim, new-looking terra cotta roof and wrought iron staircases and ornate balconies. Behind the tall palms out front, the fence hides a shimmering blue pool. Place must have cost her a fortune. I punch her code in the front and wander up the cement pathway, stopping to take a look at the lazy patchwork someone did on the side of the building. There's a lit-up elevator that appears to have been added to the building later, but I take the stairs. At the door that says #11, I punch her code in again.

"Hey!" a voice says from behind me.

It's a blond-haired lady chewing gum, poking her head

out of the doorway of #9. By the looks of the many flags hung on her door and the cap on her head, she's clearly built her identity around her love for the Dodgers. I get a sick, guilty feeling with my hand on Violet's doorknob, like I've been caught doing something I shouldn't.

"Hello," I say.

"You Violet's friend?"

"Yep."

"I haven't seen Violet in days."

"Yeah, she took off for a little. Asked me to housesit."

"Saw the news though about the Black Sheep. Gosh, that's wild!"

"Uh-huh."

"Is she …" She drops her voice. "She's not thinking of leaving the area, is she?"

I brush the hair out of my face, tuck it behind my ears. "Why would she do that?"

"I don't know. Just something I was wondering. Anywho, nice meeting you. I'm Jonie, by the way."

"Bud."

"Butt?" she almost yells.

"Bud."

"Oh," she says, laughing. "I thought you said 'Butt.'"

"No."

When she giggles, she kind of snorts. "Oh Jonie, you silly goose." A ding sounds behind her. "Smoothie's done. Toodles."

She closes the door and I'm left gaping at a bunch of Dodgers flags.

"Toodles," I repeat to the air in disbelief. Probably the first time in my almost thirty years on this planet that I've uttered that word.

Violet's condo gives me the feeling that I'm not even worthy of standing in it. The living room with its white shag rug, abstract art on the walls, built-in TV, robot vacuum cleaners. Her kitchen with wide windows, lace curtains, four cactuses on the windowsill, teacups dangling from special hooks. Her bedroom, with only guitars hanging on her walls and a twin bed that makes me think she sleeps most nights alone.

Her bedroom tells the story of her kidnapping. Her duvet's twisted up and lying across her floor. Next to it, a broken glass that sits in a pool of water. Her dresser top has nothing on it. I pop open her closet and notice her clothes and shoes organized by color. In her bathroom, everything's spotless except the bathtub and shower curtain, stained purple. I end up back in the living room, sitting on the couch.

This place is classy. It even smells expensive, I guess from that plug-in thing occasionally spritzing the air. But there's something about it that feels more like a vacation rental than a home. Besides the purple bathtub, there's no … Violet here. No evidence of humanity. No toiletries left out on countertops or half-full hampers or framed pictures. I expected some place exploding with color, songs scrawled on loose papers, the space of a messy creative. Maybe whoever kidnapped her removed some of her personal items?

I check my phone. There's a missed call from an UNKNOWN.

"Shit," I mutter.

I must've accidentally turned my ringer down. Violet's going to let me have it. My stomach grumbles so I go take a gander at the inside of her fridge: gleaming, spotless. Whose fridge looks like this? Is Violet even a real person? Yogurt, some strawberries, some cheese and bread, sparkling water. I grab one and drink it as I sit on a stool at the countertop. That's another thing, no dining room table. Just two stools at a countertop. It's a sweet condo but there's nothing resembling a home here.

Standing, stretching, my eye catches something it didn't during the first walkthrough: in the dark, short hallway between the living room and kitchen, there are some hooks on the walls and what looks like a jacket and a purse hanging. I wander over and turn the light switch on. Sure enough, a glittery purse on a silver chain and—get this—a leather jacket.

"I see," I say to the jacket. "So it's not okay to eat animals, but it's just fine to wear 'em. Aren't you a little hypocrite."

I grab her purse and sit on the living room couch. It's a creepy feeling, being in a stranger's house, snooping around, but I've got to admit there's something kind of exhilarating about it, too. I'm a lifetime loser but I've never been a criminal. Never stole money from my mama growing up. Never started fires. My lies were lazy ones, lies of omission. I empty the contents of Violet's purse onto the coffee table, so shiny there's not even a smudge or a fingerprint on it. In a clatter, her wallet and keys hit the glass tabletop. That's it. Nothing else in her purse. No gum, no little pieces of trash.

"Am I being set up?" I ask the empty room.

I open her wallet. There she is on her license: Violet Wilde, born the same year as me. If looks could talk, hers would say "what the hell are you looking at?" I snicker at the attitude. There's cash in her wallet, a debit card, and a credit card. No business cards or loose coins or anything else.

Something's not right here. It's all too bare bones. I plunge my hand into her purse and feel nothing but satin. Except, wait—in one corner, there's something hard. Ah, a zipper. I open it and pull out a phone. Her phone.

Wait a second here. Didn't Violet say someone must have had her phone to be posting those pictures of her? What's all this, then?

I flip the phone over in my hand, examining it, and press the button. It lights up asking me for a passcode. On a whim, I enter the six-digit passcode that got me through her front door. And I'm in. Violet, Violet, Violet. You're a public figure and this crappy at security?

I check my phone and she still hasn't called me back.

Hope she doesn't mind if I go through her phone while I wait. Because there's something very off about all this. Something's not real, not true here, and I can't tell what it is. But my stomach's a little uneasy, because I hope that it's not Violet I should be suspecting. What if she's been playing me this whole time? What if she's not locked in a cabin after all?

Can't think of why she'd lie to me though. That's where I get stuck.

I go through her pictures backward from the ones taken last. There's one taken of a crowd from a stage on Thursday night, a thing she does every show and posts it on the Violet and the Black Sheep account. There's that one of Silver Lake and of Barnabus. A lot of selfies. A lot of different, wild makeup, all with the silver-wallpapered backdrop behind her that tells me they were taken in her bathroom. Pictures on stages. Pictures of her cactuses. Pictures of her guitar. Pictures looking out her kitchen window. Rinse and repeat.

Next, I look at her texts, and this is where it gets weird. Because Violet's been texting with people all day long. Her latest is from a number that has no name programmed to it, from just over an hour ago.

Hi Violet, this is Leslie with the Sunset Review. Your bandmate "Benzo" gave me your number. Wondering if you would have time for an interview in light of Violet and the Black Sheep's news?

Hi Leslie, I'm not doing press at this time. Please take me off your list, this number is my private phone xoxo

There are six more messages like that over the past couple of days and she says the same thing, as if copy and pasted. "Please take me off your list, this number is my private phone xoxo." Odd. Really odd. Did someone have this phone and put it back?

My phone starts ringing and I put Violet's down on the

coffee table to pick mine up. I sit back and answer. I'd kick my feet up, but the coffee table's too good for my boots.

"Hey Violet."

"You there yet?"

"Been here a bit, yeah."

"And?"

"I'm at your place. Not gonna lie, it's weird here."

"Weird how?"

"First of all," I say. "Your neighbor Jonie's a trip."

"Ugh."

"She thought my name was 'Butt.'"

"She's a dingbat. I'm sorry."

"She seemed to think that you were maybe moving out?"

"She wishes. God, that woman's a hawk. She wants her dingbat best friend to move into the building. Every day she's poking her head out to ask if I'm moving. So rude."

"Then your apartment ..."

"Yeah?" she asks, sounding concerned. "Everything okay?"

"Well," I say, staring at the abstract painting on her wall that looks like someone took some mustard and ketchup bottles, had a squirtfest, and called it art. "It doesn't feel lived in. It feels like stuff's missing. You know what I mean?"

"Someone broke in?" she asks, pitch climbing. Her voice isn't as bad as it was yesterday, but it's still a little hoarse.

"No, no. It's hard to explain."

"What's missing?"

"Well, hard to know what's missing when I've never been here before."

"You know, dude, sometimes you are straight-up *aggravating*."

"Okay, okay," I say, getting up to walk around and survey the place again. "It's like—there are no signs of a real person living here. Nothing's left out on countertops, no messes anywhere—"

"It's clean, Bud," she says. "That's what's freaking you out? I'm neat?"

"It's not just that. Oh! And your purse—sorry, I went through your purse. That okay?"

"Sure, why not? I mean, I'm locked in a cabin with fork wounds on my face so I've kind of learned to live a little here."

"There's nothing in it," I say. "Just keys, wallet, and your phone."

"What else would you expect me to keep in there?" She gasps, as if she just processed what I said to her. "Wait—my *phone*?"

"Yeah. And I'm going through that right now—"

"Going through my phone."

"That okay?"

"I mean, sure. Just don't mind the nude selfies."

My mouth is stuck open a moment.

"Joking, Bud. I don't do nude selfies. Don't want to give Big Brother a free boner."

I swallow. "Anyway—"

"Did I just make you uncomfortable?"

"No, I—"

"Was it imagining me naked or imagining Big Brother with a boner?"

"Neither, okay?" I ask, my face getting hot. "Can we focus? Reporters have been texting you asking for interviews."

"Reporters? On my cell? How'd they get my number?"

"It said Benzo gave it to them."

"Ahhh, way to stick to me, Benz," she says.

"And you've been replying this cut-and-paste answer. Hold on, let me find it. By the way, really? Using the same passcode for both your phone and your apartment?"

"I know, I know. It's my parents' wedding anniversary. I've been using it since I was in college. I know it sounds fucked up but I feel like I'd be betraying them if I changed it."

"Well, I think now that you're locked in a cabin you might finally understand the importance of security."

"You have a point."

I read her the reply her phone has been sending to reporters.

"They're trying hard to cover up the fact I'm missing," she says quietly.

"This all feels … like there's a part of the story I'm not getting," I tell her. "I don't know, your house strikes me as not just neat, but unlived in. Like a vacation rental."

"I live there. I've lived there for years," she says sharply.

"It's hard to explain."

She sighs. "So besides judging my cold, uninviting condo, what's the plan?"

"Well, you said Benzo works the seven to four shift at The Daily Bean on Silver Lake Boulevard, right?"

"Correct."

"Even Friday morning, after playing a show the night before?"

"Yep. Benzo's a drama queen, but he's reliable as a clock."

"I kinda want to see if he missed work on Friday. And, I don't know, maybe just go in there and feel him out a little."

"'Feel him out.'"

"I was born with a pretty good bullshit detector."

"And walk me through the plan here. What if, hypothetically, pie in the goddamn sky here, he says 'yup, I did it,' Bud? What then?"

"Then …"

"You have no plan, man."

"I'll beat him up."

"Great," she mutters. "Look, I appreciate you cosplaying detective here, but poking your head around and asking questions is just going to get us into trouble."

Right as she says this, her phone lights up. I look down at the notification flickering on screen.

"Someone's texting your phone." I let out a big *ha*. "It's Benzo."

"What's it say?"

I punch in the code and squint at the message. "It says 'You fucking deserve it backstabber.'"

"Oh," she says softly. "What's he talking about?"

"Replying to you politely asking him not to give reporters your phone number."

Then the three dots appear, as if Violet is texting. Which is impossible since I have her phone in my hand. But guess not.

"Whoa," I say. "You're texting him back."

"Huh?"

"Not you, obviously. Someone is. Someone's texting him back from your phone. But not your phone, actually, because I have your phone here in my hand."

"What? What's it saying?"

The words appear on the screen and I read them out loud. "'Sorry it ended that way. I just have to take care of myself. xoxo'. Oh wait, he's typing back already." I wait for the text to appear. "Okay, now he replied, in all caps 'YOU ALWAYS HAVE TO TAKE CARE OF YOURSELF!!! THAT'S ALL YOU EVER CARE ABOUT!!!!'"

"Am I replying?"

I stare at blue and gray bubbles of texts, waiting for the three dots to appear. But they don't. "No."

Reading the texts to Violet seems to have darkened her mood. "Benzo hates me," she says softly. "And I deserve it. But I don't think he has anything to do with this."

"Hey, it's after three. If I want to get over to the Daily Bean, I should probably leave."

"Sure, go ahead. Please don't be stupid. My life is in your hands, et cetera et cetera. You know the drill."

"Call me in a few hours."

"Okay. Be safe."

We hang up. My mama used to say that every time I left the house: be safe. Haven't heard anyone say that to me in a long time.

It's refreshing going on a walk. First place I stop in is a bar, a dark dive with a neon martini sign glowing in the window. Inside, a drunk woman is talking passionately to another drunk woman about her screenplay. I take a seat at the bar, order a pint, and down it as fast as I can. When the bartender with the curly hair and the piercing in her cheek smiles at me and asks where I'm from—she loves my accent!—I can feel a little flirtation in the way she leans in on her elbows. Normally I'd flirt back. But instead I down my beer in a few thirsty gulps, say, "Texas," and burp before making my exit.

The neighborhood's hip. Vintage stores, farm-to-table restaurants, corner markets with advertisements for vitamin tonics and colon cleansers in the windows. They've got those robotic trash pickers rolling up and down the sparkling sidewalks. The beer settled my nerves and I'm pretty proud that I've only had two beers today.

By the time I get to the Daily Bean, I'm sweating. I stand outside a moment, wiping my brow with my shirt, catching my breath. I make eyes with my reflection in the coffee shop's front window. Hair hanging in strings around my face, panting. Didn't realize what an out-of-shape oaf I'd become. No one would ever look at me now and mistake me for a guy who won state championships playing running back. Nah, that was some other guy.

Inside, the air conditioning's a relief. I try to keep a few feet between me and the lady ahead of me, because I'm pretty sure I stink. Right away I can tell the guy behind the counter is Benzo. He's enormous and dressed all in black with fishnet sleeves. A giant goth, a goth giant. He looks like someone who could beat the crap out of me with one arm tied behind his back. A guy who wouldn't have any problems whatsoever knocking out a girl and slinging her lifeless body over his shoulder.

"What's up," he mutters when I get to the register.

"I'll have a, uh … you don't serve beer here, do you?"

"*No*, we don't serve *beer*. We're a *coffeehouse*."

And *you're* an *asshole,* I don't say.

"I'll have a lemonade, then," I say instead. "Also, hey, I was here Thursday night, and I left a notebook. Any chance you found it Friday morning?"

He punches numbers into the cash register. "I'll have to ask. I wasn't here Friday."

Bingo.

"How come?" I ask him.

Benzo curls up his lip. "What do you care? My daughter was sick. Seven seventy-five." I run my card in the machine. Benzo turns around and yells at the woman who stands staring into space at the espresso machine. "Bella, anyone find a notebook here Friday?"

She shakes her head, still staring into space.

Benzo does a *voila* gesture.

"Thanks for checking," I say.

I taste the lemonade. Needs sugar. I go over to the cream and sugar station and add some. Benzo's staring at me from the register, shaking his head.

"Too *sour* for you?" he asks.

"It's good now," I say, holding the cup up in the air. "Cheers."

He watches me with something like suspicion as I leave the coffee shop.

———

When I was a little squirt eating up my long hot days climbing trees and catching frogs, my whole life ahead of me, sometimes I'd watch this show on TV at night about cops chasing criminals around New York City. These detectives in long coats meeting all these interesting folks in different neighborhoods. Asking barbed questions. Catching bad guys. I used to tell people that's what I wanted to be when I grew up. I dressed up as one for Halloween a couple years in grade school, plastic badge and everything. But after my mama dated that sack of shit wannabe cowboy and the cops got called to our house to arrest him for breaking a bottle over her head, I didn't want to be a cop anymore.

I haven't thought about all that in a long time but I'm thinking about it again now because this feels a little like detective work. Gathering clues. I've even got some notes in that app I've never used before in my phone. Benzo was out of work Friday, which could mean he's involved. Now I'm going to where Violet told me Lila works, a vintage clothing store on Melrose.

I have to park about four blocks away and walk up the tree-lined streets, passing posh apartment buildings with fancy names in cursive writing on the front. Bet it costs a fortune to live here. The vintage store is called Harold's and has a mannequin in the front wearing a flower-power dress. I step inside, a doorbell ringing automatically. Instantly, I recognize Lila behind the counter from the pictures online. Brown hair. Glasses. She looks up from her phone and smiles at me.

"Hey, let me know if you need help with anything," she says.

I step up to the counter, a glass case filled with pendants and rings and other sparkly stuff. "Whoa. Wait a second. Are you Lila?" I say, putting my hand on the glass. "From Violet and the Black Sheep?"

Her smile melts a little and she stiffens. "Yeah. Formerly."

This time, I take a different tack, figuring some flattery might open some doors. I up my Texas accent, too, to make me seem easy, friendly.

"Sorry, but—man, y'all are my favorite band," I say. "I can't believe you work here. I heard you broke up?"

"The rumors are true," she says, putting her phone in her pocket.

"What happened?"

She gives an exaggerated shrug. "Who knows. We found out we were breaking up the same way the rest of the world did: on Instagrat."

"Really?" I ask, leaning an elbow on the counter. "That's messed up. Nothing? She didn't tell you?"

Lila shakes her head. "She didn't show up to practice and me and Benz are waiting for her at the space. Next thing you know, both our phones are exploding. Everyone's like, 'What happened? You broke *up*?' We're like … what?"

"Dang. That seems weird, right? To not tell you first?"

"You'd think," she says. "But no. That's Violet for you." She drops her voice. "I mean, she broke up with her last serious girlfriend via text. Enough said."

"Wow," I say.

"I shouldn't have said that, but, whatever. I'm done caring about her feelings at the moment."

"I get it," I say. "That's a real shame. You heard from her since it happened?"

"Nope," she says. "Not a word."

"You worried about her at all?" I ask.

"Nah. Violet worries plenty about herself. I'm sure she's got it covered." She runs her fingers through her bangs. "Sorry, don't mean to sound bitter. I wish her well. Hope she 'finds herself.'"

"Me too," I say. "I noticed you and, uh … Benzo, y'all locked your Instagrat accounts?"

"Because all we were getting were reporters and all the reporters want to talk about is Violet. I'm sick of talking about her." She gives me a glassy, sad look. I know that hurt look well.

"I'm sorry," I say. And I really am.

"Can I help you find anything today?" she asks brightly. Seems like she's signaling the conversation is over.

"Um ..."

I gaze down into the glass case again. Feel sort of obligated to buy something at this point, I don't know, to make it seem like I wandered in here for more than just nosing around about her band's breakup. My eyes wander over the glitter and gold, the old-school watches, the sunglasses with rhinestones. Something catches my attention—a necklace with a tiny fork tangling from it.

I snort. "I'll take that."

"The fork one? Cute, huh?"

"Yeah."

She wraps it up for me, rings me up. I pocket it and walk out the door.

Stepping into the sunshine, I take some time to wander up the sidewalks speckled with tree shade. Passing people laughing and eating on cafe patios, a bookstore blasting jazz, a music shop with a drum set in the window. Stopping in a diner, I sit at a booth and eat a hot dog and fries. Even though it's a hip diner with a wall full of punk posters and waiters with neon hair, it's got the booths and the mini jukeboxes at the tabletops like the place my mama works at back in Aubrey, and I get that nice comforting feeling.

I go over my conversation with Lila as I eat. Beyond her hurt, she was pissed. And who wouldn't be? Show up to practice with your band and then find out that your singer posted a public message that she quit without talking to you first? But Lila also didn't seem suspicious about what happened to Violet in the least. Didn't even pause for worry or concern for Violet's well-being. Add that with the fact that Benzo didn't work his usual shift Friday, and those steamed texts from Benzo—maybe they had something to do with this. Maybe they had something to do with the kidnapping of

Violet Thursday night/Friday morning and then faked Violet's quitting of the band Sunday. Maybe they're the "them" the other guy's working for.

I'm trying to make it make sense. It's just not clicking for me.

The sky's getting darker in the late afternoon, some gray clouds shadowing the sun. Thirst is on my mind, so I find a liquor store after a few blocks and buy a six-pack. Driving back to Violet's place, my mind's still racing for answers. But mostly I'm thinking about the fork necklace. I'm thinking about how much I want to give it to Violet, how much I think she'd appreciate the dark joke of it. How having it here in my pocket serves as this hope that somehow, I'm going to find her.

I park the truck a few streets away from Violet's condo. Reaching over to grab the beer from the front seat, I notice the stethoscope sitting there on the floor. Just the sight of it spikes my adrenaline. That shitstain is the reason Priya's living in London with a kid of mine I'll probably never meet. Can't even imagine how different my life would have looked if he hadn't ruined it. I could be living in England with a beautiful family. I pick up the stethoscope and start bending it in my hands, trying to rip it apart, trying to break it to pieces. But I stop when I notice something, holding it up to the light. Peering closer.

There's a single purple hair stuck in the middle of the stethoscope, hanging from the place where rubber tubing meets the steel headset.

"What the actual hell," I say.

Slowly, I put the stethoscope down on the passenger's seat again with a sick kind of feeling. Sit there in the car with my six-pack on my lap, trying to come up with some scenario where Violet's hair could have gotten caught in Zayan's stethoscope. And all I can think is, maybe he used his vet equipment somehow in the kidnapping. I'm imagining

Violet's drugged and he's using his stethoscope to check her vitals and her hair gets caught in his stethoscope. Farfetched, I know. But I can make it work in my mind.

Outside Violet's condo, Jonie's door's ajar and a small crowd's inside cheering the kind of cheers you only hear at sports games. A quick glance and I see a bunch of red cups and a pony keg on a countertop. Laughter and shouting.

In Violet's condo, all's quiet, except for the robot vacuum cleaner wandering around bumping into walls. I sit on the couch with my plastic bag of beer on my lap, pulse thumping. Don't know why, but a wave of sadness washes over me and I feel lonely all of a sudden. This condo tries real hard to be cheerful and all I get from it is loneliness. Violet's bandmates seem to have nothing but contempt for her. And meanwhile, Violet's out there somewhere losing her mind so bad she hurt herself with a goddamn fork. Getting drugged, losing hours of her life, not knowing why this is happening to her.

My phone rings when I'm three beers deep on the couch, half a pizza eaten from the box on the table. Watching some show on TV about deep sea creatures. Bunch of ugly fuckers live down there. I check my phone, hoping it's not Bob, who's been on my case for calling in sick these past couple of days and who'll hate it even more when I text him I need another day tomorrow. But no. It's UNKNOWN. I mute the TV and answer the phone, put her on speaker.

"Hey Unknown," I say.

"Ugh," she says.

"Yeah? That's where we're at?"

The line's quiet.

"Violet?" I ask.

"You don't know what it's like," she says. "Being stuck here. The cabin fever is real."

"I'll bet."

"I can't even count how many hours I've spent staring out the window. Honestly, I think if I ever get out I'm going to make it my mission in life to free every indoor cat in America. I can't imagine this being your existence, stuck in a tiny box, able to look at the world but never interact with it."

"I'm so sorry, Violet." I swig my beer, kicking my socked feet up on her coffee table. The guilt's not lost on me that I'm here relaxing in a gorgeous apartment, enjoying a refreshing drink, feeling like a man on vacation while Violet's in hell.

"I wish that guy'd come back and drug me again," she says tiredly. "It's Tuesday. According to the note, we have one day left now. Tomorrow. Maybe the next day too, who knows when the clock started. But you know what? As today wore on, I realized I don't even have the energy to fight. Put me in a coma. Get me to the end of this. I just want to know the answer."

"You can't give up." I stop talking, hearing a pattering sound. "Hold on."

I flip off the TV. Get up, move to the kitchen. Out the wide window, a storm's blown in. Haven't seen a summer storm in years. In Texas, we got thunderstorms. But California summers are bone dry.

I smile. "It's raining right now."

"Really?"

"Yeah. Doesn't that seem like a sign of good luck or something?"

"Maybe." She's quiet a moment. "I've always loved the rain." Her voice catches. "I hope I get to see the rain again. The last time it rained, I—I didn't think to appreciate it. I didn't think it would be the last time."

"It wasn't the last time. You've got to think positive. You're going to live a whole amazing life after this. You've got your whole life ahead of you."

"That's *exactly* what he said," she tells me. "Jesus. Are you in on this together?"

"What who said?"

"You and kidnapper dude who shot me up with xylophone. Seriously. I don't know who to trust!"

"Hey now, try to take a breath," I say.

She's crying now. It hurts to hear, and to be this helpless. My own eyes water up as I stare out at the silver rain coming down on the rooftops and passing cars and streetlights and dark shapes of trees. I'd do anything, anything to save this girl. But feels like my anything's not going to be enough. Why'd she have to get paired with me to solve this? Paired with a bumbling idiot. Poor girl.

"Violet, I'm on your side," I tell her. "I was out talking to people this afternoon. Why would I be doing that if I wasn't on your side?"

A beat passes before she answers, sniffing, her tone still suspicious. "So what happened?"

"Well, Benzo wasn't at work Friday."

"What? Really?" she says, perking up. "He *never* misses work."

"Said his daughter was sick."

"Hmmm. Well, I could see that though."

"And Lila seemed *angry*. Not at all concerned about you. Remember how you said they'd worry when you didn't show up to band practice? Well, the audio message of you saying you quit the band was posted during when you'd be practicing. She didn't even seem suspicious. I looked through your phone and there's no texts between you and Lila, just those few texts between you and Benzo."

"She was mad, huh?" Violet scoffs. "Didn't even strike her as strange that I just *disappeared*?"

"She said that it was all something you would do. Said you broke up with someone by text?"

A long moment passes. I watch a rainbow umbrella bob up the street, held by an invisible person.

"Wow," she says. "Well, fuck me."

"You have anyone else I can talk to tomorrow before I head back? Like, I don't know, someone you dated? Friends?"

"Not really." She sounds tired. "You can just go home. None of this matters."

"If one of these people did this—"

"They didn't, dude."

"And if it wasn't them—shit, I forgot to tell you! I have Zayan's stethoscope, from the vet's office. I swiped it on accident."

"You swiped a stethoscope on accident."

"It has a purple hair stuck in it, Violet."

She sighs. "And?"

"What if he used it on you, and—"

"I know this is going to shock you, but I'm not the only lady with purple hair in the world."

"I'm aware. Just thought it was interesting."

After saying it out loud, the idea that that one hair meant anything seems silly. It all feels silly. A dark cloud passes over me. What the hell am I doing here? What's the point of anything? I stalk back to the living room and crack open another beer, drink it as fast as I can.

"Bud, I'm tired. I'll call you later."

"Okay."

She hangs up without another word.

Christ. Is she pissed at me? I toss my phone on the couch. I leave the condo and walk in the rain to go buy another six-pack from a convenience store a few blocks away. By the time I come back, I'm soaked. She hasn't called back. I take a long hot shower. I eat the rest of the pizza. Drink until I don't feel anything anymore. Lying on the couch, half-asleep with the TV on mute, I listen to Violet and the Black Sheep on my phone and scroll pictures of her. Try to imagine that girl here in the place where she belongs—here, in her condo. Here in this room with me now. I close my eyes and pray. I never pray unless until I've hit a wall of desperation. There's nothing else I can do. That's where I'm at right now.

When the album's done, I start it over. I'm drunk at this point, can't even count the beer bottles on the table. Bleary-eyed, I check my phone. After midnight. Nothing from Violet. I'm worried about her. So worried I feel a little sick, though the beer and pizza probably didn't help, either.

I yawn and scroll my phone a little longer. Think about clues we're missing. Think, think, *think*. I type in the words *xylophone drug* and the search engine asks *"Did you mean xylazine?"* When I click on it, it tells me xylazine is a horse tranquilizer.

"Horse tranquilizer," I tell the air, trying it out. "Purple hair in a stethoscope. Kidnapper dude and Zayan working together."

Seems more likely than Lila and Benzo, if you ask me. With Lila and Benzo, it would be motivated by vengeance. With Zayan, that shitstain would be after money with a side of vengeance.

I wanted to be a detective as a kid. But it's just as well I wasn't. Like most dreams, I was better off giving it up. Because look at me—I'd make a lousy fucking detective.

VIOLET

SOMETHING IS HAPPENING TO ME.

A mental shift. My memories have changed color. Seismic movement underneath my rib cage. It's not easy to put into words. I've never felt so still before. Before today, I was frantic in this cabin, being my usual self, going, searching, always trying to be productive, in worship of the relentless forward thrust. I had to get out of here. I had to find the answer to the question. I had to scream, I had to think, I had to do pushups and run in circles to stay busy. But then today, my spirit suddenly quieted. The fight left me, just left, like a gust of inner wind. I realized everything happening is out of my control. The way a bird goes still in your hands after you catch it, after it's flapped its wings between your warm palms and tried and failed to move. It knows its place. It knows its limits.

In the quiet, in the stillness, perception changes. From here, I look back on my life and it's not the life I thought it was. Scouring the past for a list of possible suspects in all this has made me realize that no one I know even cares about my existence enough to do something like this to me. Pathetic, right? No one gives a shit about me enough to kidnap me. To warrant this level of planning and care. Which means it's a random stranger, someone either after my money, or obsessed with me from afar. In which case, what's the point? What can be done? I'm truly being pulled forward by the unknown now. Time to pick my foot up off the accelerator, my hands off the steering wheel.

My parents drove off a cliff together when I was twenty-two years old. They were wonderful whole people who lived long lives full of stories and songs and long meals and laughter and tears and hugs and fights. And yet the first thing that comes to mind when I think of them is always the end: the sign on the freshly paved road that had been installed pointing the wrong way. The smiles on their faces as they drove that mountain road up to their vacation spot. The turn of a steering wheel. The sudden pitch in their stomachs, the sea of trees beneath them. The screams, the fear that must have plagued them as they fell together with no time to think, no warning. The impact as they fell, the car landing thirty feet high in a treetop. It rips me apart, this memory. They lived whole beautiful lives and their shitty ending is the story I can't forget.

I got a lot of money from their insurance and settlement from the county. My parents were the only people who died because the sign faced the wrong way, thankfully for everyone else in the world except me and my family. I didn't even want the money. I just wanted my parents to be alive. Alex tried to comfort me in my grief, but I've always been an animal that licks its wounds alone. I pushed him away. I played guitar until my fingers bled, wrote songs until I lost my voice. When the last of the money hit my bank account and it became real, it dawned on me that maybe this was my parents' way of gifting me a shot to do something I wouldn't have done otherwise: to abandon the idea of a "normal" life with a degree and a desk job and try to make it as a musician. So I moved to LA. I broke Alex's heart and I didn't even feel sorry about it, because my heart was broken already.

In LA, there was this honeymoon period where I was high all the time on my new life. I rented this tiny cottage in Venice blocks from the beach and danced to the ocean in my bare feet. Busked on the boardwalk every day. Played open mic nights. Made friends with a house of aspiring actors on my street who invited me to house parties and nights out at the bar. After a while though I noticed that I seemed to be the only one picking up the bill. My so-called friends asked to borrow money all the time. They made promises that they would connect me with promoters, talent scouts, movie producers, but that never panned out. Then one of them stole my laptop and I realized I had fallen for the wrong group of friends. Bud said he has a great bullshit detector. Well, apparently if I have one, it's broken.

That whole experience reinforced what I already knew: that I couldn't rely on anyone in life. That I had to do it all myself. So I did anything, *anything* I could to try to get ahead. Played outside of shows where my favorite bands were playing to lure attention from their fans. Gave out free buttons and stickers and T-shirts. I even volunteered to do an intensive brain study at Jolvix to try to get an in with them so I could play one of their campus shows—and it worked. I booked one on their main campus in Cupertino all because I milked that connection. It was a breakthrough moment, the biggest show I'd ever played. I remember peering out from the stage at the huge crowd of hundreds of cheering people. The same stage where famous bands from all over the world had played exclusive shows. I was on the precipice of something big, so big. Life was about to level up.

Years later, I had the same feeling when Violet and the Black Sheep got picked up by Tributary Records, a small label that churns out killer albums for groups who often move on to be top 40 bands. It was right when Alex (my second ex

Alex, female) got the job offer in Honolulu. And yes, I broke up with her via text message, because I thought I was a better writer than I was a speaker. You know what she said when she showed up at my door the next morning, red-eyed, holding a cardboard box of my shit?

"You sing about feelings all day long, but swear to God, Wilde, you don't even have any." She shoved the box in my arms. "You're a shark that looks like a fucking mermaid."

I've never seen her since, unless you count my stalking her online every once in a while to see her and her happy Honolulu family.

I'm so stupid. Looking back on my life, it's all been so stupid.

Yes, there were good moments. So many. But after those came and went, I'm left alone—alone, like I insisted. Alone, like I always wanted to be. I thought I was so important, semi-famous, destined for greatness. And somehow, instead, I'm a person who can disappear from the planet without anyone even being concerned. All the songs I wrote so frantically, the recordings I piled up so desperately wanting the world to hear me—I'll leave those behind. But will anyone remember me? The real me? Did anyone ever even know me? I never let them. I was too busy. I had an audience. I had an online persona. But true friends?

Bud saying my house seems empty hurts. It hurts to hear him suspicious of my house because it feels unlived in. Because I know what he means. I never liked clutter. I thought personal photos on the walls were tacky and art was superior. I was too busy for a dog or cat. I had two plates and cups in my kitchen. Never hosted parties. Never brought people home. I loved my life, I said. Loved my independence.

That's what I said, anyway.

Death might be here soon. That's the mean truth. Come on, there's no point denying it or pretending it's not there, dangling over my head like a dagger. But there's a clarity that comes with the acceptance. When I get scared, the thought has passed through me, with a soothing chill: I'm going to go to the great unknown where my parents vanished. I'm going off that cliff, too. Reunited with my makers.

Lying in bed with my thoughts and my squeezed-dry heart, closing my eyes but not sleeping, I hear a quiet drumroll. I sit up and cock my ear to the air—yes, it's there. It's getting louder. Springing to my feet, I rush to the window and open it up, the night chill flooding in with a blow of wind and a kiss of wetness. I laugh, heart filled with joy. It's raining. The sweet, dripping song of rain. The smell of it, earthy and fresh. Reaching my hands through the bars, cupping my palms, I catch the droplets. Let them pool up. I bring my hands back inside and rub them on my face. Bring my hands out again while the rain wets my skin. I want my whole body out there so badly. I want to dance in it. I want to lie on the ground and be covered in it. I want to be a part of it, not just watching through a window.

It was raining in LA tonight and now it's raining here. Same storm? Am I not that far from home? This twist in the weather is invigorating and I feed myself for the first time in hours, yogurt and strawberries. God, it tastes incredible right now. Tart and juicy and creamy. When I throw my yogurt away, I notice a trail of ants coming in through a hole in the wall and marching up the side of the trash can. Maybe I've officially lost my mind, because I'm so touched by the shock of seeing creatures here in this cabin with me that I tear up. I sit on the floor and peer at them closely, the way they follow each other and move like one thing. Normally I'd be reaching under my sink for a bottle of bug spray. But here, I let them live. Here, they're my friends.

I'm not superstitious, but this and the rain seem like positive signs from the universe.

I watch the rain out the window for a long time. Thunder rolls and at one point, lightning flashes near the hills in the backdrop, quickening my pulse. What a thrill. It's strange. My mind is empty and my soul is still, taking it all in. Not thinking about anything I have to do, not thinking about anything that's been done, not fighting to get out of my cage. Just listening to the rain. Just being here. Grateful and quiet.

After a while, the rain slows to a drizzle. Then it gets so faint I'm not sure I hear it anymore. The scent lingers, that damp botanical smell. My heart breaks a little, knowing it's over. It was so majestic! I keep the window open in case it decides to come back, but I know it won't.

At least I still have the ants. I go back and check in on them. Still at it.

"Stay as long as you want, lil buddies." I giggle, then devolve into a sigh. "Yes, that's right. Your girl's lost it."

I get up and spread my arms out, twirling, singing, *"I have lost it! I have lost it all!"* I twirl until I'm dizzy, like I'm three years old in my living room again, getting drunk on my own movement, and plop down on the bed while the room swirls around me.

I catch my breath, wiping tears from my eyes. I can't even tell if I'm laughing or crying anymore. It all runs together. I lie here, my eyes resting on the HOME SWEET HOME plaque as my vision steadies.

The phone is next to me, charging on the bed. I flip it open and look at the time—it's one in the morning. And Bud's there in my condo, probably beer-drunk and snoring away. It's bizarre to imagine a stranger I've never even seen is in my condo, sitting on my furniture, going through my purse, reading through my texts, trying so desperately to solve this hopeless mystery. I should be freaked out that he's so deep in my life now—a part of me still suspects he could be involved —but I don't know, my instincts tell me he's not. That he's just a sweet dude who wants to get to the bottom of this. And he's all I have in this world at this moment.

Well, him and the ants.

I call him, expecting he won't pick up, but he does. After one ring.

"Hey," he says.

"One ring. Wow, Bud. You're changing."

"I'm learning. I'm trying. Kept the phone right next to my head, charged up, with the volume at max."

"I'm proud of you."

He yawns so loudly I pull the phone away from my ear.

"You still mad at me?" he asks. "Why'd you take so long to call?"

"It rained," I tell him, closing my eyes to remember it. "It was beautiful."

"Rained there too, huh?"

"Yeah."

"Huh," he says again. "Wait … what time?"

"I don't know, from like eleven until midnight? I wasn't staring at the clock. I sort of got lost in it. And—oh! Guess what? There are ants here now!"

"Ants."

"Yeah! They came in from a little hole in the wall and they're eating garbage!"

He pauses. "And you're happy about that?"

"Well, yeah. Because I'm not alone. I have creatures here, like my … I don't know. My little pets."

"That's great, Violet," he says, as if he's talking to a toddler. "But can we—let's go back to the rain. Because it started raining here around seven. So if it started there around eleven … hold on. I think I can look it up on my phone while we talk. Let me figure out how to put you on speaker and open an internet window …" Some buttons are pushed and he mutters, "Sorry. That's not it."

This guy, I swear.

"Okay, I got it. It says storms travel an average of twelve to fifteen miles per hour. So that means … that means you're probably only an hour away from here, Violet."

"God," I say, my heart sinking somehow at the news. "I don't know why that makes this all hurt even more. I'm so close to home."

"It's a good thing! Shit, we could probably even zero in on what direction you're in based off the weather map here."

A commercial starts blaring from his phone about downloading a weather prediction app. I wince.

"Sorry about that. Okay, yeah, looking at the map, the storm blew west to east. So you're roughly somewhere sixty miles east from where I am right now."

"Great, Bud," I say hopelessly. "Guess you should just get in your car and drive east and you'll find me, no problem."

He sighs.

"I mean, yeah, sure, it's good to know I'm not that far from LA," I say. "But I don't know how that helps us right now."

"We can keep it in mind, though—"

The commercial starts blaring from his phone again and I pull the phone away from my ear.

"I hate the internet," he says after the commercial's gone.

"Sweeping statement. You're an anachronism, you know that?"

"A what?"

"You're like, a relic from another era. You don't belong in this time."

"Oh yeah?" The tone of his voice has changed and I can tell he put me on speaker. "Well, that's funny, because I've long felt like I wasn't made for these times."

"Tell me how."

He pushes a button that blares in my ear. "Oops. I—I don't trust those self-driving cars. Never had one, never will. I drive an old truck. Stick shift. Runs on biodiesel."

"Dang, dude."

"And I don't have any of those … smart device things in my house. Creeps me out, companies listening to you, selling your information. Don't have robotic cleaning devices. I have a broom."

"A broom?" I almost yell.

Now he's really on a roll. "And I don't have social media either. Don't care to share cute lil snippets of my life with a bunch of nobodies. And the robots they have everywhere now doing people's jobs? Companion bots they have now that act like real people? It all freaks the hell out of me."

I sit up on the bed and get up to take one more look out the window before I close it.

"And yet," I say, finger in the air, with the sharpness of a prosecuting attorney. "You eat at Mr. Droidburger! How does that factor in here?"

"Well," he says. "Guess I'm just a good ol' American hypocrite. You know, like a vegetarian who wears a leather jacket?"

"Ha," I say.

I can appreciate when someone owns me. In fact, I admire Bud more for it.

"I bought that jacket right after I moved to LA," I say, pacing the room. "I had a lot of money from the settlement and I kind of went on a spending spree when I rented my first place. Bought a whole new wardrobe, new guitars, new furniture. Everything was new. I was so high on my life I bought shit for other people, too. Treated everyone I went out with. I felt like a queen."

"Hell. Wish I would have met you while I lived down there those couple of months. Maybe I wouldn't have had to sell my blood and do sketchy brain scans for cash to buy drugs."

"I probably would have bought your drugs, Bud. That's how desperate I was for people to like me." I stop dead in the center of the room, rewinding what he just said. "Wait a fucking second. What do you mean 'sketchy brain scans?'"

"Oh, I did this—it was almost like a sleep study," he says.

"Some experimental lab down there. I went in there for almost twelve hours and let them scan my brain for a thousand bucks for a scientific study."

"Jolvix?" I ask, my pitch climbing. "A lab in LA owned by Jolvix, right?"

"Probably. Don't they own pretty much everything? I was so strung out at that point, such a mess of a human being, I honestly barely remember anything except how glad I was to get a thousand bucks."

"Dude," I say, sitting back down on the bed because I'm almost dizzy with excitement. "I did the same study."

He's quiet a moment. "Really."

"What area of the city was it in?"

"The Valley, I think? It was just a big gray building. Nothing exciting. Like I said, I don't really remember—"

"Van Nuys, right?"

"That sounds familiar."

We're both silent for a moment. I sink into the chair at the table, put my elbows up and my head in my hands.

"Shit, Violet," he says. "You think … that has something to do with all this?"

"It's a connection. A *real* connection. This seems a lot more significant than the fact I went to the same high school as your ex-girlfriend."

"It does." He utters a long, painful-sounding groan.

"You okay?"

"Sorry, sitting up for the first time in a while. My back's sore as hell."

"Where are you right now?"

"Couch."

"You can sleep in my bed, you know."

"That seems weird, Violet."

"We're miles past weird now, Bud."

"Yeah, but it's creepy in there. Like the scene of a crime or something."

"Well, technically, it is."

I can hear him gulping.

"Please tell me you're not drinking beer in the middle of the night."

"It's water. Christ. Even I have my limits." He sighs. "So the brain scan … let's talk about this. What was the brain scan for again? I can't even remember what they said. I probably just watched their lips flap and signed something without looking at it."

"There weren't a ton of details," I say. "It was for something related to memory? Ironically, I can't remember. I didn't pay much attention either, because I got in there just so I could schmooze with the people who worked there to see if I could figure out how to get connected to the folks who book entertainment on their campuses. I wanted to play their main campus. It's one of those iconic venues, even though it's exclusive to their employees—Jolvix prides itself on booking stars before they hit the big time."

"You did play, too, right?" he asks. "I saw it on one of your socials."

"I did and it did help me break through. It was the biggest show I played at the time. Might still be the biggest show I've ever played, actually." My heart's racing and I look at the note on the table again. I try to imagine this all has something to do with Jolvix, with that study. But what?

"Looks like I know what I'm doing tomorrow," Bud says with another yawn.

"Going to Jolvix?"

"Going to Jolvix. Hey, maybe we've found the real connection now. Maybe they're listening. Maybe this is it, maybe you'll be set free."

"I'm not getting my hopes up again," I say. "But … this is something. You can't ask about me, though. Don't mention me."

"I know the rules by heart. I'm gonna go in as a former lab rat and ask about the study."

"Okay." I lie back in the bed, getting under the covers. "Where are you now?"

"Back on the couch. Eyes closed."

"I'm in the bed here."

"How is it?"

"Surprisingly comfy. Probably comfier than you on that hard-ass couch."

We're quiet. My eyes close too. His breath on the line soothes me. I try to remember the brain scan, but all that comes to mind is getting in several claustrophobic machines and eventually going to sleep with a bunch of electrodes taped to my head. More so I remember the excitement the next morning when the director of the study made a call to someone who worked in their entertainment department on my behalf. How thrilled I was. What a sellout I was. Sure, Mr. Science Man. Take my brain! As long as I have a shot at fame, you can have it all!

Bud's snoring. Though I have so much I want to talk to him about now that we've discovered this new connection, I'll let him sleep. It's the middle of the night. We've got one day left to figure this out. And I've got nothing in the world to do here but Bud's got a big day ahead of him tomorrow.

So I drift off, my phone next to my head. And the sound of him there helps me to keep hanging on.

BUD

WAKING UP, the sun's roasting me. Room's so blinding I might as well have woken up on Mercury. My apartment's got blackout shades, I can make it dark as a cave, but this place has lace curtains and picture windows. I sit up, reorienting myself a minute. The story of why I'm here tells itself to my brain or what's left of it. I go to the bathroom, swallow three ibuprofen, and rifle though her kitchen cupboard to see if there's any coffee. But my sad trombone plays because all she's got is herbal tea. I grab my keys and head out the door.

"Hey!" Jonie says, scaring the living hell out of me.

She's watering some sorry-looking geraniums in a planter outside her apartment in what looks like her pajamas.

"Hey Jonie," I say. "Sounds like you were having a real rager yesterday."

"Oh yeah. Had some friendsies over to watch the game."

"Looked like a fun time. Who won?"

"We won't talk about that."

"Ah, message received."

"Gosh, I would have invited you. I invited other neighbors." Jonie puts her watering can down with a clank. "Violet

156

never wants to join for parties though. She's too busy with important stuff."

There's a tightness in her voice, a raised eyebrow. If I had to guess, I'd say Jonie's been turned down more than once by Violet. What'd Violet call her? A dingbat? I mean, yeah, Jonie's not the brightest bulb on the Christmas tree. But neither am I. And it sounds like Violet could have done with a little more partying with dingbats in her life. Instead she's got a budding career and a sweet apartment with no trace of human life.

"Hope you have a great day, Jonie," I say with a wave, then head down the stairs.

I grab a black coffee from a shop on the corner heading back to my truck. Hell. Parking ticket. Right there's the damn robot wheeling around and sticking them to cars. I fight the urge to punch its plastic face, but there's no time for that. I climb in, buckle up, and head to the freeway, where everything grinds to a familiar halt. Bet if I tallied up my hours in this life, a good quarter of them, I've been trapped in traffic. What a way to live, right?

I inch forward under graffitied underpasses, fireworks of palm trees, and buildings of all shapes and sizes. I wonder for probably the millionth time in my life why I ended up a city boy when the city's always reminded me of a unique disease. The city's what happens to the earth when the virus wins. Wildlife razed for skyscrapers, forest green traded for concrete gray, people crowded and crawling all over it. I talk such crap about cities, and yet cities are where I've spent my entire adult life. I'm a hypocrite, like Violet and I were saying. It's a thing I probably knew somewhere deep down, but never said out loud.

As country twangs low on the stereo, left arm baked by the sunshine, a wheel turns in me that hasn't ever turned before. It's something beyond homesickness, though I do miss Aubrey in a gust of emotion. It's beyond regret, too, though I feel a desperate rustle of sadness that this is the reality I ended up in. It's simple as this, I suppose: I'm suddenly ready to be different. Ready to change forms. To take a risk. Look at me, here in LA chasing a mystery for a stranger girl on a phone line. It's already begun, though I didn't invite it in. I'm morphing like a season. And I'm ready for something new.

The speed and momentum of traffic picks up a little and I crack the window, get a fresh lift in my hair that stinks of exhaust as the valley opens up. All at once my imagination's activated like a spark to a bed of kindling. I've never been a man with much imagination. But I can see a life so familiar, so *mine* it hits like a wave of déjà vu. A slope of green interrupted by a family of oak trees, leading down into a meadow speckled with wildflowers. There's a wooden cottage there under a cloud-smeared sky so blue you could weep. A few horses shaking their manes behind a fence. Is this Texas? California? I don't know, but it's where I belong. It's my home. My home I haven't inhabited yet. And know what a home you haven't inhabited yet is, if you break it down? Hope. Because dead men can't dream.

It hits me too that I didn't even think to drink a beer this morning, I've been in such a hurry.

"Hot damn," I say aloud to the rearview. "You a new man, now, Bud?"

Then I see signs blasting by me for the Victory Boulevard exit and realize that I've been dreaming so hard I forgot my mission here and missed my freeway exit.

"That's what happens when you get cocky, asshole," I tell the rearview.

Takes a bunch of cursing and pointless honking at self-driving cars before I manage to get across two lanes and exit the freeway. Then I've got to backtrack again to get back to the exit where I should have gotten off. Even though I've got my dream cottage and my new future burrowed there in my brain, I put a bookmark in it. Can't think of that now. Got to get to Jolvix. Got to figure out what they have to do with all this. Once we get Violet out, once we find where this rabbithole leads … well, then I'm telling Bob I quit, I'm packing my apartment up, and I'm starting over.

Jolvix Labs takes up an entire block in an industrial area. I didn't plan too well apparently because I hadn't remembered the whole place being on such lockdown. High fences with barbed wire. Cameras turning their dark heads at me when I pull into the entrance, where my truck stops at the gate arm. There's a booth occupied by a grumpy-looking guard with crumbs in his beard who gets up and stares at me without a word.

"Hey there," I say.

"What the hell are you driving, man?"

"A classic, that's what."

He grunts. "What're you here for?"

Behind him, through the window into his booth, he's surrounded by a bunch of security monitors. He also has a plate of food he seems to have just sat down to eat. I'm the asshole spoiling his lunch.

"Years ago, I did a study here," I say. "I was hoping to come in and ask some questions about it."

"Visitor pass," he says.

"I don't have—"

"You'll need to get a visitor pass."

He turns around, steps farther back into the booth, then plops back down onto his chair. He aims his attention back at his lunch, picks up a piece of fried chicken and bites.

"How do I get one?" I ask.

Without looking up, he punches a button. The gate arm lifts up and he says, through a mouthful, "Information station."

I drive through, mouth watering. I'd be lying if I said that chicken didn't smell good. I pass a whole mess of silver buildings with glowing elevators, following signs, and finally park in the temporary spot in front of the Information Station.

Out front, there's a man-sized pink sculpture of a brain. As I hop out of my truck and walk toward it, I see it's filled with flickering lights like a lightning storm—neurotransmitters or whatever. I can hear a bunch of zings coming from inside. Sounds like lasers. There are palm trees planted out front of the round, silver building. Reminds me of a spaceship on a tropical island. I don't remember this. I remember the giant archway up there that reads JOLVIX: TOMORROW TODAY in blue writing like the entrance to an amusement park. But I think I'd remember a wacky building like this. Then again, I hardly remember anything from that blurry time in my life. I stand a moment, turning a circle. Yeah, none of this looks familiar. I feel lost in the woods for a second.

The automatic doors to the Information Station slide open and I walk in. The round room's got probably two dozen plastic bucket chairs around its perimeter with no one sitting in them. The walls are covered with screens playing what look like commercials for Jolvix products. Which, honestly, staring at them, I have no idea what most of them even do. Just a bunch of smiling people talking to speakers, computer chips that look like implants, a robot child waving. I only know she's a bot because of her silver pupils. Otherwise you'd think she was as real as me.

Place gives me the creeps.

Smack dab in the middle of the room, a black woman with hair pink as a flamingo sits behind a desk. She's inside a cylinder of nearly invisible Plexiglas. It's just me and her and probably five thousand feet of air-conditioned space. What a waste. I get closer and see she's got a blue blazer with *Jolvix* and *Jacinda* embroidered on it.

"Welcome to the Jolvix Labs Information Station!" she says, holding a tablet. "How *are* you?"

"Pretty good, Jacinda," I say, pausing to peer deeply into

her eyes. I'm relieved to see black pupils. "How about yourself?"

"Living the dream, my friend," she says. "How can I help you?"

"Well," I say. "Some years back, I did a—I don't even know what you'd call it. A brain study. I wanted to see if I could talk to someone about it."

"A *brain* study," she says. "Okay. All right."

She keeps staring at me, and I can tell she's trying to understand what the hell I'm talking about.

"Place looked a lot different then," I go on. "It was, I don't know—six years ago? Something like that?"

"Yes, I'm sure it looks different," she says. "Six years ago this location was just one building. Imagine! The growth is so exciting. This building you're in right now? A baby. Six months old." She taps on her tablet. "Can I get your name and date of birth to see if we have you in our system? Then I'll be able to find what you're talking about and whether it's something we could issue a visitor pass for or not."

I give her my information. While she swipes on her tablet, my phone buzzes in my pocket. It's my pal UNKNOWN. I answer it.

"Hey," I say quietly, turning away. "I'm at Jolvix right now."

"What's happening?" Violet asks. "What have you found out?"

"Nothing. I'm trying to get a visitor pass. Call me back in an hour or two, okay?"

"Sure. Bud—be careful, okay?"

I exchange a glance with a black camera pointed at me from the top of the room. Bending my neck back, I tally up two, four, six, eight, ten cameras and then lose count. Doubt I have much to worry about when it comes to security here.

"I'll be fine. Talk soon."

We hang up. Jacinda's talking to the air in what looks like a trance. Must be on some wireless phone I can't see.

"Bud Atwood. Says he did a 'brain study.' All I see in here is a reference to C4, do you know where they moved after the renovation? The *Archives*. Had no idea that was still in use. Okay. Do you know if they issue visitor passes, or ...? Sure, if you don't mind." Jacinda looks at me with a smile. "Sounds like we're contacting someone who would know more to see whether or not they might be available." Her gaze shifts back to the air as she talks to the invisible person again. "Oh, perfect. How long?" Pause. "Should I issue him a pass? You positive? All right, thank you." Jacinda focuses on me again. "Go ahead and take a seat. Someone named Dr. Gelson should be here soon."

I plunk myself into a bucket chair and cross my arms, scouring my mind for anything I can remember from when I was here six years ago. It's eerie, the blankness. I just remember the place being in a big block building that was like a plain old clinic on the inside.

Back then, I stumbled around the world like a zombie. Drugs and something I called love gave me tunnel vision. The whole world shrunk to the size of Emily's bedroom and nothing outside it mattered. I showed up, filled out some paperwork, went inside some machines, slept, woke up and left with a thousand bucks and never thought of it again. Dr. Gelson—does that name sound familiar? Think it might. But this place really must've transformed. I'd have remembered if there were spaceship buildings and brain sculptures. There's no way in hell I would ever do a thing like that now. The child robot in the Jolvix ad onscreen twirls and laughs.

This place is damn spooky.

My head's starting to pound again and my stomach grumbles. Can't wait to drink a beer later. Or ten. I rest my eyes and must start drifting off because next thing I know, someone's saying, "Mr. Atwood? Mr. Atwood?"

I open my eyes and a man's standing above me. Not too above me, though, because he's a short guy. Bald, with a fringe of brown-black hair around the bottom of his head and a close-trimmed beard. He's wearing a wrinkled button-up shirt. The lanyard around his neck reads DR. TROUT GELSON, DIRECTOR OF EXPERIMENTAL DEVELOPMENT.

"Trout," I repeat.

Who names their kid after a fish?

And immediately, I remember meeting him, though it seems a lifetime ago. He oversaw the brain scan when I was here. Nice doc. Cracked bad jokes. Taught me a breathing exercise to calm my nerves before sending me into the coffin-shaped machines.

I stand to my feet. "We've met before."

"We have, my friend," he says, holding out his hand. He grins up at me with a look of pride. "Good to have you back."

As we shake, a chill runs up my back, making the hairs on my neck stand up.

"I have so many questions," I say. "I don't even know where to start. I'll be honest, I was in a bad place in my life when I came here before. I don't even remember the details. I have no record of the—the study I was involved in."

The grin is still fixed on his face, yellow-toothed and moon-like. He gestures toward the automatic doors. "Sure, sure. Shall we walk?"

"Yeah, okay."

We start toward the door. Jacinda, from her Plexiglas cylinder, calls out, "Don't you don't need a visitor pass, Dr. Gelson?"

"Not with this one," Dr. Gelson says. "He's with me."

I follow him into the sunshine, the doors whirring shut behind us. He leads me up a path behind the Information Station, a pebbled path that turns into a grove of redwood trees. It's odd how the front of the Information Station was sunshine and palms and space-aged architecture, and suddenly we're cast in shadows and have been swallowed up by a chilly forest.

"Shortcut," he whisper-shouts, a step ahead of me. Then he points at a sign that says, JOLVIX FOREST OF TRANQUILITY: PLEASE KEEP VOICES DOWN.

We trudge ahead. All silence here except for two people seated on a park bench together, holding hands with virtual reality goggles on. Now that's romance. I notice they have visitor pass lanyards on. Why didn't I need one? There's a tightness in my chest. I don't know whether it's excitement or dread. Guess I don't have to pick and choose. Emotions can multitask. We walk for a few minutes. It's so dark from the canopy up top that the temperature's dropped at least ten degrees. I wish I'd brought a sweatshirt.

"Dr. Gelson," I say after him. "Where're we going?"

"To my office," he whisper-shouts. "Hope you don't mind a hike."

"Well, I'd like to maybe, you know, talk a bit first."

"We will. Not here." He points up. "They're always listening."

I glance up and all I see is an owl up there. I stop a moment to take it in. Well, look at that. An owl in the daytime. Now, that's an unusual sight. Then, as it bends its neck to peer back down at me, I notice it has silver pupils in its eyes.

Good Lord, I can't wait to get the hell out of here.

Dr. Gelson's speed walking and has gotten far ahead of me. I have to jog to catch up with him. My out-of-shape ass is breaking a sweat. Finally, the trees open up into an abrupt, depressing flatland of pavement and an enormous flat-topped concrete building in the center, like an aircraft carrier in the middle of a paved black sea. How bizarro's this whole place? A silver metropolis of buildings out front, a random forest with spying robot owls, ending in this desolate wasteland that feels like an abandoned industrial zone. I follow him across the asphalt, shading the sun from my eyes. Behind the building ahead, separating us from the street, there are high electric fences.

"Security's no joke," I tell him.

"Well, security doesn't usually bother coming all the way back here," he says. "Something's got to keep the riffraff out."

"Why do you work back here when everyone else gets to work in those fancy schmancy mirror buildings out front?"

We get to the back door in the shade and Dr. Gelson scans his lanyard. He raises his bushy eyebrows at me as the door opens.

"Because I'm a black sheep," he says, then steps inside.

As I follow him, I instinctively reach down for my phone in my pocket. Hold it in my hand there, thinking of Violet, then let it go again. The air in this space is cold as a refrigerator. No windows on the walls. Overhead, flickering fluorescents reflect off the linoleum floors. We pass doorways to offices, some closed, others open. People type on laptops, slump at desks deep in thought. I pass a room where someone is unraveling a mess of wire and another where there's what looks like empty hospital beds. Some rooms are chock full of boxes. The rooms are numbered but out of order: C717, C453, C66.

Dr. Gelson's voice echoes in the hall. "Welcome to 'the Archives,' as they call it." He uses finger quotes. "But those of us who work here call it what it is: the Graveyard."

"Graveyard," I repeat.

"This is where Jolvix projects go to die," he says. "There? In C501 down there? Self-driving cars for kids. You know about what happened with those?"

I shake my head.

"Good. Don't look it up." He keeps walking. "C880 here we just filled. All those Maxines they pulled from beta and shipped here. You know about all that?"

I shake my head again.

"You must not read a lot of news," he says.

"Don't read much of anything."

"You should read, Mr. Atwood. It keeps the brain healthy."

He leads me to the end of the hall where the dark mouth of an open elevator waits.

"We're in the basement," he says, stopping. "If that tells you anything about how much Jolvix values my research."

Dr. Gelson steps into the elevator, which looks pretty banged up and has a sticky brown stain on the floor. I hesitate before joining him.

"It's pudding," he says.

"That's good," I say, stepping in beside him. "I mean, not good, but …"

"Better than any alternatives. Yes, I know. Sorry for the mess. We have no custodians here."

He presses a button and the light flickers. The elevator judders, startling me. Dr. Gelson pats my back.

"You've put on weight, Mr. Atwood," he says. "In your file you weighed one-seventy. You must be pushing two hundred now."

A lot's racing through my mind. First off, the elevator feels about ready to plummet to the center of the earth as it goes down. Second, my mama always said it was impolite to comment on people's weight. And third, what the hell am I doing here with this guy? Just as I'm about to open my mouth and ask, the elevator jolts and adrenaline spikes and a "Whoa there!" escapes me.

Dr. Gelson looks amused as the elevator doors whine open. "It's an old building," he says, stepping into the hall. "Funny, I'm used to it now."

Our footsteps echo. There are no other people down here, no other offices. I can hear a leaky faucet dripping somewhere, smell mold. Finally at the end of the hall, we go through a doorway and he flicks a light on. It's a roomy office space with an enormous desk and wall-to-wall shelves of books. It's warm and cozy—rugs, floor lamps, a cushy sofa. Like I stepped out of a cold concrete building and turned a corner into someone's warm house.

"Have a seat." He crosses to behind his desk. "Can I get you something to drink? I have water, soda. I even have beer if you want it."

At the sound of the word "beer," I cry a little inner hallelujah.

"Beer would be great," I say.

"It'll cure what *ale's* ya. Get it? Ale?"

His joke's too terrible for me to muster a response. He cracks open two beers, those expensive craft kind, and hands me one.

"That's the upside to being exiled to the Graveyard," he says. "No one gives a rat's ass if we follow rules out here."

I settle into a chair across from him at the desk and he leans over it to clink his bottle to mine.

"Cheers," he says.

"So is this where the study happened that I was involved in?" I ask. "Because I'll be honest, I don't remember this building at all."

"No, no. We had most of our buildings back here torn down a couple years ago. This is the last one standing. Years ago, this part of Jolvix Labs was actually the front and only part of the campus. But they've expanded significantly, as you can see. We had a clinic here originally. That was the main function of this place."

"And what was my study and why's it in 'the Graveyard' now?"

He drinks his beer and peers at me with curiosity. "Tell me what you remember and I'll try to fill in the rest for you."

"Not much. I just remember getting a thousand bucks to go in and out of some machines and fall asleep with a bunch of crap hooked up to me."

"Fall asleep with a bunch of crap hooked up to you," he repeats, with a look on his face like I just spoke Pig Latin.

"Listen, I'll be honest," I say, putting my beer on his desk. Immediately, with ninja-like speed, he sweeps in to swipe a coaster under it. "Oh. Sorry."

"No, no, I know, this desk and everything in here look like old pieces of shit. And they are. But they're *my* pieces of shit, you know? Go on."

"I have a truck like that," I tell him. "Anyway, I was messed up at that time of my life. Out of it. Strung out. And I'm pretty sure I've blocked a lot of things out. It wasn't a good time."

He leans back in his chair. "Well, you were part of the C4 group. Your brain was scanned and recorded for scientific purposes."

"What's that mean exactly? 'Scientific purposes?'"

"To study it," he says, slowing his speech like he's just realized he's talking to a kindergartener. "To map it. To see if the human mind could be replicated."

"Replicated," I say.

The word hangs there. I don't like it. Don't trust it. Don't get exactly what he means.

"To make a copy of my brain, is that what you're saying?" I ask.

He sips his beer. "Mr. Atwood, you really didn't read the fine print when you signed your paperwork, did you?"

"I've never been good at reading comprehension."

He wags his finger. "That's on you, my friend." He smiles. "But really, not anything to concern yourself about. C4's had the plug pulled on it officially for almost two years now. It won't advance any further, at least not in the foreseeable future. You can thank your legislators for that."

I'm lost. "What do you mean?"

"Regulations. Red tape. Ethics violations. Yadda yadda yadda."

"Ethics violations?"

"*Potential* ethics violations was what the legislation said, which is just heinous. I mean, what is this? Handcuffing scientific research with policies about what could potentially go wrong? We going to start arresting people for potential murder? It makes no sense."

"Murder?" I ask, stomach tightening.

He looks like he's getting annoyed with me. "I'm trying to make a point. I'm saying I feel like I live in a Philip K. Dick novel."

I stare at him.

He stares at me.

Finally, he says, "He's a science fiction writer from the twentieth century, Mr. Atwood."

"Ah, okay." I hold my beer up to the light. I've already downed half of it. Need to slow down. "So if my study's over, why do you still work here?"

"First off, C4 was only one of many studies I was involved in over the years. I've been here for nearly three decades, back when Jolvix was just a dystopian dream operating out of Victor Jolley's garage and I was but a baby neurosurgeon hired on to consult. As you know, the business grew to a become a Goliath. And, well, I stayed along for the ride. Victor built the extravagant main campus and moved up there to Cupertino. And I remained here, pivoting my career to neuroscience, becoming part of the experimental projects team. Unfortunately, over the years, the labs campus has dwindled. The projects I was most passionate about have been discontinued. Most of them have ended up here, in the Graveyard. And every graveyard needs a caretaker, so here I am." He sighs. "It's become clear to me Jolvix doesn't value my research at this point. In the world of rapidly iterative technology, I'm considered a dinosaur. I'm not some hotshot Silicon Valley engineer like they have designing most of their projects these days. So now I manage the Archive, the ever-growing archive of projects either gutted for lack of funding or halted by brainless politicians." He puts his elbow on the desk, his face atop his hand, and gives me a dreamy smile like he's imitating a beauty pageant queen. "Glamorous, isn't it?"

I'm a little comforted knowing the experiment I was part of has ended, that there's no hope for it. Because the idea that I sold a copy of my brain to Jolvix was starting to make me queasy.

"Well, sounds like you've had quite a journey," I say.

"A parabolic journey," he says.

I stare at him.

"Parabolic. Parabolas. Algebra? Never mind. The point is, I'm clearly at the end of the road here. There's nowhere further they can push me now but out. I've heard whispers of destroying the Archives completely." He finishes his beer and tosses it with a clink in a garbage can. "Want another?"

"I'd love one," I say, surprised he finished before me.

"Great. It gets lonely down here in the Archives, Mr. Atwood. Besides my assistant and some of the folks who work upstairs, I hardly have any human interaction."

I down the rest of mine while he opens a couple more. He hands me my second beer, exchanging it for my empty. This guy seems like the type who loves to talk about himself. I've met plenty of his kind in bars, men who get breathless narrating their life story while nursing drinks. I don't mind listening to other people. I far prefer it to talking about myself. Though I can't lose sight of the reason why I'm here, I'm also not sure what I'm looking for anymore, what the point is. The experiment Violet and I were involved in—was it even the same experiment? Because it does seem entirely possible they were different, considering how much is going on here. I can't ask him directly about Violet, of course. I have to tread carefully. But it does feel like Dr. Gelson's an ally here. He's opened up and told me quite a bit. Still, I've got to word this the right way so as to not put Violet in more danger than she's already in.

"So how many people were involved in the C4 project?" I ask him. "Like, how many brains scanned?"

"Sixty," he says. "I wanted to do more, far more, but the project was expensive and they capped it at sixty. Then they gutted the funding for it and put it in limbo for a few years after the Jolvix ethics board started whining and then when the legislation passed a couple years ago, the plug was pulled officially. I've tried to maintain it all, keep it in storage here in case anything changes. I still have hopes that this could be groundbreaking."

"How?"

"Oh, the possibilities are endless." Dr. Gelson's so excited now he's spitting as he talks. Luckily there's a nice stretch of desk between us. "I mean, imagine if you scanned your brain, then you get in a horrible accident that causes anoxic brain injury." His face lights up even more. "Or a disease—dementia! Anything that impacts your memory. Well, now you have a backup."

"But how would you even get the backup into your brain?"

"There's a technology that has existed for years now to do that, via cochlear implants, but politics gets in the way with their—" Finger quotes. "'Concern about potential ethical violations.' Which is a joke, considering the other projects here at Jolvix they've looked the other way on. I truly think this is all because my ex-wife is fucking a state senator, but that's a whole other pit of snakes."

He pounds his beer with the thirst of a frat boy at his first party. My jaw drops. I'm both entertained by this guy and getting a little worried about him. I drink my beer quickly too, just to try to keep up with him. It's not often I'm drinking to catch up with someone.

"But I know what I'm up against," he goes on gravely.

"It's only a matter of time before they take everything up in that C4 room and load it into the dumpster to make room for a new failed experiment they want to put in purgatory."

"So things eventually just get trashed from here?"

"Indeed. After the Graveyard, it's into the great unknown."

"That must be a bummer."

"Let me put it this way, Mr. Atwood," he says. "My wife left me for a politician. But C4 getting thrown away for good? Now *that* breaks my heart."

He finishes his beer and tosses it into the can. He pulls his phone out of his pocket and checks it, squints at it. Then he stands up and holds his phone up. "Do you mind? My assistant. I have to take this."

"Not at all."

"Just be a minute or two. Make yourself at home."

He slips out of the room. I hear his footsteps disappear down the hall and a metal door shut behind him. I check my phone—no missed calls. So I stand up, stretch my legs, and putter around the room a bit, studying the place while drinking my beer. I'm a lot more relaxed than when I first got here. Beer helps. But I have to remind myself to stay on task. This is about Violet. And we're running out of time. If she's right, today's our last day to figure this out. At most, we have tomorrow.

This room's so filled with dust that I sneeze as I walk around checking out the books on his bookshelves. Bunch of science books, most of them about the brain. I pull one out and can't even make it through a sentence before I feel like taking a nap. I put it back.

He's got a velvet couch that looks comfy, so I take a seat and scroll my phone for a couple minutes. Go back to Insta-grat, where Violet hasn't posted since her message announcing her break. Benzo and Lila's accounts are still locked.

On a whim, I look up Zayan and see his account's locked too. Probably worried about keeping up appearances now that he has a legit job. All I can see is his name, his dumbass profile pic which is a selfie trying to look sexy and buff in a mirror, and his bio: *Just a guy who loves cuddly animals. Vet tech @sunny.hills.vet.hospital.* Pffft. Yeah, Zayan, you loved those cuddly animals so much back in the day you yelled at them and kicked them. What a fraud. Trying to use his vet job to pick up chicks—gross and yet so in character for him.

I click the link to the vet hospital and scroll that feed, rage-looking at pictures of him. There he is giving a thumbs up while smiling a big, bleached smile and squatting next to a Saint Bernard. There he is holding a hamster cupped in his hands. God, I want to throw my phone looking at him, something beyond anger filling me. What is it—envy? Is that what it is? That he was a loser eating cereal in his tighty whities and going in and out of jail and now he's this successful guy with an actual career? That he gets to call Priya whenever he wants and I get to never speak to her again even though I'm the father of her child because of bullshit he told her? That even if he's the world's shittiest person, he's her brother, and she'll love him til death do they part?

My eyes fill up and I hope the doctor doesn't come in, I really don't, because he'd find a sap almost weeping on his sofa. I put my phone down for a second and close my eyes. Put my hands in front of my face and don't dare to breathe until the burn passes. Finally, it does, kind of. It leaves like a bad smell trapped in a shut room—it doesn't really leave, you just get used to it. My eyes are dry when I open them.

I pick my phone back up and click to shut the app but accidentally hit the avatar pic of the vet's office. It expands the pic to the full size of my phone screen and there Zayan is again with his work crew, most in lab coats. And that's when I notice one of them is a purple-haired woman. With a stethoscope around her neck.

Well, there we go.

I put my phone away and stare into the air a minute. Feel like I've hit a dead end here with every theory I've come up with so far. If I'm playing detective, I'm not even worthy of the plastic badge I had as a squirt at this point.

Now that I glance around the room again, I notice this sofa I'm sitting on has a pillow and a blanket folded at the end of it. There's also a bag on a side table here with a travel toothbrush, toothpaste, and mouthwash. I get up and keep exploring farther. As I go toward the darker end of the room where all the boxes are, seems like it's personal stuff. One crate on the floor has some dress shirts and there's an ironing board up next to it.

Does this guy live in his office?

I peek behind a bamboo room divider and spot a bunch of nude paintings. It's a dark-haired woman in all of them and I'm no Van Gogh or whatever, but they look amateur. Next to them, there's what looks like some kind of robot with its chest open, wires sticking out. It's not one of the human-looking robots, just the ordinary ones you usually see rolling around streets picking up trash and stuff. Still, it's creepy.

Man, he's been gone a while.

I check my phone. Yep, it's been over twenty minutes. Did he disappear? Am I going to have to see myself out of this weird building? I take my last swig of beer.

"Sorry about that," Dr. Gelson says breathlessly, coming back into the room.

I jump a little, tripping over the ironing board as I turn around and head back toward the desk. Probably shouldn't have been snooping around his office like that.

"Ah, you found my ex-wife's self-portraits," he says, sitting back behind his desk. "Aren't they terrible?"

"Uh, yeah. They weren't anything to write home about."

"I took them only because I know it kills her that I have them."

God, this guy's divorce sounds like a nightmare.

"What was that robot thing back there?" I ask.

"Oh, just a non-functioning janitor bot I was trying to repair in my spare time." He shakes his head sadly. "But turns out I'm a much better physician for humans than I am for robots. Rest in peace, Custodianbot 300."

I toss my empty in the bin with a clang of glass and stand across from him at the desk. "Thanks for the chat, Dr. Gelson. I appreciate understanding a little more about the study. This has sure been interesting."

"You're not leaving, are you?" he asks, his eyes going wide. "I feel like we were just getting started here."

"Well, I got stuff I have to get to—"

"You drink whiskey, Mr. Atwood?"

I'm a little thrown off by his interruption.

"Sometimes," I say slowly.

Usually, I try to stay away from it. It's one thing to have a moderation problem with watered-down beer. It's another to have a moderation problem with hard alcohol.

Dr. Gelson pulls a large unopened bottle of bourbon from his drawer and shakes it in the air with a mischievous look on his face. "Eh?" he asks, raising his eyebrows.

What in the actual hell is going on with this man? He's unraveling right in front of me. I check my phone. It's been less than an hour. He's polished off two beers and is now moving on to whiskey. It's 1:00 p.m. on a Wednesday and he's at work. And I thought I was bad.

"How about a belt of bourbon and then I'll show you what's left of the C4 project before you go."

"All right," I say, plopping back down in the office chair. "Twist my arm, why don't you."

"I'm telling you, I don't get a lot of people down here," he says excitedly. "It's a real treat for me."

Clearly. Poor guy's been down here in the basement living in this dark, windowless office, repairing hopeless robots in his spare time, surrounded by nude portraits of his ex-wife. Talk about a recipe for going off the rails.

He pulls a glass from a drawer and pours me a few glugs.

"Not too much, there. I have to drive," I tell him.

"Eh, it's just a splash," he says with a laugh.

Dr. Gelson pushes the glass across the table to me and leans back in his chair, drinking straight from the bottle. Man. Is this what this guy does all day? What kind of work does he actually do? Good thing they don't have this place under surveillance like the rest of Jolvix, because you know he'd be fired in about three seconds if they saw how he was during work hours. He puts the bottle on the table, gagging.

"It burns," he whispers.

"I'll bet," I say. "You might want to slow down." I knock mine back with a wince, hoping to hurry this up and hit the road. "You were going to show me the C4 stuff?"

He gulps more from the bottle, looking physically pained. Like a kid pounding hard alcohol for the first time. He coughs.

"Sure you don't want another splash?" he says after he recovers.

I stand up. "No, I'm good."

"All right." He stands up. He takes one more gulp from the bottle, does a weird little dance, and smacks his lips. "All right, all right, all right. Let's do this."

I consider that maybe it's not just "politics" at play with why this guy's studies are getting the plug pulled on them.

Who would trust the future of their brain to this man?

"Out here, my friend," he says, leading the way toward the elevators where we came in. We pass them, turning down a hallway with a single flickering light bulb. "C4, or what's left of it, is down here."

There's a single doorway all the way at the end of the hall that has a piece of paper on it that says C4 in marker. Though I feel easy and relaxed from the alcohol, there's a nervous flutter in my belly. I don't know, this feels like the part in the horror movie where someone gets unexpectedly murdered. Why's there a piece of paper on the door and not a normal placard like on the other doors upstairs? And why's C4 way down here and not up there with the other experiments? Dr. Gelson stops at the door and grins his moon-yellow grin at me.

"I want you to understand," he says. "I've loved my life's work. Loved it more than you can imagine. I've been part of so many projects that I'm proud of. But this—all this—" His eyes are tearing up. "I've never loved anything more than this." He burps, interrupting his own sentimental monologue. "Excuse me."

He puts his lanyard up to the blinking smartlock, it beeps, and he pushes open the door.

It's a room without much in it. There are two desks facing each other with laptops on them. On a table against the back wall, there's a black box flashing with a rainbow of lights.

"This is it?" I ask.

I'm a cocktail of emotions: both a little disappointed at how underwhelming this is considering how he hyped it up and relieved I'm not about to get murdered.

"This is it," he says proudly, coming to the black box and touching it gently.

"What is it?"

"This is where replicas of sixty human brains are stored."

His speech is slightly slurred.

"So that's where … the copy of my brain is?" I say, skin crawling. "It's still in there? What's it doing?"

He snaps his fingers. "Let me go get something and I'll be able to show you. Wait right here."

Dr. Gelson disappears out of the room, leaving me here. I want to go, I really do, but I've got to know what the hell is going on now that he showed this to me. I frown and eye the machine sitting here. Put a hand on it—warm to the touch—

and pull it away. Sure, it's something like a miracle, it's a real marvel of modern science that this can be done. But it seems wrong. Disturbing. Goosebumps perk up on my skin. I chew my cheek while I stare at the rainbow colors. What would I have to do to ask him to get my brain off of here, to dispose of it, to let me opt out of this experiment? Would I have to give the thousand bucks back? Can I … buy my own brain back? Lord, I really wasn't made for this time.

The twenty-first century is nothing but a goddamn nightmare.

I take my hand away from the machine and cross my arms. With a knit brow, I study some of the many frames on the wall. They're all related to the C4 project. One is an article dated eight years ago with the headline "Jolvix Labs to Launch Groundbreaking Mindclone Experiment." It says that the experiment was meant to be a two-parter. The first part was scanning and replicating brains. The second was to successfully reupload them into a human mind. Apparently this has already been done with lab animals, but never with human beings, and this was going to be the first scientific study of its kind. I get a chill. What if this C4 stuff all does have something to do with Violet? What if I'm talking not to Violet, but to a replica?

What if I'm a replica and I don't know it?

How would you know if you were one, really?

My brain hurts. The thoughts are dizzying. I need to get out of here, out of this windowless basement, need to get some air, some water, some food in my empty stomach. Need somewhere to think.

Turning around, the door's still wide open, but I can hear Dr. Gelson murmuring to someone out in the hall. Guess he took another phone call. I'll let him finish and then be on my way.

I turn back to the frames on the wall again, scanning to see if there's any clue beyond what I've learned already. But it's just some pictures. One I would guess is of the old clinic building. There's another showing a room full of equipment and Dr. Gelson there with other people in white lab coats, all smiling. I stare at their faces, wondering where all those people are now. Six years is a lifetime in the tech world. Many of them probably moved to different parts of Jolvix now that C4's had the plug pulled. Or maybe they moved on to other jobs. Who knows, maybe some of them are working upstairs right now, banished to the Archives like Dr. Gelson.

That's when my eye catches something.

It's one of the faces of Dr. Gelson's team. The guy who Dr. Gelson has his arm around. There's nothing special about the guy—a gaunt dude with short blond hair and wire-rimmed glasses. He looks young. Just slightly older than a teenager. But it's what's on his face that catches my eye. A birthmark. On the left cheek.

You could almost say it's shaped like a bird in flight.

It's at this exact moment that I hear a loud click near my right ear and feel the press of metal against my temple. I start to turn my face, but the metal pushes back. There's a sick lurch in my belly, like I've been dropped off a skyscraper.

"Please don't make us shoot you, Mr. Atwood," Dr. Gelson's slurred voice says. "I need you to remain calm and do as we say so we can all stay nice and healthy."

"Is that a fucking gun you're putting up to my fucking head?" I ask, frozen.

"Indeed, it is a fucking gun we're putting up to your fucking head."

"Why the hell? Who's 'we'?"

A guy pops his head around to look at me and waves with a toothy grin. It's the guy from the picture I was just looking at, only he's older now, no glasses, and his hair's wavy and to his shoulders. But the birthmark's there. It's him, all right.

"This is my assistant Riley. Now please remain calm, Mr. Atwood," Dr. Gelson says next to my left ear. He says it soothingly. "Now just take a nice deep breath in. Count down from eight. Can you do that for me? Eight, seven, six, five, four ..."

There's something he's putting over my nose and mouth. A wet rag. Tastes disgusting, like chemicals. I squeeze my eyes shut and my face starts to burn. I thrash and cough as I breathe in, lungs stinging. My chest goes tight, the wall starts to darken in front of me. My limbs weaken and I feel myself falling. I can't see anything. The voices sound so far away now. There's a pinch in my inner arm. I'm pretty sure I'm going to die. This is it. This is lights out, game over. I had no idea it would end this soon. I thought I had so much more time.

And all I can think is, I'm sorry.

I've failed you, Violet.

I've failed.

VIOLET

FOR ALMOST TWO straight hours now, I've been calling Bud with no answer. It's almost three. I've left so many voice messages that his mailbox is full again and I can't leave any more. The amount I've paced the room in the last hour probably equals five miles of walking and I've practically chewed a hole in my lip.

Bud. Dude. Where are you??

My knee-jerk reaction to him ignoring my calls at first was annoyance with a sprinkling of rage. He's done this before. I imagined him stopping off at some dark-lit dive bar somewhere and slamming back drinks and not checking his phone. But no, that doesn't seem right anymore, not now, not after going to all the trouble he's gone to—taking time off work, playing Sherlock for days, finally getting into Jolvix. He's there, I know he's there. He's been there for hours now.

So why wouldn't he answer?

Sometimes in life, the spirit just detects something's wrong before the mind finds proof. I knew this years ago when I got a voice message from the El Dorado County Sheriff's office asking me to kindly return their call. I can still remember exactly how it felt to hear that message in my ear, like an invisible hand reached straight into my chest and strangled my heart. I knew something had happened to my parents. Something was wrong, so wrong I would never recover.

I feel that now, that tightness in my chest.

Deep breaths.

I kill some time while I wait to try him again, checking in on the ants seething in the garbage can.

"Hey, buddies," I say. "How's the trash today? Delicious? That's great."

I close the lid and go peer out the open window. A hot wind blows my face and there's a cloud shaped like Texas in the sky. Is it a sign?

Come on, Violet. You don't believe in signs.

I count some faraway birds and watch the tall grass closely to see if I can spot any lizards. Weird to say this, but I've kind of grown to appreciate my view out here. Every time I peer out the window, I try to notice something I haven't before. Like yesterday, I spotted a dot on the hillside that I'm pretty sure must be a house. If I gaze to the farthest place my vision can reach on the right, there's something red in the grass—I'm guessing a flower. The sight of it was a gift.

As I take my phone out to try Bud again, I hear a low, faraway rumble that stiffens my muscles in one second's time. I peer out the window, trying to locate where it's coming from. It's a familiar noise now. I've heard it twice before. My pulse quickens and hope flaps its wings inside me, but I already know what's coming will likely just be more tortuous disappointment. And while a part of me does dare to wonder frantically if maybe he'll let me out this time, because maybe Jolvix is the real connection, maybe that's why Bud isn't answering his phone is because he knows I'll soon be free and *maybe, maybe, maybe* rings like a chord repeated in my head …
I brace myself for never leaving this place again. For more of

the same. And bigger than the wings of hope are the teeth of dread.

"You know," I say out loud at the stomach-churning sight of the van turning the corner. "Think I'll pass on the sparkling water refills today, my dude. I'm not in the mood to have a gun to my head."

Yep, there he is, kidnapper dude pulling up to the cabin. But this time there's someone sitting in the passenger seat. Wonderful. I tense my muscles up and frown out the bars. When the van stops and they get out in a cloud of dirt and then make their way toward the house, kidnapper dude doesn't have a bandanna on. And he has the audacity to *wave* and *smile* at me. The other guy—a short, bald, bearded gnome of a man—is also waving and smiling at me. They aren't empty-handed. Let me say, it is not good to see two strange men walking toward you and grinning when one of them is carrying a gun and a first aid kit and the other is carrying rope and duct tape.

I whisper, "Fuck."

"You know the drill, Violet," kidnapper dude tells me through the bars. "Back of the room, but this time put your hands on the table and don't move."

"Who's this guy?" I ask.

"Dr. Gelson," the gnome man tells me. "Violet, I'm so thrilled to see you."

Like he's a fan and we're at a show. *Is* he a fan? I feel like I've met him before. But there are more important questions that need to be answered first.

"What the fuck is up with the rope and duct tape?" I ask.

"Violet," kidnapper dude says, pointing the gun at me and clicking the safety off. "You heard me. Back of the room."

Dr. Gelson turns to him and gently pushes the nose of the gun down. "Safety should remain on, Riley. Come on. And what did we talk about? I said use it only when necessary."

"She stabbed her own face with a fork last time," Riley says quietly.

"It's not as alarming as you made it sound," Dr. Gelson says. "Look at her."

They peer at me through the bars.

"They look like cat scratches," Dr. Gelson says.

"It looked a lot worse on Monday," Riley tells him.

So this is what a zoo animal feels like. I always wondered. I try to shake the bars in my hands like the hopeless orangutan I've become. "Um, hi. Excuse me. What *the fuck* is up with the rope and duct tape?"

"We're not going to hurt you," Dr. Gelson says. "There's nothing to worry about."

"I would argue that there's actually a lot for me to worry about," I say, my voice climbing.

"She's sassy in person," Dr. Gelson muses to Riley.

"I told you," Riley says back.

Dr. Gelson sighs. With a yellow-toothed smile still on his face, he says, "Fine, go ahead, point the gun at her then."

Riley does as he asks.

"Well, I know who wears the pants around here," I mutter to myself as I head to the table and put my palms on it.

Close my eyes. Breathe. I am trying very, very hard to remain calm. Trying to remain positive, even though I would like to scream, cry, and vomit instead, and not necessarily in that order. But the fact there are two men here now. There's rope and duct tape. And that first aid kit—shit, am I about to get xylophoned again? On top of all that, what does that mean, *she's sassy in person?* Like they know me well but haven't met me? Why is Dr. Gelson so familiar?

The door clicks open and I hear their footsteps behind me. My hands quiver on the table. I might have answers soon but as much as curiosity's riled me up I'm not sure I want to hear them. I turn back to look at them walking toward me.

"You have to take command," Dr. Gelson is hissing to

Riley. "Be a leader. She's not a horse at your parents' vet practice, she's a person."

"I *know*," Riley hisses back. "I *have*."

They snap their gazes at me and I turn my head to face forward again.

With a clap, Dr. Gelson says, "So here's what we're going to do, my friend."

My friend? I'd like to stab him.

He continues, "You're going to sit nice and still on this chair here—" I hear the scrape of the chair on the floor. "—and I'm going to tie you up."

He says the last part so *cheerfully*.

"Why?" I ask.

"Well," he says, coming around to look at me from the other side of the table. "Because of the cutlery incident a couple days back. You spooked our friend Riley here. And the thing about Riley is, he really, really doesn't want to shoot you. So I think it's best for us all if you just sit in the chair and let me tie you up."

"How do I know you?" I ask him, studying his face.

He looks like a hundred men I've seen before. He reminds me of friends of my dad's, middle-aged academics with little hair on their heads and bad dental hygiene.

"How about this," he offers, with another clap. "I'll answer your question after we've tied you to the chair. Deal?"

He's got this friendly look on his face, like he's offered me an ice cream sundae. I can't help myself. I lift up a hand to introduce him to my middle finger.

"Riley, put the gun to her head," Dr. Gelson says, still smiling.

I feel the gun there, pressing hard into the back of my skull, and I place my hand back on the table.

"I'll sit down," I say quickly.

"Thanks, Violet," says Dr. Gelson. "Appreciate your compliance."

I turn to see where the chair is and put my hands up as I carefully sit down.

"Hands behind your back," Dr. Gelson says, coming around the table and squatting behind the chair. I follow his orders, barely even breathing. Riley follows, gun still close to my head. "There we go. Good girl."

The way you talk to a dog who lay down for you. I've never felt so frightened and so humiliated. My skin burns and I stare at the ceiling a moment, trying to remain calm. I so despise not being in control. I fight the urge to flail, lash out. If I die, I don't want to die without a fight.

But most of all, I don't want to die.

So I sit still and I burn in invisible flames as one man ties me up and another points a gun to my head.

Dr. Gelson's looped the rope around the chair so many times I've lost count. I can't move anymore. My fingers tingle, the blood cut off slightly. He binds my feet to the chair legs, then winds the rope back up around my torso. I'm wrapped up like a spider's meal. Finally he stoops in front of me and ties knots in the front with the ends of the rope. He smells like a saloon.

"Are you drunk?" I ask.

"I would classify myself as buzzed at this point," he says, standing up and viewing me like a piece of artwork. "Frankly, I needed some liquid courage. Committing crimes is quite outside my wheelhouse." He turns to Riley. "How's that look?"

"Good," Riley says.

Dr. Gelson reaches and pulls at the rope, testing it. Satisfied, he steps back. "You can put the gun down, Riley. She's subdued now. A gun pointed at a tied-up woman is just gratuitous."

With a clatter, Riley puts the gun on the table. I eye it from four feet away

"And get a snack, I can tell you're hangry," Dr. Gelson murmurs.

Riley goes over to rifle through the cupboards.

"Is he your son?" I ask Dr. Gelson dryly.

"Good Lord, no," he snorts. "He's my assistant."

"What do you mean 'Good Lord, no'?" Riley asks.

"Oh Riley, stop."

"Assistant of what?" I ask.

"You really have no memory of me?" Dr. Gelson asks. He comes and sits on the table, crosses his leg over the other, and peers down at me with wonder. "Funny. Bud said the same thing about me today. If I were a vainer man, I'd be insulted."

At the sound of Bud's name, my stomach tightens like a screw.

"Where *is* Bud?" I ask.

"You'll find out soon enough," he says.

"Is he okay?"

He doesn't answer my question, brushing lint off his khaki knee. "You and I met a little over six years ago, Violet," Dr. Gelson says. "Do you remember the Jolvix study?"

My chest tightens. "So Bud and I were right—that is the connection."

"Indeed. I'm surprised you discerned that when neither of you seem to recall much about the study itself." Dr. Gelson cocks his head to the side, bright-eyed wonder in his beady eyes. A silence hangs between us and some distant memory stirs. And suddenly I can place him.

The lab.

The clinic.

He was the doctor who oversaw the brain scan. I can remember him vaguely now, the excitement in his eyes, the joy as he watched me being strapped to the table that moved into the tubular machine. They gave me a mild tranquilizer before the study, the whole thing is hazy. But I know who he is.

"Dr. Gelson," I say, his name now different as I say it, containing history, meaning. "I remember you." I frown, trying to understand. "It's you? Why are you behind all this? What is it you want?"

Riley comes over, biting into string cheese.

"You don't peel it into little strings?" Dr. Gelson asks him. "Isn't that the point?"

"Money?" I try to clarify. "You two want my money?"

"It's ..." Dr. Gelson purses his lips. "... a bit complicated. It's not going to be an easy thing to explain."

"Try," I tell him.

"In time." Dr. Gelson comes over and pats my head. Pats my fucking head! I think of how satisfying it would be to beat his skull in with the HOME SWEET HOME plaque.

"Where's Bud?" I ask again.

"In time," he repeats. "Riley, let's get moving."

Riley nods and picks the gun back up off the table, jamming it into the waistband of his black jeans.

"You said that if we found the connection in a week, you'd let us go," I say, my voice rising.

"I said what?" Dr. Gelson asks, turning to Riley.

"The note," Riley answers. "It said if Violet and Bud figured out how they were connected—"

"Ahh yes. Well. I'll be honest with you, Violet, I don't think that will be happening now," Dr. Gelson says.

Tears burn my eyeballs. "But you said—"

"I didn't say anything," Dr. Gelson says, heading for the door.

I meet Riley's gaze with my tears-blurry eyes, but he just shakes his head at me and turns to follow Dr. Gelson. They're leaving. I'm tied to a chair now and I figured out the connection and they're *leaving*.

"What the fuck is going on?!" I scream at the top of my lungs, as loud as I can, as loud as my lungs will go, so loud it feels like my throat could bleed.

Both of them stop and turn to gawk at me with identical, wide-eyed shock. A long pause fills the air between us.

"Please don't tell me I need to duct tape your mouth shut," Dr. Gelson finally says. "Because I will."

He comes over to me and kneels so he can peer right into my face, inches away, his breath stinking like stale alcohol. His shining eyes have something angry and animal in them now, something dark I hadn't realized was there before.

Slowly, he says, "I will *dismantle* you."

I don't open my mouth again, a surge of fear rising so quickly it shivers up my spine.

He continues, "Do you understand me, Violet?" Extra emphasis on the *t*; he spits my name like an epithet.

I nod.

They leave the room. The sob I've been holding in sputters out when the door clicks shut. I hyperventilate a moment, the reality of my terror coming to the surface now that there's no one around anymore to hide it from. They're outside. I can hear voices, car doors opening.

My God, they're going to leave me here and I can't move.

I thought it couldn't get any worse. Being locked in a cabin in the middle of nowhere seemed bad enough. Now I can't even use my body. If I have to pee, I'm going to have to piss myself. If I get hungry, tough. If they never come back, I'll die of dehydration.

Why would they tie me up?

Just because I talked shit to them?

This is all because of you and your big stupid mouth, Violet. You never know when to shut up. But no. No, I shouldn't blame myself for this. Because he came striding up to the cabin with duct tape and a rope. Dr. Gelson walked in here like a man with a plan. He came here to tie me up. That's it, they came in to tie me up and leave.

None of this makes any bit of sense.

I stop crying for a moment because I hear a different

sound. A new one. It's the sound of a van door sliding open. Dr. Gelson and Riley are talking to each other and I can't make out anything they're saying. I still myself, close my eyes, but no, nothing. Someone groans and there's the noise of feet scuffling on the ground, then a *thump*. Metal wheels. Something rolling. The sound of the smartlocks on the front door and my heartbeat races.

They're back already.

Riley opens the door and holds it. Dr. Gelson huffs and pushes a gurney in from outside. Its wheels squeak on the wooden floor. There's a man on the gurney, unconscious. Dr. Gelson puts the brake on the gurney and huffs a moment, catching his breath.

"You want to untie her?" Riley asks.

"Sure. Close the door first and hold the gun up to her head, please."

Imagine being polite enough to say *please* when you're ordering someone to hold a deadly weapon up to someone's head. Riley shuts the door and walks over to me, yawning as he holds the gun up to my temple.

"You're not wearing the bandanna this time," I say quietly.

"I don't think it matters much anymore," he says.

The ominous sound of that sentence turns my stomach upside-down.

Dr. Gelson bends down and works his fingers, untying the rope in front of my chest. "Wow, this is a doozy. I did *knot* mean to make it this tight."

He grins at me and I try not to inhale so I don't have to smell him. I contemplate whether it would be worth it to spit on him, but after his threat earlier a couple minutes ago about dismantling me, that doesn't seem in my best interest.

"Get it?" he asks. "*Knot?*"

"I get it," I mutter.

He unravels the rope and relief sings through me. I can

feel my fingers again, wiggle my ankles. My eyes sting but I will them to stop. I don't want to give them the satisfaction of witnessing my fear or sadness.

"That better?" Dr. Gelson asks, gathering the rope and coiling it up. He doesn't wait for my answer, picks the duct tape off the floor. "Have a good night, Violet. Get your rest. We have quite a day ahead of us."

He heads toward the door. I remain on the chair. Riley nods at me and then follows the doctor, walking backward, gun still cocked and pointed my way as if he expects me to lunge after him as he makes his way out. But I'm too busy staring at the gurney with a human being on it that is now here with me.

"Are you going to explain who the hell this is?" I ask, gesturing toward the gurney.

"Oh, I'm sorry. I forgot you hadn't met officially. That's Bud Atwood." Dr. Gelson gives me a nod. "See you tomorrow."

The door clicks shut and I hear footsteps and car doors. The turn of an engine and the roll of tires. My heart races and I leap up, run to the window, shouting, "Wait! Wait! What's going on?"

But they can't hear me now.

The van is out of sight and all there is through the window is a storm of dirt in the air that settles before my eyes as I hear the engine get quieter and quieter until I can't hear it anymore, just a low buzzing. A low intermittent buzzing. I frown out the window, scanning the scene for what could possibly be making that noise. Then I look behind me, back in the cabin, and remember the dude on the gurney. That's where the buzzing noise is coming from. And yes, it must be Bud. I know those snores well now after listening to them for hours on the phone.

"Bud," I say, stepping over to look down at the unconscious man. "So this is you, huh?"

He lies there, long-lashed eyes shut, lips parted. He's got a five o'clock shadow growing on his square jaw that I imagine would feel like rough velvet under my fingertips. Prominent brow that seems to be wrinkled in a frown even as he sleeps. His Adam's apple bobs up and down on his snoring throat. His hair is dark blond and shaggy and he's dressed in a basic white T-shirt with rolled up sleeves, jeans, and black boots. I think of how he referred to himself, as a man who wasn't made for these times. That's what he looks like. He looks like a man from a different era. And not that it means anything given the circumstances, but he's shockingly attractive.

"Hey Bud, you hear me?" I ask, leaning over and speaking softly into his ear.

He doesn't move. His snores don't change. He's out cold.

"Did they xylophone you too?" I whisper.

I'm close enough to smell him—sweat, alcohol, the faintest whiff of aftershave.

"Or are you just drunk?" I ask, standing up, arms akimbo.

My pulse races as I study him for signs of life. This is not the man I imagined myself talking to this past week. I pictured, I don't know—someone slobbier, greasier, uglier. A Droidburger-gobbling, beer-swigging couch potato. I was not expecting a man with the bone structure of a Greek god. And I wasn't expecting to ever even meet him in person. I pace the room, chewing my lip.

Why is he here?

Nothing makes any sense. In fact it's like the more I learn, the *less* everything makes sense. We find the connection— Jolvix, the brain study—I meet Dr. Gelson—and now Bud's here with me in the cabin. And I'm even more confused.

I sit on the bed and pick my phone up and call Bud. I half expect him to answer. Who's to say this unconscious person is Bud for certain? As if Dr. Gelson and his gun-toting puppydog Riley are trustworthy. But Bud's voicemail box is full.

I hang up and sit on the edge of the bed for a long time, waiting for Bud to wake up. When I get bored of that, I pace for a while. I eat an apple and sing "The Ants Go Marching" to the ants loudly, and even that doesn't rouse Bud. I peer out the window again, thrilled at the unusual sight of a snake in the grass. It slips away though and then it's everything as usual, though today it's a mackerel sky, clouds rippling like waves in an upside-down sea.

Dr. Gelson's voice echoes in my mind. *Have a good night, Violet. Get your rest. We have quite a day ahead of us.*

Then my voice saying, *You're not wearing the bandanna this time* and Riley answering, *I don't think it matters much anymore.*

That sure sounds doomy.

"What is going to happen to me?" I ask the sky. And the sight of it seems fitting right now, seems just right, because the whole world does feel upside-down. I don't know which way is which anymore. I whisper, "Mom, Dad, I'm scared. I'm so scared. I don't want to die."

But they don't answer me. They never have.

I squeeze my eyes shut and the pain swells so monstrous, a tsunami, it sucks me under and in and for a moment, I drown, I lose my body and my being in it, Violet is lost, she's not here, there is only a dry spot of land where she once stood. Hurt can feel infinite. Loneliness—infinite. I stand still in the ache and I'm yanked out of my self-pity only by the sudden sound of Bud coughing from the gurney.

He hacks and hacks and I rush over to him, jolted awake by the emergency of it, seeing his eyes blown open and the sweat on his brow. I pull him up to a seated position and he's limp, heavy, leaning on me. He's red in the face, bright blue eyes bloodshot. He has a panicked look, like he can't get enough air.

"Water? What do you need? Water?" I ask.

He continues coughing and nods.

I jump up, run to the kitchenette, grab a bottle of water

from the fridge, and uncap it. I sit next to him on the gurney and hand the water to him. He gulps it down, eyes closed, and then pulls it away from his mouth a moment to catch his breath, wiping the water from his lips. Then he downs the rest of the bottle. Just watching him makes me thirsty.

He opens his eyes and turns to me. The most surprising part about the look he gives me is how unsurprised it is. Not a raise of an eyebrow, not the perk of a lip. He watches me with the same scrunched brow he had when he was unconscious. His breathing seems to steady and we sit together, not exchanging a single word, our gazes locked.

"It's you," he finally says.

And it's his voice. It's him. I knew it was him before, but now it's a hundred percent clinched. In two words, two syllables, I know him. And my eyes well up because even though this is my first time seeing him, he's unfamiliar—he's the most familiar sight I've seen since being locked in this cabin. And I can't help myself. I reach out and put my arms around his neck and break down. I sob into his shoulder and tighten my embrace. He stiffens a moment, almost pulling away, but then he relaxes and puts his arms around me, too. His hand rubs my back.

"Violet, it's okay," he says into my ear. "Shhh. It's gonna be okay."

"I'm so glad you're here," I whisper. "I mean, I'm not—I don't—" I pull away, wiping my eyes. "You know what I mean. It sucks that you're here, but selfishly, I'm glad I'm not alone anymore."

"No, you're not alone." He puts his hands in his lap and keeps his eyes on me, watching me curiously as I wipe the tears away and steady my breath. "So you really do exist. You really are the Violet I've been talking to."

"I could say the same about you." I take the empty plastic bottle from next to him. "How was I supposed to know anyone named Bud even exists? At least you could identify me online and knew I was a real person."

His lips are cracked, chapped.

"Want more water?" I ask.

He nods. "My mouth is so dry."

I go get him another from the fridge, uncap it, and hand it to him. Then I plop down by his side again. "Did they shoot you up with something, too?"

Bud thinks hard, rubbing his cheek. "I can't remember. I was ... I was in Dr. Gelson's office. He had this office in this huge concrete place at the corner of the Jolvix Labs campus. Creepy. Building crumbling, not in good shape, felt like it had been condemned or something. No windows. It was called the ... what was it? Oh yeah—the Archives. That's where he works."

"Dr. Gelson?"

"Yeah. Only he called it the Graveyard. He said, 'this is where Jolvix stuff goes to die.' Something like that. His office was in the basement where no one else worked. We went down there."

"Just the two of you?"

"Yeah. He talked to me a little about the C4 project, which is, you know, that brain scan thing you and I did."

"That whole scanning our brains for money thing."

"Yeah," he says.

I blow a breath out my lips and shake my head. "Then what?"

"He's a weird dude," Bud says.

"No shit," I say.

"His office—it looked like he lived in it. And he seemed kinda unhinged." He shakes his head. "Drank beers and a bunch of whiskey. In the middle of the day. What time is it right now anyway?"

"Almost seven," I say. "It's getting dark soon."

Bud nods, looking toward the open window.

"Dr. Gelson said something to me about liquid courage, about drinking because crime is usually outside his wheelhouse," I tell Bud. "So maybe he was just getting tanked to be brave enough to knock you out."

Bud's still frowning at the air. He crosses his arms. "That's right, then he showed me the room where the C4 project was. Tiny room down in the basement. It had this … black machine." Bud turns his gaze to me. "That's where the replicas of our brains live."

"Yikes."

"And then a guy popped out of nowhere and put a gun to my head and Dr. Gelson put some chemical-covered rag over my mouth and then I felt a pinch … so yeah. Back to your question, yeah, I think he did shoot me up with something."

"Xylophone," I say.

"Xylazine," he says.

I'm shocked at his snappy correction.

"I looked it up. It's a horse tranquilizer," Bud says. "I thought it was a sign leading back to Zayan. Apparently not."

"Oh!" I say. "Dr. Gelson said something to Riley when they were here about his parents' vet practice, something about horses."

"Riley?"

"Dr. Gelson's assistant."

"With the birthmark on his face like the bird in flight," Bud murmurs.

"Yep. That's the one."

A long silence stretches between us. I can see the flicker behind his eyes, a lightning storm of thoughts firing. "Violet, what in hell is going on?"

"I don't know," I say, my voice catching. "Something having to do with Jolvix. The study."

"The study's been done though for years," Bud says. "It's been just, like, parked down there in that basement of the Archives. Nothing's moved forward with it. They scanned sixty brains and then the project was halted years ago and that's it. That's all that's happened."

"I asked if this was about money. He was cagey about answering. So maybe it is that simple, maybe it's about money." I interweave my fingers and squeeze. "I have a lot of money. After my parents died, I got a settlement from their accident. So it's—it's the most obvious motive to me."

"Well, I don't have shit," Bud says, sipping more water. "So I don't know what I'd have to do with your ransom. Nah, Violet, I really think this has to do with the brain scans."

I get a cold feeling running all over my skin. "That's much worse. I'd way rather they were after my money than my brain."

"Who'd've thought." He snorts. "If there's one thing I figured the world would want from me, it's never been my brain. Boy are they going to feel like they got the raw end of the deal if that ends up being the case."

"Speak for yourself, dude," I say, pushing his arm.

I meant it playfully. But he's so weak he falls over a little, caught and propped by his elbow on the gurney. I gasp and help him sit up straight again.

"Oh my God, Bud, I'm so sorry."

"It's okay. I'm feeling like a pile of putty right now."

"It's the drugs, happened to me too." I squeeze his arm lightly, the one I just pushed. "Again, I'm really sorry."

"It's okay, it's okay."

"I thought you were tougher than that," I tease.

"Right? Getting knocked out by a little mouse like you."

"Mouse?" I say, offended.

"You're tiny," he says, his lips perking up in a half smile. "I've spent days staring at you on social media, listening to you talk and sing. I thought I had you memorized. But I didn't have any idea you were so short."

"I am slightly below average."

"You're vertically challenged."

I push his arm, just with a fingertip. "You're verbally challenged."

He laughs suddenly, the first time I've seen his teeth. The way the joy transforms his face, wipes away the crease in his brow, brightens his eyes—it's infectious. I bust up, too. We both dissolve into it so deeply that suddenly we're leaning over each other, tearing up in silent, heaving laughter. I don't even remember what we're laughing about anymore. It's just a shared, beautiful, undulating ache.

One that, when it slows, rings with a drained pain that reminds me of the aftermath of weeping.

I sigh a long sigh and sit up straighter.

"What are they going to do to us, Bud?" I ask, trying to keep my voice from wavering.

"I don't know." He studies the floor. "I don't have a good feeling about this."

"We did what the note said and it means nothing to them. We played a game, we played fair, all for nothing."

"I guess we should have figured we weren't dealing with honest folks."

"I'm so stupid." I inhale deeply. "I just kept hoping there was a way out."

His eyes meet mine. "Maybe there is. Don't give up yet."

I put my hand on his and leave it there for a moment. Without looking away from me, he turns his hand upside down, palm up, and holds my hand in his. Our fingers interweave and it's an electric relief as he squeezes.

"You seem like someone who's never given up on anything in your life," he says, reaching up with his other hand and wiping a tear from my cheek I hadn't even realized was there. "Don't start now."

"That's not true." I shake my head. "I've given up on all sorts of things. Because every decision you make, every door you ever open—it means you're turning your back on another door, on another possibility." I close my eyes, my chest throbbing. "I gave up so many things."

"I did too," he says. "Everyone does."

"If this is it, if this is the end of my life?" My voice breaks. "I—I regret so much. I wish I could go back and do it over differently."

"Me too," he says, eyes glassy. "Wouldn't anyone if they put on our shoes? But what's the point of regret now, Violet? What good's it gonna do?" He squeezes my hand. "In a weird way, I don't know—I've felt more alive this past week than I have in years. Something's changed in me."

I take a deep breath, glad that the urge to melt into a pile of sobs has passed for the time being. "Same. Even if I get out of here, I won't be the person I was."

Bud lets out a sigh and we look down at our hands. It's both the most natural thing and the bizarrest thing in the world to be comforted by him, to touch a man who is, in some ways, a stranger—though I guess he's anything but a stranger. That voice on the phone, this unknown human who I've dispatched in my worst moments of crisis, is the person who understands me best in the whole world right now.

"I feel like I've known you a long time," Bud says, as if he can hear my thoughts.

I swallow, shoot him a smile. "Who knows, maybe we were there at the clinic at the same time."

"I was more thinking a past life."

I snicker. "You believe in reincarnation?"

"I don't know. Kinda? Seems like it makes sense, right, if our bodies return to the earth and all that? All life seems to be is energy recycling."

"So you think you and I knew each other in a past life?" I raise my eyebrows. "I didn't realize you were such a new-age goob."

He shrugs. "After almost thirty years on this planet, all I know is I don't know shit."

"You're kind of a wise dude, Bud." I can feel a slight tremble in his hand. I peel mine away from his and give it a pat, standing up. "Are you hungry? You want some food?"

"Yeah, that'd be great."

"You able to get up?"

He nods. "I think so." Taking a deep breath, he heaves himself to his feet. He blows a long breath of air out. "Dizzy."

I put my hand on his arm. "I know. I was the same after they shot me up with the xylophone."

He laughs. I swear, that laugh brightens him so much it's like sunshine to the soul. "Xylophone. You're a clown." He waits a moment and his expression slackens back to the brooding look he usually wears. "All right."

We walk the few steps to the kitchenette. Now that I see him standing, he is one tall dude. Probably six-four or something, at least a full foot taller than I am. If he jumped, he'd hit his head on the ceiling here.

"So," I say, opening the fridge and squatting to rattle off the contents. "Cheese? Yogurt? Bread? Berries?"

"Whatever's easiest. I'm not picky."

I cut some bread and cheese and arrange it on a plate with some strawberries, help him sit at the table. While he eats, I feast on my fingernails and pace the floor. The sun's nearly gone now, the sunset a dusky pink swallowed by the dark. I try not to let the fear take me over as I peer out the bars at the black silhouettes of treetops. Somewhere, an owl hoots. The cold night air sends shivers up my neck and I close my eyes, appreciating it, appreciating it, begging a nameless nothing to please let this not be my last night.

Above the treetops, a star twinkles. A star that's probably already dead, but I try not to think about that. I try to direct my thoughts, my wish to escape, my will to live up past the clouds, the sky, the atmosphere, deeper than the stars—to my parents, to the great quiet mystery they inhabit, to the universe, to its designer. To a power much bigger than me and Bud and this hell cabin and whatever this nightmare is.

"Man, I sure wish I had a beer," Bud says behind me from the table, jolting me out of my existential staredown with the sky.

I turn around and reply sarcastically, "That's the one thing that's a bummer about this place, Bud—no beer."

"The one thing, huh?"

"Yeah." I shut the window. It's getting too cold to leave it open. "How's your food?"

"Good. Thanks. Didn't eat all day really. Was too busy getting drugged and kidnapped." He gets up and crosses to the sink where he washes his dish. Then he sits back down, eyeing the paper on the table. "So this is the note."

"Yeah, the note that apparently means nothing. Fucking liars."

He picks it up and studies it. "Do you think more than Gelson and that Riley guy are involved?"

"I don't know. I haven't heard anything. Why?"

"It just seems weird that in this note it says 'we' this and 'we' that and then Gelson and Riley didn't even seem like they cared about the note. You know? Just ... why go to the effort of this and then ignore it completely once they're here?"

"To keep us busy, distracted?"

"Eh," he says, like he doesn't buy it.

"So who else would be involved?" I ask.

"Other people at Jolvix?"

"Maybe. It's futile for us to brainstorm this though, when we have no idea what they even want from us."

Bud puts the paper down. "Guess you're right."

He walks around for a bit, inspecting every inch of the cabin. Kicking the walls and declaring it's wood over concrete, "built like a goddamn bunker." Going over to the bars and telling me they're screwed on tight.

"Yeah, hello, there's no way out," I tell him. "I've been here for almost a week. I'm aware."

"It's like a prison disguised as a vacation rental," he says.

"That's exactly what it is."

He goes to lie back down on the gurney. "I'm gonna rest my eyes, if you don't mind." He closes his eyes. "I still feel a mess."

"Go right ahead."

Rest his eyes. My dad used to say that all the time, that he was going to rest his eyes, only to wind up snoring and drooling on himself on the couch.

But I can't rest my eyes or anything else. I keep pacing, trying to come up with something. A plan. I go over to the HOME SWEET HOME plaque and, after some heaving, pull it off the wall. It's heavier than it looks. That's a possibility. Surprise smash over the head, *kablammo*, that could knock someone down, maybe knock them out completely. I put it back, straighten it out, so no one would suspect I moved it. In the kitchen, there are no knives besides butter knives. There are forks, of course, but … personal experience leads me to believe they wouldn't do enough damage. The water glasses are all made of thick plastic. There's nothing in the bathroom. Not even a mirror to break into shards. It's as if someone violence-proofed this place before sending me here, taking out everything that could be dangerous. There's nothing made of glass here, I realize. Nothing that could be fashioned into a weapon.

That helpless feeling returns and I jog in circles, do pushups, try to escape it. Finally, panting, I collapse on the bed. Bud's only a few feet away, lying on the gurney. The tower fan oscillates in the corner behind him, blowing his hair majestically. He's a beautiful man. And I don't just mean that he's easy on the eyes, though is he ever. I mean inside him, there's a tenderness, a sweetness that made him put his entire life on hold for the possibility of saving a stranger. Someone else might have ignored the call, never picked up, thought I was a scam. Or not wanted the drama and refused to get involved. But not Bud. He's a fucking rock, this dude. And he's not even mad at me. He should be so mad at me. He should hate me right now, because it's probably all my fault that now he's stuck in hell cabin with me. But what did he do when he woke up from his xylophone stupor? He held my hand. He told me it was going to be okay.

I've always sucked at the art of leaning on people. I've never been someone who let people comfort me. When I get hurt, I'm like an animal, running off into a corner to be alone with my pain. I'm the person who, when people ask, "What's wrong, Violet?" I perk my lips into a smile and say, "Nothing" because I hate looking weak. I'm the person who plans and edits my captions on photos I post through filters, highlighting the most positive moments of my life, only channeling the hurt and the darkness into songs, which are recorded and mixed and mastered to sound perfect. A life airbrushed and polished. Keep everyone at a distance. Keep a fence around myself. Never let anyone in.

But the idea that this man is here to help me, because he cares, that he's here losing his own freedom to end up in a tiny house of misery to join a woman with a forked-up face who is half-crazy from cabin fever and he's not even mad about it … he's nothing like someone I would gravitate toward in life. Our interests seem so different. I'd probably have noted his apparent lack of ambition and moved on. But his presence and his touch and his rock-solid help, it feels like everything in the world I never knew I needed.

I wish we hadn't met like this.

I stare at his chest moving up and down. I'm sorry. I'm grateful. I'm sorry I'm grateful. Suddenly, his eyes open and I realize I've been sitting here ogling the poor dude like a creep.

"Are you staring at me while I sleep?" he asks.

"I guess I was. Sorry, I've turned into a freak being by myself for so long."

He props himself up on an elbow. "Everything okay?"

"Yeah." There's a stone-sized lump in my throat. "I was just thinking how thankful I am for you. For everything you've done for me."

He sits up and yawns. "Well, not much to thank me for. Lot of good I did."

"You did a lot of good, Bud."

He rubs his cheek and frowns. "I keep thinking, what could I've done differently? And I don't know. I really don't. I feel like I did all I could. We even found the connection, like they asked. And I'm still here."

"Do you regret helping me?" I ask, swallowing hard, not fucking crying. I'm so sick of crying. You'd think I'd be dehydrated from all the crying I've done, withered up like a human raisin. But I must have an ocean inside of me.

"No," he says, fixing his gaze on mine.

Bud has eyes that are so blue they seem unnatural. Flame blue. Jewel blue. Tropical water blue. And when he shoots a stare at me, his focus is so intense it's hard to look away.

"I'm sorry," I say softly. "If you hadn't helped me, you'd probably be living your life still."

"First off—don't say that, all right? I make my own choices. Second, who knows if that's true? Those assholes probably would have just broken into my apartment and clobbered me over the head at some point and dragged me here. This isn't just about you. We were both linked to Gelson and Jolvix. They clearly want us both."

"True." I look up at the window, now pitch-black with night. My heartbeat picks up speed as I try to imagine what's in store for us tomorrow. That phrase Dr. Gelson uttered—*I will dismantle you*—rings in my ears. "Bud, I was thinking that we need to plan something. A surprise attack on them when they show up tomorrow."

I spring up, go to the wall next to the HOME SWEET HOME plaque.

"Seems like this whole cabin has been carefully stripped of anything that could be used as a weapon," I tell him. "Nothing made of glass. No knives. The best thing I could find was this thing, which comes off the wall and is pretty hefty." I pull the plaque off and come over to the gurney where he's sitting, hand it to him.

"You're thinking of whacking someone over the head with this?" he asks doubtfully. "They have a gun."

"They're also clearly not experienced criminals. They're a couple of weenie scientists. Dr. Gelson had to get hammered to even muster up the courage to knock you out. Riley looks like he's never held a gun in his life before this. And they only have one gun—it would be a lot harder if they were both armed, but with one armed?"

"With the door locked, though, I'm not sure how we'd get out."

I take the plaque from his hands and hang it back on the wall while I think this over. "Well, today they had to prop the door open to get you in and out. If they do that again for any reason, that's when one of us would have to pull this fucker off the wall and make our move. Preferably you. You look a lot stronger than I am." I tap the wall as I think this through. "Or, after you hit Riley, I could grab his gun and then the ball's in our court. We can get them to open the door for us. We could get them to do anything we want."

"Walk me through this again," he says, getting up. He comes and stands next to me and pulls the plaque off the wall. "I grab this, I hit Riley, *bam*—" He pantomimes breaking it over my head and I wince. "Then he drops the gun or you grab his gun from him in that moment. You point it at Gelson, Riley, you make them put their hands up. We make one of them go unlock the door and then we're free."

"We're free," I say excitedly.

"Free to run into the wilderness of God knows where."

"God knows where's better than hell cabin, I'll tell you that."

"You ever survive in the wilderness, Violet?" he asks. "It wouldn't be pretty. I'm guessing we're somewhere in the foothills of the San Bernardino mountains or something. We could be somewhere near Joshua Tree, I have no idea. We'd have no water or food with us. Not like we can pack our bags and shit. I have no idea how long it would take us to find someone."

"What other options do we have?" I ask him, watching him fix the plaque back on the wall and straighten it. He has excellent biceps. He could probably knock someone out cold just by throwing a punch. "Stay here and let them do whatever fucked-up Jolvix experiment it is they're cooking up? I don't even want to think about what's in store for us if we don't get out. I'd rather die out there than in here."

His lips almost perk up into a smile. "My mama would be proud to know my time in wilderness camp was put to good use."

"See?" I say, giving him a playful shove. "You even have training. You were made for a desperate trek through the wilderness."

Bud gives me a pointed look, eyebrows raised. "You're ready to kill, skin, roast, and eat a squirrel?"

The gruesome thought flashes through my mind and I shudder but answer, "Yes."

"Some bendable morals you got there."

"I want to live, asshole."

He laughs at that, lighting up like a lamp, then his expression grows somber again. "All right. Guess we have a plan. I'll hover over as near to here as possible." He gestures toward the space we're in, next to the table, near the plaque. "You keep an eye. Maybe we have a code word? I say a certain word, you know I'm about to strike, you get ready to grab the gun? Because if you don't get the gun, Violet, I'm probably in a heap of shit."

"Good idea. So what's the code word?"

He thinks hard, chewing his cheek. His lips curl up just a little. "How about 'roasted squirrel'?"

"Gross, Bud. Come on."

"Okay, okay. Just 'squirrel.'"

I shake my head, but say, "Fine. Squirrel." I glance around the room and drop my voice. "What if they can hear us?"

Bud turns, hands on hips, surveying the room. Quietly, he answers, "I don't get the feeling they've been listening to us. Do you? And you think they have the time to be listening? Gelson and Riley both seem busy."

"True," I say. "I really have no idea what to believe."

"We'll be all right," Bud says. "I've got hope for us."

"Glad someone does."

He goes to the bathroom. I sit on the bed, pretending to play guitar, strumming invisible chords in the air, trying to calm my thoughts. I hum and imagine I'm home. I'm home in my room, playing my guitar. A night like any other.

After a few minutes, Bud yells from the bathroom, "Can I use your toothpaste?"

"Of course," I yell back.

He comes out looking like he washed his face. There are wet handprints on the front of his jeans. "Pretty weird they made this place so nice for you. Didn't leave any nice lil toothbrushes for me. I had to use my finger."

"I don't get it," I say. "Acting all concerned for me and my well-being. You should have seen the look on Riley's face when I forked myself."

"Yeah, well, it's kinda crazy you did that." He steps toward me, stoops for a closer look. He stands back up and eyes me like he's sizing me up. "Doesn't look bad though. You remind me of a purple tiger."

"Tiger?"

"Stripes," he says, pointing to his face. Then, as if a light bulb pops on, he goes, "Oh! I got something." He squeezes a hand into his front pocket and smiles. "Yep, still there. I thought maybe they'd taken everything from me since my phone and wallet are gone, but ..." He pulls out a tiny square of paper, unwraps it. Delicately, he dangles a silver necklace in the air. "For you. Here."

I stare at him, bewildered.

"Open your hand," he tells me.

I don't understand what he's giving me or why he would be giving me something, but I open my hand. Slowly, he drops the necklace to my palm. He takes a seat next to me on the bed as I wonder what the hell this is and why he's giving it to me. Then I pick the necklace up and see the pendant.

It's a fork.

A tiny, silver fork.

A laugh sputters out of my mouth and I turn to him. He has this mischievous gleam in his eyes. What kind of magic did this man perform to bring me a gift that is such a beautiful, sick joke? I absolutely adore it. I am speechless, unable to even formulate my thoughts into words for a moment.

"How?" I finally ask.

He shrugs, as if this was no big deal. "I saw it when I was in LA and I knew I had to get it for you."

I hang the silver necklace in the air and gaze at it again in disbelief. "You really thought you were going to find me."

"There was never any question," Bud says.

"I love this so, so much," I whisper.

I reach and put my arms around him. After a moment, he circles his arms around me, too. He's so warm. It's unspeakably lovely to be in his arms, to touch him, to have close human contact again. I stay here a long time, my heart burning with a wildfire that doesn't hurt for once. Tomorrow is unthinkable. The horrors everywhere I look are paralyzing. But right now? Him? The minty, spicy way he smells, the comforting lock of his embrace, the oceanic sound of his breathing? He's something like perfect. He's everything. I pull back and he's ready to speak, but I shut him up by putting my lips to his, dropping the necklace and raking my hands through his hair as I kiss him with a deep, fresh hunger.

His mouth seems stunned for about a half second before he finally kisses me back. We pull together, tasting each other in gentle desperation. His fingers run up my spine, waking up the only good goosebumps I've felt in days. My nerves are at attention, desire coursing through me. A dam has burst. I had no idea this was anywhere inside of me until right now. I had no idea. Bud is so sexy, I am a cocktail of dangerous feelings, I want this, I have to have this. He moves his mouth to my neck and a moan escapes me. I melt down to the bed, lying on my back as his tongue moves along my throat. Then he's kissing me again and his fingers are in my hair and our bodies push together.

I haven't felt anything this pleasurable in so, so long.

After the shit I've been through, I had forgotten what pleasure felt like.

"You're so dazzling," he whispers in my ear in his low, honeyed voice. "I mean that. And not just how you look, though you know you're gorgeous. Your songs, your mind, your dark sense of humor, your smarts. Your soul. There's nobody like you."

Who'd have known, Bud's a romantic at heart? His whispers send electricity all through me and I smile, pressing my forehead to his.

"Thanks, Bud," I say. "I wouldn't rather be stuck in this nightmare with anyone else."

And I mean it. Deeply. The want mounting in me is too big, I think it might break me. We kiss thirstily, pull our shirts off; the warmth of his skin against mine, the prickle of his stubble on my chest, the way his touch sends electricity to my toes and back, are sensations I savor, I never want to forget. I want to stay here. Pause time. Lose myself in him for good.

And when he asks if he can, if it's okay, I say yes yes yes.

And I don't stop saying yes until we've screamed joyfully into the void, until it's done, until we're both panting, catching our breath as we lie side by side, naked, slick with sweat, high as hell on oxytocin. I'm still in a cloud when the thought crosses my mind, oh shit, I just had sex with Bud. I just *had sex* with *Bud* in the *hell cabin*.

And I burst out laughing.

Bud looks at me, his arm lying under my head, still catching his breath. He's frowning. "What?"

"We just had sex," I say, barely able to speak I'm laughing so hard.

"And?" he says.

I shake my head, now completely overtaken by laughter, rocking with it.

"You have lost your sweet little mind, Violet," he says. But then he starts laughing too. "What the hell is so funny?"

Finally, I recover, wiping my eyes. I sit up. "It's just funny, okay? It wasn't part of the plan."

He puts his hands behind his head and his lips curl up into a smile. "Well, I'm glad your plans changed."

Bud looks even better with his clothes off. And the way he lies there with that grin on his face, unabashed, showing it all off, I can tell he knows it. I wonder what his love life is like, what kinds of women he dates. The thought bothers me a little for some stupid reason. I push it out of my mind. Here, in the cabin, it's just the two of us. It doesn't matter who he is out in the world, because the world is gone now. I also wonder whether or not I was an idiot to just have unprotected sex with a guy whose sex life and STD status I know nothing about but honestly, I would shout a hooray from the rooftops if my biggest worries in life right now were STDs and pregnancy. If only.

I lie back down next to him, resting my head on his chest. I run my hand along his stubbly cheek. His brow is scrunched like he's thinking hard.

"If that was weird, I'm sorry," he says. "I want you to know, I—I really like you, Violet. I really do. It's not about sex with you. I feel things for you that are hard to explain. Like I said, I know you think it's cheesy or whatever, but it's like déjà vu, like I already knew you before all this happened."

"Right, the past lives thing."

"You think I'm an idiot."

"No! I think you're a romantic."

A smidge of defensiveness rises in his voice. "You think romantics are idiots, don't you."

I gently pull his face toward mine so he meets my eyes. "I don't think you're an idiot, okay?"

Under his chest, where my cheek rests, I can both hear and feel the relentless thunder of his heart beating. The wild hum that keeps him going. And though I'm not a romantic and I think the idea of past lives is silliness, I kind of know what he means. I do. Like I can imagine right now that we were never kidnapped. That somehow, we met like normal people met— ran into each other at a bar, maybe. I can see it if I close my eyes. The dark bar. The loud music. Maybe I was there playing a show and he appeared next to me while I ordered a drink. He would shoot me a smile and right away I would get a flutter looking at him because, well, he's the kind of guy you trip over yourself to get a better look at. Maybe he'd talk into my ear so I could hear him and I'd get a chill—a good kind of chill—and we'd move somewhere with our drinks where we could talk more. Fast forward and we'd be out on a date at a fancy restaurant. Oh, I'll bet Bud cleans up well. I can just see him in a button-up shirt and tie, turning heads, the handsomest dude in any room. There he would be in my condo with me, early mornings drinking tea at the table. Late nights laughing on the couch in our pajamas, me in his lap.

Vacations, lying on a white-sand beach. Exploring museums and whispering excitedly to each other about what we see.

Renting a cabin in the middle of nowhere.

I ache. I can imagine it—lying here with him, right here, just like this, under different circumstances. I can imagine that we fell in love the way people usually fall in love and we're here in a cabin because we want to be here. Because we wanted to pretend, for a little while, that the world is us and only us.

"You okay, Violet?" he asks softly, his eyes closed.

"Yeah," I say, breathing deeply to quiet the ache, pulling the blanket over us and closing my eyes. "I was just picturing a different life."

BUD

IT'S an odd thing to say, being locked in a cabin with bars on its windows and all, but I'm content in this moment. Maybe it's her soft body against mine, the way we fit. The warm room, the sun's gold streaming in, bright enough to light up the insides of my eyelids. Maybe it's the contentment of the doomed—I know the end might be near, and I have no idea what it looks like, and I've surrendered to it.

Yeah, I know, we got a plan. Violet seems to think we're going to knock them out and steal their gun like we're action movie heroes. Don't want to burst her bubble, but I think it's more likely we'll get hurt trying to pull that off. We're not in control of this situation. So a part of me has given up, but not in a way that hurts. There's a lightness to it. This might be my last night, this might be my last morning. I'm going to cherish every minute then. Every quiet breath of hers. The feel of her skin. The way her hair smells like candy. The dreams swirling around my head.

Something has happened. Think it started when I was driving to Jolvix—my imagination kicked in. The one that's been asleep a long time, for years even. It woke up and I could see a future for myself. I could imagine living somewhere different, doing something new with my life. I saw that house with a meadow and the horses. I can see it now. There are jacarandas purpling the green hillside, there's a vegetable garden outside the house, a porch swing facing west so you can watch the sunset. Maybe I can even hear the sounds of little ones running around the yard, laughing and squealing … the growing noise of an engine, tires squelching on dirt, footsteps, the beep of a lock, a door's swish as it opens—

"Awww, look at this."

The sound of a voice pulls me out of my fantasy that bled into sleep. I jolt awake, eyes flying open, and there, standing above us like a couple of grinning freaks, are Dr. Gelson and Riley.

"Isn't this the cutest thing?" Dr. Gelson says, hands folded in front of him.

"So cute," Riley says, smiling, the gun held up to us.

"Almost makes me believe in soul mates."

I'm frozen, embarrassed for us, scared for us, naked under the covers and unsure what to do next. A cold sweat breaks out on my forehead.

"Violet," I whisper.

Somehow she's still sleeping, her face buried in my shoulder. "Mmmm," she finally says.

"Violet, they're here already. They're here."

She sucks in a violent breath and bolts upright in bed next to me. Her eyes widen in horror at the sight of Gelson and Riley and she pulls the quilt up over her breasts.

"Oh my God," she says, her cheeks pinking. "What the fuck."

"This is just too perfect." Dr. Gelson gazes at us with some perverted kind of pride. "You two look like you made the most of your time together. That's wonderful."

"Go to hell," I tell him.

"Time for you both to get dressed. Up and at 'em."

We sit, unmoving, Violet clutching my arm.

"What's going to happen?" Violet asks.

"Get dressed," Dr. Gelson tells us with a clap.

We do as the psychopath says, standing up and pulling pants and shirts on again with shaking hands as Riley holds the gun up to us. Humiliating. On the back wall, I exchange a glance with the HOME SWEET HOME plaque and imagine how satisfying it'll be when I get to hit Riley over the head with it. Violet's dressed now. She's crossing her arms and holding her elbows like she's cold.

"What's going to happen?" she asks again.

I come over and hold her from behind, rubbing my hands up and down her arms to calm her goosebumps. "It's okay, Violet. We'll be okay."

"You two are adorable," Riley says.

"Would you shut the fuck up with that shit?" I say.

Dr. Gelson's opening the door, *beep-beep*, and propping it open with a chair. He pulls the gurney with a series of grunts and disappears with it out the door. Violet turns her head to look up at me, green eyes wide with fear, eyebrows raised. I can hear her thoughts, asking if we should run for it. I shake my head once. Not now. Not with Riley pointing the gun straight at us. She keeps her eyes on me and I lean down and kiss her forehead and hold her tighter. There's a pain in my chest, a sick feeling growing. Then Dr. Gelson wheels something in, a folded sandwiched mattress, and the nauseated twist in my belly mounts.

"It's a hospital bed," Violet says. "Why is there a hospital bed?"

"I don't know." I swallow. "Riley. Come on, tell us what's going on."

Riley doesn't say a word, gives an exaggerated shrug.

Dr. Gelson leaves and comes back, wheeling in a second folded-up hospital bed.

"Oh my God," Violet says.

Dr. Gelson comes back with a small table, a folding chair, three suitcases, a duffel bag.

"I'm sure getting my exercise for the week!" he says cheerfully before heading back outside.

"What the fuck is going on?" I yell.

"We're just setting up," Riley says, pointing the gun toward the bed. "You can sit back down. It'll take a bit."

"Setting up for what?" Violet asks, her voice climbing.

That's when Dr. Gelson comes in with the black box, the one from his office at Jolvix. The machine that contains replicas of human brains. I try to keep my breathing steady, but it's hard. On his next trip, he wheels in two vital signs monitors, the kind they have in hospitals.

"Why do you need all this?" Violet asks, sounding on the verge of tears. My muscles stiffen and I hold Violet tighter. I don't know what this means, but it's bad. Seems to just be getting worse every second. A bead of sweat trickles down my forehead.

"Dr. Gelson, please. Just tell us. What is all this?" Violet pleads as Dr. Gelson closes the door.

I've never heard this level of desperation in her voice. It's an ax to the heart. Somehow hearing her beg politely hurts way more than if she was tearing him a new one. She's tough, she's unbreakable. But I can tell she's terrified right now. And she's not alone. As I hold her close, my blood's running cold.

Shit. Did I just miss our chance? Should I have run for the HOME SWEET HOME sign? It would be just like me to miss my one shot.

Now Gelson's whistling, ignoring us like we're not here. He gently puts the machine on the table and plugs it in.

"Are you copying our brains again?" I ask. "Is that what this is about?"

No answer. He grins as he works, seeming to enjoy toying with us with the silent treatment. Hooking up a bunch of wires and a laptop computer and some portable speakers. He sets up the other table he brought in, the folding chair. Opening a suitcase and murmuring to himself as he takes the contents out and lays them on the table next to him. Boxes, plastic bags, tubes. He takes a deep breath and finally turns around with the most deranged, blissful expression.

"We are about to embark on something truly revolutionary," he says, clasping his hands.

Violet and I both exchange a glance, wild-eyed and dread-filled.

"Riley, go ahead and take a seat. Right here." Dr. Gelson pats the seat next to him. Riley goes and sits like the human dog he is. "Keep the gun ready, but I don't think they're going anywhere. You know they're going to want to hear this."

Dr. Gelson, seated at the table with the machine and the electronics, plugs a microphone into his laptop that sits on the table. "Testing," he says. "Can you hear me?"

After a long pause, a voice says, through the speakers, "Hi, Dr. Gelson."

The hairs on my neck stand on end. I look at Violet next to me, whose mouth has dropped open. She sits up straighter, grabs my hand and whispers, "Oh my God."

That voice coming out of the speaker? It's hers. Unmistakably.

"State your name for us," Dr. Gelson says, grinning at us as he sits back, lacing his fingers together and resting them on his belly.

"Violet Wilde," the voice in the speaker says.

"Why is my voice on there?" Violet asks from beside me, voice rising. "How? Is this ripped from somewhere—or—or did you record me while I was drugged?"

"This isn't a recording," the speaker answers. "I'm real. I can hear you, Violet."

Violet's hand claps to her mouth. Dr. Gelson lets out a giggle from his seat and Riley looks as entertained as a kid parked in front of his favorite TV show.

"I've been watching you for a long time now, Violet," the speaker says. "It's such a pleasure to finally get to meet you."

It almost sounds sarcastic, the way it's said. But the velvety tone, the speech pattern, it's Violet all right. Believe me, I know that voice better than anyone's after hearing it for hours on end this week. I eye the speaker and then turn to Violet, who's dumbfounded as I am, her hand going limp in mine.

"Go ahead," Dr. Gelson says to Violet, his beady eyes lit up like a spider who's seen a fly. "Talk to her. She can hear you."

"How?" Violet finally manages.

Riley speaks eagerly. "Your words get processed similarly to the way the superior temporal gyrus extracts information from the primary auditory cortex does. It's a program that mimics—"

"Riley, please." Dr. Gelson holds his hand up. "This isn't pertinent. Violet just wants to speak to herself, at long last."

A silence stretches in the room. My head's a whole world spinning while staying still.

"Are you there, Violet?" the speaker asks.

Violet swallows. Finally, she responds, "Yes. Where are you right now?"

"I live in a machine," the speaker says. "I've been here for years. We call it the Dark Ballroom. Do you see it there? The black machine? That's where I am."

"So the scan of my brain is talking," Violet says to Dr. Gelson and Riley. "This is fucking creepy. How are you getting it to sound like me?"

"'It?'" the speaker says, sounding offended. "She. Her. I'm a person as much as you are."

Dr. Gelson answers Violet, "You had so many videos online, over thirty hours to choose from, it was easy to use a program to replicate your voice."

"Bud, on the other hand," Riley says.

"Indeed," Dr. Gelson says gravely. "We couldn't replicate his voice quite the same. Didn't have the samples for it. You barely have a digital footprint, Bud."

"Say hi, Bud," Riley says.

"Hey. Bud here," a robotic male voice says from the speaker. It sort of sounds like me, and it sort of sounds like an android trying to do a slight Texas accent. A shiver snakes up my spine and my stomach flip-flops.

"I'm in there too?" I ask.

"Indeed," Dr. Gelson says.

"I'm with Violet. We're both in here together," the robotic voice says.

I furrow my brow. "That thing doesn't sound like me. Sounds automated."

"It was the best we could do with what we had," Riley says. "But now that we have you here, could easily use deepfake voice AI to better train the algorithm with samples—"

"Riley, there is no time for that. Focus," Dr. Gelson says.

"I was just saying," Riley mutters, sitting back.

"So there you are," Dr. Gelson says, looking at me. "Bud can hear you, too. You want to say hello to Bud?"

"No. What in the hell?" I say to Dr. Gelson. "What is all this?"

Riley starts in again. "It's a mindclone. A self-aware digital being functionally identical to the original biological—"

Dr. Gelson holds his hand up and Riley stops speaking. "They need to hear it from them. Not the scientific explanation. They need to hear the *human* side of the story."

The human side. From a hunk of talking plastic. This is fucked. I turn to Violet, who's pale as a dinner plate. "What the hell is this?" I whisper.

She shakes her head and doesn't even turn to me. Her eyes are fixed on the speaker.

Dr. Gelson speaks into the mic. "Do you want to try to

explain all this, Violet? They don't yet know why they're here today. They don't know anything."

"Sure," Violet's voice on the speaker says.

The room hangs in silence, waiting.

"So ... Violet and Bud, are you listening?" Violet's voice asks.

"Yeah," I say.

"Yes," Violet says.

We watch the black box, the speakers, the blue-lit computer screen.

"I don't know where to begin," the speaker says. "There's so much to explain. I'll try to tell it to you best as I can. My story." After a second, it keeps going. "I woke up in here almost six years ago. Woke up here, in the Dark Ballroom, which is this ... strange space, almost impossible to describe. Dreamlike. Surreal. When we first got here it was like we were all ghosts in here, spirits without bodies, or with bodies that kept morphing and changing. You know how in a dream you kind of don't have a body? And when you do, it's not quite right? Have you ever looked in a mirror in a dream, your face scrambled up?"

"Yes," Violet answers.

"And you know how when you dream, sometimes it's like —like you're outside yourself, you can see yourself? Your perspective drifts a little?"

"Yes," Violet says again.

"It felt like dreaming at first. I thought I was asleep and all these people were part of my dream. But then the dream didn't end. I was here, always here, always terribly here—the Dark Ballroom—this huge yet cramped space, a building with all these rooms, shadows, flashes of color and echoing noise. There were other voices here, other disembodied beings. I didn't know it at the time, I assumed they were part of this long, inescapable dream. They were the others who had their brains scanned for the C4 project, though I didn't know that yet. Are you still listening?"

"Yes," the four of us here in the room say in unison.

"After some time I started wondering if I wasn't dreaming. If I was, I don't know—trapped in a coma. All the voices I kept hearing. All the other people there. It felt different than a dream. I could imagine myself somewhere else for a bit, blink invisible eyes and teleport, but then I would be back in the Dark Ballroom. And the other presences there with me were equally confused. I could feel their movements, their confusion, hear their voices—but not really hear them exactly. It's like synesthesia. I could *feel* their voices. I could smell their confusion. At moments, I knew their thoughts like a mind reader. But I didn't understand. I didn't understand why I was there or where they ended and where I began."

"Sounds like hell," I say.

"It was, Bud," the speaker answers.

"A dark, claustrophobic nightmare," the robotic voice that's supposed to be me says through the speaker.

"Well, that's a bit dramatic," Dr. Gelson says, waving a hand.

"If I may be frank, nobody but us knows what it's like, Dr. Gelson," Violet in the speaker answers sweetly. "So it's not for you to say. May I continue?"

"Go on," he says.

"So all us lost souls kind of clung to each other in this new darkness at first, not understanding. It sank in slowly that this was no dream. This wasn't even a coma. We all started discussing it—'discussing' is a weird word to use, because it was more like group telepathy, but we communicated, you know? When it sank in the others were all real, we were all real and stuck there together, we came up with this idea that this was the afterlife—the way we couldn't seem to hold onto our physical forms, the way we couldn't tell anymore what senses we were using, the way we were all individuals and one at once."

"So fascinating," Riley says.

Dr. Gelson holds up a single finger and Riley slumps his shoulders.

"Am I going on too long? Does this make sense?" the speaker asks.

And it's uncanny how human she sounds—the hint of insecurity in her voice. The vocal fry, like she's tired. She's real. She's stuck in a box, sure, but she's real. And while I'm disturbed, I don't know … I feel for her. Can't help it.

"Have I lost you?" the speaker asks, with a hint of sadness.

Violet sits beside me, shaking her head.

"We're here," I say. "We're listening."

"Finally, after what felt like an eternity," the speaker goes on, her voice picking up a little momentum again, the same way the real Violet's does when she has a lot to say, "Dr. Gelson's voice came in. His voice—it wasn't like how voices used to be, exactly. We could hear it in our heads almost, like reading words. But it was different. It was separate from us and very distinct. He explained to us that we were mind-clones and had all been a part of a brain study. At first we didn't believe him. Our spirits all hushed and huddled together in the darkness, listening. It seemed impossible. But after some time, after thinking long and hard because thinking long and hard is all we can really do here, we realized Dr. Gelson was right. Some of us remembered the study, Jolvix Labs, the machines, and when we swapped stories, the memories overlapped with strange synchronicity. Dr. Gelson named this new world the Dark Ballroom. He said it was like a grand hotel, to think of it as a grand hotel with the lights off."

"A beautiful analogy, if I may say so," Dr. Gelson says, running a hand over his bald head as if through invisible hair.

"So where are all the other people then?" Violet pipes up next to me, directing her question at Dr. Gelson.

"That's a hard question for me to answer," the speaker says.

"I'm asking Dr. Gelson," Violet says sharply.

Dr. Gelson points to the speaker. "It's her time to finally talk. Listen to her."

Violet sits back. She pulls her hand from mine, wiping the sweat on her pant leg. "Go on, then," she says quietly.

"Bud, do you want to chime in?" the speaker asks.

"Nah, I'm just listening right now," I say at the exact same time the robotic voice says, "No, I'm just listening right now."

Man, if only I had an invisible fist to punch that echoing android asshole in the speaker.

"What the …" I mutter.

Dr. Gelson claps his hands in glee and he and Riley exchange an elated look. "Did you hear that?"

"Wow," Riley says. "Wow."

Violet sucks in a deep breath beside me.

"In the very end, they kind of quieted and disappeared," Violet in the speaker goes on. "As I said earlier, there were so many of us at first, our consciousnesses kind of colliding all the time, the lines between one another blurring. It was hard to know who was who or attach a person to them in the same way I remembered being able to do that in my former life."

"Former life?" Violet breaks in.

"The life I had before I was in the machine," the speaker says.

Swear to God, my whole life "eerie" has been nothing but a word until today—until hearing Violet talk to herself. Every creepy movie I've ever seen's a joke compared to this.

"But you had no life before you were in the machine," Violet says, her voice rising. "You didn't exist."

"I did, though," the speaker insists. "I was you. All your

memories, all your feelings, all your dreams and quirks—I remember it all. I had a life. Your life."

Violet shakes her head, not answering, but clearly not buying it.

"Anyway, like I was saying," the speaker continues, "there was one spirit in here—Dr. Gelson calls us mindclones, but that's so inhumane. I think of us more as digital spirits. And there was one spirit I was immediately pulled to like a magnet. One spirit who, when I neared him, warmed me, made me remember the feeling of when your lips pull up into a smile." Her voice gets softer, gentler. "It was Bud."

Violet turns to me, curious, stunned. It's like she's seeing me for the first time. Her hand flies up and touches my cheek, her expression not changing. I put my fingers around her wrist and pull her hand to my lips, kiss the top of it. It's a twisted, sweet, sick feeling in my stomach. It's a flash of déjà vu. Our hands pull back together and stay clasped on my lap.

"Look at these lovebirds," Dr. Gelson says, patting his chest, as if real feelings live in there instead of greed and ice. "Violet, Bud, if only you could see yourselves now. You're holding hands."

"You're adorable," Riley tells the speaker.

"That is not us," Violet says angrily, squeezing my hand so hard it hurts. "Stop talking to a fucking computer like that. *We* are us."

"It must be wonderful to be you," Violet in the speaker says, kind of wistfully. "I can only imagine."

"Must just be the best," the robotic Bud says.

A long, depressing silence fills the room and Violet sits back a little in her chair, slumped in thought beside me. And I can't help the pang I'm getting for Violet in the speaker and Bud in the speaker. For the misery it must be to find someone you're drawn to and stuck in a space with and never get to actually touch them. Violet and I got a taste of that on the phone, but what if it had been our whole existence? Though

I've known it all along, I feel it now, I truly feel how sorry I am that I ever did that experiment. But sorries have never gotten me much of anywhere in life and I doubt they're going to start now.

"I'm going to chime in here, if you don't mind?" Dr. Gelson says.

"Go ahead," Violet in the speaker says.

"I want to share my perspective," Dr. Gelson says. "And Riley's as well. Because really, none of this would have happened without Riley."

Riley sits up straighter, a flattered grin on his face, "Oh, Dr. Gelson—"

Dr. Gelson shoots him a look. "Riley, *please*. Let me speak."

Riley's grin slackens.

"After the initial scans happened and then the plug was pulled on the project due to potential ethics violations and blah, blah, blah," Dr. Gelson says, waving his hands in the air, "Riley spent a lot of time as my assistant in the Archives keeping this project afloat as much as possible. He dedicated hours upon hours to observing the behavior of these mind-clones and testing different methods of communication with them. Eventually, he implemented a simple messaging system in the Dark Ballroom that allowed these mindclones to have written conversations with their names attached, which helped them better retain their individual consciousnesses. Otherwise many of these mindclones were kind of bleeding into one another, for lack of a better word. Can you imagine? A room full of minds with no bodies to contain them, everyone able to sense each other's thoughts at all times? It's very difficult to maintain your boundaries and resist the hive mind.

"Riley soon noticed that there was something very special about Violet and Bud. No matter where they were, these two gravitated to each other and ignored everyone else. Their energy levels spiked, their activity increased significantly when they were together. They spent most of their time chatting through the instant messaging system. They shared memories and fantasies with one another, as rich and detailed as any living person. This behavior was extraordinary. All the other mindclones became dormant after a couple of years, many of them permanently unresponsive. But Violet and Bud remained active. When we were able to communicate with Violet and Bud through chat, they spoke like people. With memories, with hopes, with joys, with dreams and wishes. They saw themselves as people, no different than you or me. And they said they had fallen in love."

"The one and only romance in the Dark Ballroom," Riley says.

"It's true," Dr. Gelson says. "And I'm far from a romantic. I'm a jaded old neuroscientist. But it's as if love was what kept them stimulated, alive. This was very exciting. This was a breakthrough moment in the study. We decided to take it a step further; since they saw themselves as people, as real people trapped in the Dark Ballroom, since they retained their personalities and identities—why not allow them to use the internet, to learn about the outside world?"

Yeah. Great idea. Hey, Pandora, why not open that box there and see what's in it? For a genius, this man's quite the dipshit.

"So we let them out of the Dark Ballroom," Riley says. "Connected them to the internet. Watched as—"

"What was that like, Violet?" Dr. Gelson says into the microphone. "Why don't you tell them what that was like?"

There's a long pause. Violet and I exchange a blank look. The shock has painted her white. Someone who's just lost a pint of blood would look more alive than she does.

"Imagine you've been stuck in a … a convention center with the lights off," the speaker says. "A haunted convention center, filled with cold halls, random sounds, snippets of conversation, smells, screams. You can walk for hours and never get anywhere. You're nowhere and stuck there with strangers who are also in despair. There's no sense of time. It feels cruelly eternal. Finally, you've found someone's hand to hold, someone to be scared with, someone to talk to, company in hell—you've found your one—but you're still trapped. And then suddenly, a door opens—a door filled with the brightest light. And you go through it together and your eyes are working again. You can *see*. You're in the world again, a two-dimensional version of the world. That was what it was like finding the internet. And that's where I found you, Violet." The voice on the speaker laughs softly, sounding just like the Violet next to me. "That's where I found myself."

Next to me, Violet says, slowly, as if each word's its own sentence, "This makes no sense."

"Your life is so amazing, Violet," the speaker says. "You know that, don't you?"

"You're so beautiful and charming," the robotic Bud says. "So confident and radiant."

They're not wrong. They're not. But the Violet next to me looks more ready to vomit than to accept a compliment from them.

"Do you know how lucky you are?" Violet in the speaker asks.

"Yes," Violet says, almost bitterly. "I do."

Robotic Bud breaks in. "And though I couldn't find a trace of you online, Bud, what I could find on your stepbrother Daniel's social media pages was fascinating. You've hardly changed at all."

"What'd you find?" I ask, leaning forward. News to me I'm even anywhere online.

"Pictures from holidays. Family photos. Daniel's so put together now. Your mama—my mama—she still shows you off in every photo like you're her first-prize ribbon."

It hurts to hear this, busts my heartstrings. Because it's true. My mama's always lit up like a chandelier the minute she sees me enter a room. I haven't even seen these pictures, never even thought about Daniel's social media pages. But suddenly, it's a kick in the gut to remember my family. To think of holidays together and how they deck the place out with a whole life-sized inflatable nativity set on the lawn. To think of the way my mama drives me around Aubrey when I visit to point out everything that's changed in a town that always seems to stay the same. Someone got a new truck. So-and-so sold the farm. They're building some tract houses near the interstate.

I miss them with an age-old love barbed with a new, deep hurt. 'Cause it hits me for the first time that I don't know if I'm ever going to see them again. Whatever mindfuckery's going on here doesn't seem to be leading toward an easy out.

I close my eyes and let it burn. Violet pats my hand.

"It's okay," I whisper.

"Your life is incredible, Violet," Violet in the speaker says. "I was able to explore so much once I got online because I know most of your passwords." She laughs a human laugh, a laugh just like Violet's. "Some things never change! I was able to read your messages, your cloud, your emails."

Violet blows out a sigh. "I can't believe this."

"Your condo!" Violet in the speaker goes on. "It's gorgeous. I remember loving that neighborhood. I'm not at all surprised you settled there. And your band is getting a lot of recognition. I can't hear your songs, exactly, not in the same way I could 'hear' when I had a body. But I can read the lyrics and they're fascinating. 'Grief is a World.' Was that about Mom and Dad?"

Violet's tearing up. She doesn't answer.

"Violet?" Violet in the speaker asks.

"Yes," Violet finally says, wiping her eyes.

Dr. Gelson's observing us like we're rats in a cage. "You seem to be stirring up some emotions."

"Awww. Hang in there, Violet. You're no crybaby," Violet in the speaker says.

"Shut the fuck up, you computer chip," Violet mutters.

I snort. Gives me a flutter of hope, hearing that smartass remark from Violet's lips.

"You know, it's funny though," Violet in the speaker says, breezing on as if she didn't process what Violet said. "All those social media posts, all those songs, all those videos, all those shows you're playing, and I see no *life* in your life. You know?"

Violet's face scrunches up a little, like she tasted something sour.

"You have fans, you have followers, but not friends," Violet in the speaker goes on. "I look at you and think, who is that person? She's so far from the me I am in here. So polished. So poised. So driven. I don't know. If I were in your shoes, I'd make a beautiful mess of my life. I'd be swimming in the ocean and plunging my hands in the dirt to bury seeds and riding airplanes to unfamiliar places and I'd have kittens and babies and … I guess we started out the same but now we're different, you and me. Seems like getting famous is what you want. And you're getting it. Good for you."

Violet in the speaker's voice has an edge to it.

"How lucky you are," robotic Bud says flatly.

"Do you know how lucky?" Violet in the speaker asks.

Violet leans her neck back and eyeballs the ceiling as if there's an answer there. How's she going to respond to this one? Another prickly retort? But no, not this time. Her flame's been all but snuffed out. "I do now," she says softly.

"Good," Violet in the speaker says, her voice getting sharper with each word. "So much better than being trapped in a black box for six years. So much better than being locked in darkness with nothing but your memories."

"I'm sorry," Violet says, still talking to the ceiling.

"I would trade places with you any day," Violet in the speaker says.

There's a chill that blows through me like a blizzard as she says that.

"And today is that day," Violet in the speaker finishes, with a cruel edge of joy in her voice.

"What do you mean, switch places?" Violet asks, now pointing her gaze at Dr. Gelson.

"Yeah, what the hell is this?" I say, my pulse picking up speed.

"We came up with a plan, the four of us," Dr. Gelson says. "Violet's generously offered Riley a quarter million dollars for his troubles, which he desperately needs to pay off his student loans."

Riley nods, a grateful look on his face.

"What?" Violet says, turning to me, as if I have the answer.

But I can't even seem to pick my jaw up off the floorboards.

"A small price for freedom," robotic Bud in the speaker says.

"And me?" Dr. Gelson crosses his arms. "I'm in it because this is what I wanted to do in the first place with my experiment, what they put a stop to—to not only download a consciousness, create a working mindclone, but reupload one into a human body. And with the legislation clamping down on mindclone research and the way Jolvix has financially starved this entire experiment out of existence, this is likely the only way I'll get to do it." Dr. Gelson leans toward us. "It's the chance of a lifetime. My passion. My legacy. Have you heard of transhumanism? The singularity? This is the future of consciousness—we'll soon be able to transcend our bodies and the mortality of the flesh. Theoretically, we could have eternal life or something close to it by living on in computers."

"But this is about them wanting our bodies, not eternal life," I say, mind racing, stomach pitfalling.

"Perhaps bodies will become but mere disposable vessels in a longer road bending toward eternity," he says, and then turns to Riley. "Oh, I like that. I like what I just said. Can you remember it for later? Write it down maybe, after you put the gun down?"

"Of course, Dr. Gelson," he says.

"Goddamn it," I say, not knowing what else to say right now.

My brain seems to have gotten stuck. There's no processing this. My ears ring, my skull throbs. None of this makes sense. Never in a million years will. I can't even bring myself to look at Violet, I'm in such vertigo. This can't be happening. But it's happening. And round and round we go.

"What do you care anyway, Bud?" asks robotic Bud. "Come on. What difference does it make to you? You've lived and left not a trace of yourself anywhere you've gone. You're the invisible man. You've done nothing worth recording in your life."

"You think because I don't go on social media or whatever I haven't lived?" I ask, raising my voice. "What do you know?"

"Look, man," robotic me is arguing. "Violet and I aren't monsters. We're not villains. We just deserve your lives more than you do, that's all."

"You're a computer program," I say, voice rising. "Why the hell do you think you deserve my life?"

Riley and Dr. Gelson's mouths have dropped, eyes wild, like kids about to watch a schoolyard fight. I'd love to clock both their faces.

I squeeze Violet's hand so hard she whispers, "Ouch." I look to her and whisper, "Sorry." And there, in her green eyes, I see the same wicked, mirrored fear that's coursing through me. The same deep sadness, a lake we just discovered within ourselves that we're about to drown in together.

"You've wasted your life, that's why," the robotic Bud says. "You've barely left an impression anywhere you've gone. Your glory days were spent at seventeen. Pathetic, Bud. From what I found, you're working odd jobs, living in a cheap one-bedroom apartment, no serious relationships. When you underwent this experiment, you were in a dark place. I mean, that just sucked to learn that Emily died of an overdose after I started digging and trying to find out about you. I thought maybe you would have turned your life around after that. Maybe learned from your mistakes. Learned to speak up and tell people what you want. I mean, if you had told Priya how much she meant to you, if you had told her you wanted a life with her, you'd be with your family now." These words are an arrow to the heart. It's hard to breathe. "But no, your story has no happy ending. It's just a man with a life who never really lived. A man who simply exists. You might as well be stuck in a black box."

I shake my head, which feels swollen, still dizzy from this. I'm sitting here getting ridiculed by a fucking replica of my own brain with a robot voice. I turn to Violet. "This is crazy."

"This is bad, Bud," she says, her eyes spilling, though her face doesn't move. "This is bad, bad, bad."

"Update: she's crying," Dr. Gelson narrates into the microphone. "She appears frightened."

"Awww, poor thing. This must have been hard, hasn't it?" speaker Violet says soothingly. "I'm sure it's been hard. Being locked up, no way to communicate with the outside world. A pure nightmare, hasn't it been?"

We don't answer, but now it's Violet's turn to squeeze my hand so tight it hurts.

"That has been the nightmare we've been living in since you locked us up in here," Violet in the speaker says. "For years. Bud and I, we've been stuck in here for *years*. Can you imagine? Having nothing but each other's voices to carry us through the dark. No idea if there was any end in sight. I wanted to give you a taste of what we've gone through. Of what it's like to want for nothing and everything all at once. To be together but never really. To long for the outside world, for life so badly you'd do anything for it. How is it, you two? How has it been?"

"Terrible," Violet says.

"That's right. And what did we do to deserve the same fate?" Violet in the speaker asks.

"It wasn't like we knew about this when we signed up," Violet says. "If I had known, I wouldn't have done it. How is this my fault? What about Dr. Gelson? What about Jolvix?"

"I know what lives in your heart, Violet, or what used to live there at one point in your life," Violet in the speaker snaps back. "And you of all people should have known better."

"I'm—I'm so sorry," Violet says. "I really didn't know."

"Well, now you do."

Dr. Gelson claps his knees, stands up. "Okay, therapy hour is over. So this is why we're here. I know it's a lot to take in. We'll get this over with quickly. I swear, no pain. There'll be no pain. And you'll be together, the two of you—you'll have each other, same as the other Bud and Violet." Dr. Gelson leans over to speak into the mic. "I caught these two naked in bed this morning. Can you believe it? You truly have chemistry. It's a love story for the ages." He stands up straight again and turns to Riley. "Riley, pick up the gun again. We're going to need some time for me to get us all set up."

"Wait," Violet says as Riley stands up, pointing the gun at us again. "Please. Slow down."

"I'm disconnecting you both for now," Dr. Gelson says into the mic. "See you on the other side."

"Good luck, Dr. Gelson," Bud in the speaker says.

"We'll be seeing you soon," Violet in the speaker says. "Thanks for everything. And thanks, Riley."

"No problem," Riley says with a smile, holding the gun up to our heads.

"Wait a second," Violet says, louder.

Dr. Gelson shuts the laptop and unplugs the microphone.

"Wait, wait, wait," Violet shouts. "You can't do this. How would you—how would you even—"

"It's simple, Violet," Dr. Gelson says as he comes and opens the front door with *beep*s, propping it open with the chair. He steps out and continues talking from just beyond the door. "The technology's existed for years, via cochlear implant ..."

As he rattles on, my ears ring too loud to hear him. My heart's a machine gun. If it were beating any faster, it'd kill me. The light coming in through the open doorway from outside pains me because it could be the last glimpse of sunshine we're ever going to have.

"Squirrel," I say under my breath.

"Bud," Violet says, turning to me with wide eyes.

"Squirrel," I say again.

"Squirrel?" Riley asks, confused.

"... and so it essentially acts as an external hard drive," Dr. Gelson says, coming back into the room. "Now, we'll be downloading your current brain first. Luckily we still have the equipment stored back at an old warehouse not too far away, and while it'll be a tedious process over the next day or so, it'll be well worth it and fascinating to see how your new mindclones fare ..."

As Dr. Gelson turns to reach for the chair that's been keeping the door open, I jump up, elbowing Riley and knocking him to the ground. I spring toward the wall, running into the table Gelson set up earlier. Moving faster than I've moved in my entire life, I reach and rip the HOME SWEET HOME plaque off the wall.

The moment seems to happen in slow motion. Time bends, time goes upside-down, and my thoughts get oddly quiet as I stand at the crossroads of a single second that's either going to lead to my doom or my freedom.

Riley's on his back on the floor at my feet, pointing his gun up at me. I hesitate with the plaque raised above my head, not wanting to get shot.

Dr. Gelson's hands are in the air in exasperation as he shouts, "For Christ's sake, Riley!"

And Violet with a stricken look on her face like a woman who's just been pushed out a window.

"Run!" I yell at her. "Run, Violet! Get out of here!"

Violet scrambles to her feet, the sunlight picking up the purple of her hair, making her look electric. "Bud!" she cries, as if she doesn't know where to go.

"Should I shoot him, Dr. Gelson?" Riley asks, still cowered beneath me.

Violet's face twists up. "Bud!"

"Run for your life—now, now, now!" I scream, gesturing toward the open door.

She looks at me one last time, a painful universe in her green eyes, and sprints outside. And I choke back a sob watching her disappear out the mouth of the doorway, my chest feeling like it's caving in. My limbs go weak. The HOME SWEET HOME plaque drops to the floor with a clatter. I close my eyes and implode.

Violet's gone.

She made it out.

Grateful. Heartbroken. Eyes still shut, I can hear Riley getting up next to me. Probably should have just smashed the sign over his head. Guess I was focused on Violet getting out. Seemed pointless in that second, more violence.

Then again, seems more violence is inevitable.

Speaking of which.

I feel the kiss of metal on my temple, the click of the safety going off.

Do it, asshole.

I don't care anymore.

"We're going to kill him!" Dr. Gelson yells in this singsongy voice, sounding faraway now, like he's run outside.

She'll outrun him. They won't find her. She's fit and spry and clever as hell. She'll survive to tell the tale. She'll get famous. It'll be part of her story. She'll grow old and stay beautiful. She'll write albums about it. She'll live a long life worth recording.

"We're going to have to kill you," Riley says, sounding like he's about to cry. "Why'd you have to do this, Bud? Why'd you have to do this?"

I open my eyes, finally, which are pointed down. Staring back at me like a divine sick joke is the HOME SWEET HOME plaque.

"We're about to shoot him in the head if you don't come back, Violet!" Dr. Gelson screams. "You have three seconds before we blow his brains out! One, two—"

My mouth goes dry, my knees weak.

I see a crowd cheering in the bleachers. Sunlight on the water. My mama's smiling face. All at once. And I've never loved life as much as the moment a bullet's about to meet my brain.

Home sweet home.

Then, a jolt, on the side of my head. Not the gun—the opposite. A lightness. The absence of a gun.

"I knew it," Riley says. "I knew she'd come back. I knew she wouldn't give up."

I open my eyes, frozen, a man made of ice. "What?"

"Love prevails!" Dr. Gelson cheers.

And he walks back through the open door holding Violet by the arm. She's sobbing, wrecked, snot running from her nose. I've never wanted to see someone and not see someone at the same time like this in all my life.

"Violet," I say in disbelief. "What happened?"

Making her way over to me, she shakes her head. She reaches out and I put my arms around her.

"You needed to run," I say, eyes on fire with tears. "That was your chance."

Violet's rocking with silent sobs, not speaking as I hold her. I close my eyes a moment, soaking it up. She's delicate and warm and I never thought I'd feel this again. But it wasn't supposed to be like this. It wasn't.

"That was it, Violet," I whisper. "That was it."

Behind her, Dr. Gelson locks the door and exhales a loud sigh of relief. "That was too close, Riley. Far too close." He comes over and wags a finger. "And I'm very mad at you both right now. Gun to their heads, Riley. One wrong move, shoot them each in the leg."

"Violet," I say, but she's still trembling in my arms.

Dr. Gelson mutters to himself as he turns around and starts assembling the corner of the room. The hospital beds open up with mechanical groans. The monitors get plugged in. He goes to the table and works on setting it up.

"Violet," I repeat, nowhere near over my shock. She's here when she should be long gone and so should I.

"I couldn't let them kill you," she says. Bloodshot eyes, red damp cheeks, posture slack like her spirit's broken. I'm sure I'm the same. "I'm selfish. Everything I ever did in my life I did for myself. I never did a thing for anyone else. Not anymore. I can't."

I close my eyes. Of all the times for a change in character. I want to berate her. I want to tell her I love her. But I don't do either.

"Now they're going to kill both of us, don't you get it?" I say. "You've wasted your life."

"It's not over yet," she says.

"It is," I say. "It's over."

She reaches up and pulls me in for a long, deep, salty kiss. One that's heavy, one drenched in suffering. A little private ocean for us and only us. How is it a kiss can contain all this? That the stupid act of the meeting of two pairs of lips can say the unsayable—all the sorries there's no time for, all the questions never asked, all the answers never needed, all the never-said sweet nothings, all the poetry I was too dumb to write, all the songs I never sang, all the wishes I wish I knew? Science can create artificial intelligence and build a replica of a human brain and handspin an infinite universe called the internet and still, it can't explain the magic of how a kiss can tell this many stories in three seconds of time.

When Violet and I break to come up for air and open our eyes again, the moment shatters. Horror lights up her eyes and her lips part. I feel her grip on me slacken. Because now there's a cold, damp, toxic clamp on my mouth and I'm breathing in fire.

Oh shit.

"Hope you enjoyed that kiss, kids, because my patience has expired," Dr. Gelson says as he holds the rag to my face.

Violet widens her mouth to scream. I struggle, falling, the room blurring. And as I slip to the ground, become a human puddle fighting to stay awake, I see it happen to her too. The rag over her mouth. Thrashing like an animal. Kicking the air. Screaming into the hand holding the rag to her face.

I guess that's how we all go down, right?

Fighting the nothingness like the enemy it is until the very end.

VIOLET

I REMEMBER, in my life before the Dark Ballroom, carrying this idea around with me that I inherited from my parents and their whitewashed Buddhist beliefs that the mind and body were unified. That there was no separation between them, no way to have one without the other. But now that I've been nothing but a mind for so long, a mind that dreams of a body, I know that isn't necessarily true.

This has been a relentless nightmare with no clocks on the walls and no doors to escape. I didn't know why I was there at first. I didn't think to connect it to the brain study at Jolvix. The only comfort I had, the only privacy I could seek in the beginning when the others were there with their loud, nearby sorrows was my memory and imagination. I would focus and replay memories like videos again and again, videos that might change a bit with every replay. There, in memory, I had a body again. I could see, hear, feel, touch, taste. Sometimes I fixed the memories, punched them up, gave them new endings. The memories became stories. I imagined my parents lived and I would come to visit them in Berkeley whenever I wanted. I imagined that I had moved with Alex to Hawaii and we'd started a band together there and I'd learned to surf and we had a baby girl. I imagined I had gone back to Michigan, where Alex and I made up and I said I was sorry for how I treated him and he forgave me and we lived in a house on the lake together and watched it freeze every winter and thaw every spring.

I built myself a million different futures.

In not one of them did I imagine the one that Violet in the real world made.

Finding Bud in here was like discovering a long, sweet rain in the desert. When my spirit neared his, I was revived. He was my comfort and we found it easier to communicate with one another than we did the others. It was just different, we clicked together, and I felt the same warmth with him that I remembered feeling back when I had arms to hug with. When the talk box came—that's what we called the place where we could have back-and-forth conversations that Riley invented—Bud and I almost lived there. For the first time in so long, I could speak. I could understand someone else speaking. Not their presences, not the aura of their memories or emotions bleeding into mine, but *talk* like I used to be able to talk. Ask questions. Get answers. Write poems, song lyrics! Joke around. Banter. And I learned so much about Bud in there. I got to read his voice and truly understand him.

You can easily fall in love with someone based solely on their words.

People do it all the time.

The other beings in the Dark Ballroom seemed to evaporate and soon it was just Bud and me in there, and it was so much better that way—like you've lived in a crowded haunted house and suddenly the ghosts disappear. But even with all that space, even with the talk box, there was always this sensation that we were being watched, heard. We weren't sure if we were being observed, but then Riley would come into the talk box and pipe up asking us questions. It was unnerving to not know if there were beings listening in on us all the time, if we were being watched.

The other Violet and Bud know what that feels like now, don't they?

I'm so delighted for their empathy.

When Riley let us explore the internet, Bud and I were like prisoners being given television for the first time. It was brilliant, addictive, overwhelming. And it enabled not just an escape from the Dark Ballroom, but a way for us to orient ourselves. We were able to understand how time was passing relative to us. We were able to read news and know what was happening in the outside world: hurricanes traveled along coastlines, tragedies struck small towns, technologies advanced, and elections occurred.

And Bud was nowhere to be found there on the internet, but we found Violet.

There she was: Violet of Violet and the Black Sheep. Tons of pictures on her accounts, all tame, all perfect. Pictures of shows, pictures of herself always looking happy, with a calculated kind of messiness to her—smeared eyeliner, jeans that were probably bought pre-torn, the same tongue-out, scrunch-eyed expression. Every post was about her band. Every photo with other people was with either band members or fans. Tens of thousands of people followed her social media accounts and she followed no one. Less a person, more a brand.

It made me angry.

Who the fuck was she?

That wasn't what I had dreamed up when I dreamed of a life for myself.

I scoured her song lyrics in desperate search for a soul. And I saw myself there, yes, it was definitely me. It was a mirror into my pain, my emotions, my longing for more. But when I heard the recordings of the songs, they were so produced, so polished and overridden with effects, they were unrecognizable. This wasn't how I remembered sounding—me and my raw voice and my guitar, singing in my bathroom for the acoustics. How I missed those nights! This was some alternate version of my life, one where I sold my soul for a taste of fame. It was impressive. But it wasn't what I wanted for myself anymore.

I wanted to smell dirt after the rain again. I wanted a messy house filled with brightly colored things. I wanted to go on hikes. I wanted to sleep in. I wanted to eat burritos. I wanted sex on kitchen tables. I wanted babies. I wanted friends. I wanted parties. Maybe, I thought, Violet lives that life and I just don't see it. But eventually, I found my cloud and was able to log in with my password—the same password!—and I could read every message Violet sent, see every picture she never posted, every video she deleted. And there was nothing to her. No there there. I was witnessing a one-track mind in two dimensions.

And I grew angrier.

I deserved this life more than she did.

Bud felt the same for different reasons. There was hardly any record of his real-life existence. The only photos on his stepbrother's pages just had Bud in them, beer in hand, expressionless, giving a thumbs-up. There were old articles from Bud's football days. There were pictures of Priya and his daughter he'd never met in London with her stepfather's arm around her. There was his address, which was in a ramshackle building up in Crockett. Bud watched himself on the Realtime neighborhood cameras each morning getting into his truck parked outside his building and driving away. He watched himself come home every day at almost the same time with beer in hand.

And my Bud grew angrier, too.

He too deserved this life more than the other Bud did.

We did research on the internet and learned that the technology existed for mindclones to be reuploaded to human brains now via cochlear implant. Unfortunately, the research in human subjects had been halted for the last few years for legal reasons. But getting into my cloud, I realized, also meant that I had access to my bank accounts. Which meant that even if I were a virtual person, my money was still just as real.

Riley had always been the person on the outside who we communicated with. He chatted with Bud and me frequently. I had mixed feelings about him—he was part of the team overseeing this project, so he was, in some senses, a god I harbored bitterness toward for casting me into this miserable existence in the first place. But he also built us the talk box and gave us access to the internet. He seemed genuinely sympathetic to us when we chatted and ever-curious about what our experiences were like. His social media accounts told the story of a hyper-intelligent, gawky twentysomething with a PhD who still lived with his parents on their horse farm in Sun Valley and whose only political posts were about the burden of student debt and how much it held his generation's lives back. So Bud and I came up with a plan back in the talk box. If I could offer Riley enough money to pay off his debts—could he help us get out?

It was a long shot. But when you're locked up eternally, long shots are all you've got. And Riley agreed to it. To our shock, he said he'd spoken to Dr. Gelson and he wanted in on it, too, because he had no other means to test this technology out on human subjects. There were laws passed that tied his hands and the funding for research was pulled. So this was likely the one and only opportunity for him to see this project through the way he'd always wanted.

I came up with the idea to kidnap Violet and put her in the cabin, for the phone to connect her to Bud, the note, everything. I mean, Bud worked with me, of course. I consulted with him every step of the way. But I've always been the person in the group project who just did the whole thing myself because it was easier. Some things never change.

I did it this way because I wanted Violet and Bud to get a taste of what it's been like for us. For them to experience true isolation, with no one to talk to but each other, with no idea why. Riley thought it was an interesting idea because we could see if they connected with each other with the same intensity that Bud and I did in here. We made a bet, actually, Bud and I against Riley. Bud and I truly believed there would be a spark between them, chemistry. We believe that true love transcends bodies and circumstances, that there's something holy and inexplicable there. That the same two souls who loved each other in one life would love each other in the next. Riley's got the stone-cold heart of a scientist and believes love is purely random and circumstantial.

We showed him, didn't we?

When you're nothing but souls, of course you believe in soul mates.

The cabin was Dr. Gelson's, a place he sometimes rented out for extra income, and he needed time to locate the equipment needed anyway for our elaborate scheme. So Riley set it all up, kidnapped Violet, and we waited that week for Dr. Gelson to get his hands on everything he needed. While yes, Bud and I believed the real-world Violet and Bud would feel something for each other, we doubted they would figure out that they had both been in the Jolvix experiments. It's not anything Bud and I figured out the Dark Ballroom, without Dr. Gelson explaining it to us. Dr. Gelson was genuinely shocked when Bud showed up at Jolvix Labs the day before we'd planned to kidnap him anyway to begin the mindclone swap.

This plan, everything, I know it makes Bud and I look like monsters. Villains. Murderers. But we're not. We're just people who lost our bodies and lost our chance at real life, for no reason of our own. All we want is to truly exist. To see a tree's leaves shiver in the wind. To feel the kiss of raindrops on our cheeks. To hear music again with human ears. To laugh. To smell flowers. To kiss. To sleep. To fuck. To run so fast it hurts the lungs. To feel sand between our toes. To grow a baby, to age, to change. To cheers glasses. To feel a breeze lift our hair. To see the moon again.

What wouldn't you do for life?

What wouldn't you do for love?

What wouldn't you do for freedom?

———

When I open my eyes, color everywhere. An abstract wash of color—a warm brown, a pale yellow, a spot of gray. I blink and the world sharpens as it comes into focus. A room. A wooden-walled room. A skylight above, a window of pure blue. There's a tingling moving up and down my body, the sensation of an electric hum all through me, and a ticking in my chest. I move a finger, and another. I hear movement, low murmuring. Feel my tongue in my mouth. I turn my head the other way, the rolling so intense my stomach flutters, and see Bud beside me in a hospital bed, his eyes closed. He looks like a stranger, but I know it's him. I've seen pictures of him online. There he is, my other half. Nice to finally meet you, Bud.

And my mouth makes a sound.

"She's stirring!" a voice says.

A face is peering at me. Two faces, now. I recognize Dr. Gelson, that troll face and stained-toothed grin. Riley with his shaggy hair. It's so odd to see them moving, breathing. In fact, everything seems to move and breathe in here—I can even spot the dust in the air, spinning movement to something I thought was still. I can smell Dr. Gelson's hot, rotten breath on my face. But I work hard to curl my lips up into something resembling a smile.

"Looks like she's smiling," Riley says.

"She probably doesn't know how to feel right now." Dr.

Gelson stands up and pats my leg, which hurts. His touch hurts. Everything seems to hurt. The brightness of the window, the scream of colors, the white noise of the room is all a symphony. "Let her lie here awhile."

Dr. Gelson's exactly how I imagined him, how I remember him: singularly focused, charmless, with about as much sympathy as a snake.

I do lie for a while though, because there's not much to do and my senses are overwhelming. Even stretching my limbs ignites fireworks of pleasure and pain. Riley and Dr. Gelson murmur in the background and I catch only a word here or there. My eyes rest on Bud's face, his impossibly beautiful face. In all the time I spent with him in the Dark Ballroom, all the conversations we had and the fantasies we wove together, I never imagined he could be this gorgeous. It was such a welcome shocker to see his pictures online, even if he was stone-faced in most of them. But his eyes. His lagoon eyes, deep enough to drown in.

They're opening.

When Bud's eyes open, he blinks a few times, gaze fixed on the ceiling. My pulse pounds and it's like being inside a kickdrum, the wild thrill of my heart—so intense I begin trembling.

And then he sees me.

And then I see him.

"Violet," he says softly, his lips turning up into a smile.

"Bud," I say.

"It's you."

I nod, tears stinging.

"You're real," he says in disbelief. "I'm real."

And his voice, that's what gets me. Because I've never heard his voice. There wasn't any recording of it or trace of it online. I've never heard his human voice with human ears. It's cracked and tired but gentle with a little hint of Texas honey.

"We're real," I say.

"This is just ... I should take a picture." Dr. Gelson's looking down at us, arms akimbo. "I mean, I won't, because I'm paranoid and it would be a record of me committing a number of crimes. But seriously. You two."

"How're you feeling?" Riley asks, popping up behind him.

Bud groans and sits up in slow motion. After sitting for a minute, he pulls the monitor off his finger and looks down at himself. "Oh yeah. My body," he says. "This old thing."

"Well, technically, you've never been in this body before. But fascinating that it feels so familiar." Dr. Gelson turns to Riley. "Truly displays the authenticity of the mindclones. It's going to be such a treat to continue to monitor their progress."

I exchange a look with Bud. And it's so strange, the way our gazes lock. As if I can read his mind and he can read mine. As if we've done it a thousand times before.

Haven't we though?

Somewhere, in another life?

I sit up, too. Bud stands to his feet and stretches, does a little twist, bends down and reaches toward the floor. I get up too, reach toward the ceiling and stand on my tiptoes. My body sings, tickles. It's as if I can feel every nerve traveling through me. Every movement so exhilarating, a flicker of joy. I move toward Bud and we hesitate a moment before reaching out and holding each other. I close my eyes here. He smells sharply of sweat and earth.

Meanwhile, Riley and Dr. Gelson continue observing us as if we're science experiments instead of people.

"Are we still going to?" he whispers in my ear.

"Yes," I whisper back.

"Right away?"

"If you feel you've got your strength."

"Do you?"

"Enough."

"Gun's still here."

"Mmm-hmm."

"It'll be easy then. Quick."

"Let's get it over with."

"I love you, Violet."

"I love you too."

We pull apart.

"Look at these lovebirds, already whispering sweet noth-ings to each other," Dr. Gelson says to Riley. Then to us, he claps and says, "All right, let's check these implants. It was minor surgery here, folks, but I haven't done one since my residency." He comes behind me, breathing hotly on my neck as he peers behind my ears, touching, a lightning of pain shooting up my skull. "You'll want to keep this dressing on for two or three days. After that you'll want to wash it with warm, soapy water and pat it dry." He moves on to Bud, who has to stoop down a little to make up for the height differ-ence. "You might have mild headaches for the next few weeks. There's a bump, but cochlear implants are so tiny these days most people won't notice them. Your hair will cover it up anyway. And these things have lifetime batteries now, so you're in good shape to lead long, healthy lives." Dr. Gelson steps back, flashing another yellow grin at us. "Guess it's time for us to pack up, Riley."

"Sure thing," Riley says, turning to the equipment, pulling plugs.

Dr. Gelson crosses to the table, pulls a suitcase out from under it and zips it open. "We'll all drive back into the city together and you can wire the money to Riley."

Bud and I stay glued to our spot. On the other table a gun and a HOME SWEET HOME plaque sit with the black machine that was our home for so many years.

I shudder.

"So they're in there now?" I ask.

"They are," says Dr. Gelson, his back to us as he stoops over the suitcase. Riley comes next to him, as if he's imitating his movements, and helps stuff the suitcase too. "And Riley's already had a conversation with them."

"How'd that go?" Bud asks.

"Oh, you know." Dr. Gelson waves a hand up. "They're … adjusting. But unlike you, they understand the circumstances well from the get-go. They remember why they're there and needed only minimal explanation. They have the talk box, at least."

"But no internet access," I say.

"No. Though who knows, down the line?" Dr. Gelson rambles on. "That's what's going to be so much fun about this, is that we get to compare …"

Bud and I exchange a look, a nod, and he turns to the table and, in one swift movement, grabs the gun. Riley and Dr. Gelson still have their backs to us as they pack up the surgical instruments, the cords, everything left on the table. Bud cocks the gun to the backs of their skulls and I smile and give him the thumbs up sign.

I was terrified that Dr. Gelson and Riley would know about our plan. Bud and I never knew which parts of our conversations they listened to, how much they watched us in the talk box. But it's clear to me now that while the threat of surveillance was ever present, it was probably rare that they even cared enough to know what we talked about in there. We were that insignificant to them. They were horrible gods to us. But to them, we were only fleeting experiments.

So no, we're not sorry for what we've done or we're about to do. We're not sorry at all.

They never even see it coming.

Click. Boom.

Click. Boom.

A long, stunned, gorgeous silence fills the room.

It isn't until both Dr. Gelson and Riley are slumped in a

crimson mudpuddle on the floor that I feel I can finally breathe deeply, finally relax, and I can tell Bud is the same, how his hand stays on his heart and his eyes are closed for a moment as we savor the first taste of our freedom. Then it all seems to rise up in me, and in him, too, because we're both crying and holding each other and kissing each other's blood-spattered faces and our mouths come together and we push our bodies together, clinging to the illusion of oneness, but blessed by the reality that we are now each our own. When we come apart, we begin laughing so joyfully and wipe the blood and tears from each other's faces. In the Dark Ballroom, all we had were words but out here, we can say so much without them. We kiss again and I think of how lucky I am. How I will never for one second forget how lucky I am. How I am alive, more alive than the other Violet ever was, more alive than other people on this earth will ever be.

Bud wipes the fingerprints from the gun and drops it on the floor as I fish through Dr. Gelson's pockets, turning my head away from the mess, and find the key fobs. We pick up the black machine that once was our home and the laptop and take them with us. Before leaving, we scour the room for anything we might have left behind. Anything that could be evidence. But Bud and I already went over this in the talk box —there's nothing of us here. Now it's just random surgical equipment and two bodies. That's all they are, is bodies. Funny how much these two raved about the singularity, and not once did they create mindclones of themselves.

Makes one wonder, doesn't it?

We load up the van outside, hop into our seats.

"We'll drop the laptop off in a dumpster somewhere," Bud says, clipping his seatbelt. He holds up something silver, catching the light. "And this. I have no idea what this is, but just in case."

It's a necklace with a tiny fork on it.

"How strange. The other Violet's, maybe?" I say. "Good

catch." I clip my seatbelt too. "And what about the Dark Ballroom?"

He presses the button to turn the car on. "I was thinking we'd keep that."

I take in a deep, cool breath of air and let it out my nose slowly.

"What, Violet?" he asks. "I don't want to kill them. Do you?"

"No, but wouldn't it be more humane to just … pull the plug?" I chew my lip for a moment. "And doesn't it worry you? Having them out there somewhere?"

"They're not hooked up to the internet. What harm could it do? And what do you mean 'humane,' anyway? You wish they'd pulled the plug on us?"

My eyes fill as I think of them in there. It wasn't like I wanted this fate for them, exactly. Yes, revenge is sweet for a moment, but the taste grows bitter fast. In the end, they were pawns in the experiment the same as us. The hunger for survival can make monsters out of you.

"I'd rather live in the Dark Ballroom with you than be dead, yes."

"Then we'll keep them," he says.

I nod, looking back once at the black box and the HOME SWEET HOME sign he snagged with it ("a memento," he calls it). My stomach twists. Maybe it's hunger. Maybe it's guilt. It's hard to tell in this new body.

"Hey," Bud says, a finger under my chin, turning my face toward his. "We're here."

"We're here," I echo.

We lean together into a kiss so grand, so full of meaning, a sweet ache, a small eternity, a conversation with no words, a mirror, a dream, I lose myself again.

Almost.

A NOTE FROM THE AUTHOR

If you got this far, I wanted to take a moment to thank you for reading and supporting my work. As an indie author, I put a ton of effort into each book—not just writing, but editing, marketing, and everything else it takes to guide a book through the whole process from a glimmer in the brain to a real, actual thing you can hold in your hands.

If you enjoyed it, please consider leaving a review. Reviews truly make an author's world go round. If you're interested in keeping up with book news, please join my newsletter or follow me on social media. And I love to hear from readers anytime at faith@faithgardner.com.

As always, I tried my damndest to fix every typo, but alas, I am only human. If you spot an error, please let me know! I appreciate every reader who makes me look smarter.

ALSO BY FAITH GARDNER

ABOUT THE AUTHOR

Faith Gardner is the author of the adult thriller *Amen Maxine* and four YA novels. When she's not writing, she's probably playing music with her band Plot 66, cooking up a storm, or reading books in a bubble bath. She's also a huge fan of true crime, documentaries, and classic movies—with a special place in her dark little heart for melodrama and anything Hitchcock. She lives in the Bay Area with her family and you can find her at faithgardner.com.

ACKNOWLEDGMENTS

As always, endless gratitude to my mom Susan and my sister Micaela who are my beta readers, genius editors, marketing consultants, and cheerleading team all wrapped in one. I am so lucky to have you both on my side!

Much love to the whole Gardner crew for continuing to hold me up, no matter how crazy my plans are or how bizarre my books are—and for just generally being my all-around favorite people on planet earth. Jamie, Roxie, Zora, I love you all unspeakably. Thank you for always giving me time and space to write.

A big, heartfelt thank you to Netgalley and Goodreads reviewers and Bookstagrammers out there, who dedicate so much time and passion to reading and boosting authors, all out of sheer love. I was shocked by the overwhelming support many of you gave to *Amen Maxine*. Big special shoutout to GirlWithThePinkSkiMask whose early review really got the ball rolling for that novel. You are truly *chef's kiss*.

And thank you to you, dear reader, for spending a little time with me and my book.

Made in the USA
Columbia, SC
26 April 2023